I0589614

DIONDRAY'S
Roundabout

DIONDRAY'S CHRONICLES
BOOK III

MARION HILL

Contents

PART 1

Adrian

Chapter 1

I departed the city of Issabella on the twenty-sixth day in the month of Coter. It had been nearly seven months since I left Charlesville. I had never been away from my home city that long. And the decision made at the hearing before the konseho of Kammbi brought my homesickness to the forefront.

"Maisa Merez has made her decision, and she will be the new owner of Silver Mine 12. This hearing is adjourned. Now, Diondray Azur, you will get the chance to prove whether you are the one to fulfill Oscar's prophecy."

Deputy Santiago's words had reminded me of how I'd been used by Mr. Cortes. The businessman wanted the silver mine the Merez family had owned for nearly two hundred fifty years, and he'd thought that Maisa's love for me would win out over her wanting to keep the silver mine as the last heir of the family.

I shouldn't have been surprised by her decision. Maisa had made it clear to me during our time in the city of Alicia that getting ownership of Silver Mine 12 would finally bring the Merez family name to prominence and get them the recognition they rightly deserved as one of the founding families who had helped discover the region north of the Great Forest alongside Oscar Ortega.

However, her decision would keep Maisa in Alicia, and I would never get to see her again. I understood her decision, but I was not happy with its outcome.

"Do not fault yourself for what has happened," Diakono Copperwith said.

I looked over at him and his wife, Annalisa, who were sitting across from me on the plane. I had been staring out through the window at the clouds, trying to manage my thoughts. Diakono Copperwith's blond hair and mustache had become a regular sight in my life. We did not have many people who looked like him back home in Charlesville—I'd heard there were a few from Terrance, but I had never seen them. Diakono Copperwith was my first direct encounter of someone who looked the way he did.

"I have since we left Issabella," I replied.

Mrs. Copperwith got up from her seat and sat down next to me. I had gotten used to her pious nature and motherly presence during the journey. Her long brown hair and olive skin were more common back home than her husband's pale coloring. But she wore dresses that seemed a size too big, hiding her attractiveness.

"We could tell," she said as she caressed my right hand. "You have not said a word since we got on the plane."

I stared into her soft, brown eyes and found some motherly comfort in them. "I have always trusted my instincts, and allowing Frederic Cortes to come felt right at the time. If I had only known what his true intentions were."

Diakono Copperwith handed his wife the copy of the Book of Kammbi they were both reading together. She released her caressing grip on my hand and opened the book. "I thought my instincts were correct in that most people in Guadharra would believe in Kammbi because of the miracles he did amongst the people," she read. "He fed ten thousand people with a few loaves of bread and meat. Replaced a woman's broken leg with just a touch of his hand. Showed that a young boy could walk on water. I thought those miracles would be enough to show people they should believe and follow Kammbi. I thought that by sharing the stories of those miracles, the people would instantly believe. But they did not. They ran me out of the city as a heretic."

"Gregory felt the same way as you do, Diondray." Diakono Copperwith said after his wife finished reading. "He was Kammbi's first disciple, and he wrote those words in the first chapter of the first book in the Ryianza section of the Book of Kammbi. The opening chapter of our sacred text reveals how our instincts can be misled."

Mrs. Copperwith added, "Mr. Cortes had his own agenda from the start. Thankfully, the Eternal Comforter allowed it to be revealed at the right time."

"What does that really mean?" I retorted. "I thought I allowed Mr. Cortes to join us on the journey to the cities north of the Great Forest *because* of the Eternal Comforter. I even started praying. And it did not work."

"Sometimes the wrong outcome can be used by the Eternal Comforter to lay the path down for a better result in the long run," Diakono Copperwith said.

He smiled reassuringly, but I did not feel reassured at all. I was still confused about the Eternal Comforter, even after reading about in the Book of Kammbi and having the Copperwiths explaining it to me since I'd met them in Santa Sophia.

"Diondray, we will have to trust in the Eternal Comforter to use what has happened so far on the journey for our benefit," Mrs. Copperwith said as she returned to caressing my right hand.

I glanced at the diakono's wife. I sensed that she was going to sit beside me for the rest of the plane ride. Her touch was comforting, and I knew that she had become my second mother for the rest of the journey. She smiled at me, and while I was not reassured about the Eternal Comforter, I did feel comforted by her presence.

"Would you like to read with me?" she asked.

I nodded.

Mrs. Copperwith released my right hand and moved the Book of Kammbi closer to me with her left hand. I looked over at Diakono Copperwith, who had pulled out another version of the Book of Kammbi from the overhead compartment. He was going to read with us. I guessed their comfort came from reading this sacred text.

We landed at the airport in the city of Adrian two hours later. The Copperwiths and I had spent the rest of the trip reading about Gregory. Kammbi's first disciple had left his home in Guadharra after a dream about Kammbi. The dream felt so real that Gregory knew he had to find out about this god. He faced more resistance than any of the other disciples in the rest of the book. Being Kammbi's first disciple had many more disadvantages than I would have expected. We had a good discussion about Gregory, and it helped with my uneasiness about the Eternal Comforter. However, I still was homesick, and as we landed, my thoughts returned to Charlesville.

Spending nearly seven months traveling to the cities north of the Great Forest had made me long for home. Despite my differences with Mother and Uncle Xavier, I thought about them and Aunt Maxina as we traveled from Issabella to Adrian. Did they miss me? Had they tried to look for me? Had Mother and Uncle Xavier found out it was Aunt Maxina who had helped me escape Charlesville? If so, had they placed her in confinement? Those questions raced through my mind as we exited the plane.

I followed the Copperwiths into the airport lobby. A couple of short and husky olive-skinned men trailed us with our luggage—or rather, the Copperwiths' luggage. I had only one suitcase and my over-the-shoulder travel bag that had come with me from Charlesville.

The konseho of Kammbi had provided the plane and given the Copperwiths enough silver to make sure the next part of this journey would be well funded. I had learned from Diakono Copperwith that the konscho had plenty of silver bars in its coffers—a good thing, since that was the only currency the people in the cities south of the Great Forest accepted.

The autobus driver retrieved our luggage from the airport employees and placed them in the trunk. The driver had droopy eyes and cheeks, and I wondered if he'd just woken up before arriving at the airport. He took off from the airport in a hurry, and his driving immediately let me know that he was awake.

The driver explained that Adrian had only four main streets, which connected the entire city. He said that the city was shaped like the letter B. We were on the city's longest road, Araceli Circle. It made a loop around the city and connected with the other three main streets: Adrian Place, Adrianna Way, and Guanna Lane. The entire city of Adrian fit inside of Araceli Circle.

Mostly residential homes and two-story office buildings passed by as the driver raced west on Araceli Circle. No tall buildings or notable landmarks met my eyes, like those common in the cities north of the Great Forest.

The driver turned right off Araceli Circle onto Adrian Place heading north. It seemed like he was driving away from the city.

He pulled into a hotel's parking lot a couple of minutes later. The hotel was the largest building I had seen so far on the drive from the airport. It was three stories high with a wooded area surrounding it.

"Welcome to Hotel Samantha," the driver said as he turned off the autobus. "The best hotel for first-time visitors to the city. The Azur family owns this hotel and wants to make sure all its visitors have a first-class experience."

"You said this hotel is owned by the Azur family?" I asked the driver as I got out of the autobus.

"Yes," the driver answered as he placed our luggage on the curb in front of the hotel's entrance. "Eduardo Azur and his family own this hotel."

"Who is Eduardo Azur?"

"Eduardo Azur is the family's patriarch and the biggest javann maker in the city. This hotel is just another piece of real estate for the family."

The driver finished placing our luggage on the curb, and I realized that he had not noticed the last name on my luggage tag. He got into the autobus and drove off just as fast as when he had picked us up.

Two sinewy, dark-skinned men wearing brown uniforms came out from the hotel to get our luggage. They had my complexion and treetop hairstyle. The shortest of the two stared at my luggage and read the tag.

"Azur," he said in a clipped voice.

I nodded.

"Diondray Azur," he said more loudly for the other employee. The second man stared at the tag and then looked up at me.

"Is there something wrong?" I asked.

"We have never seen anyone not from the city with this last name," the shortest employee said. "Are you related to Eduardo Azur?"

Before I could answer his question, I heard a growl in the distance. It must have been coming from the woods behind the hotel. The employees stood stiff as a board—like they knew the growl as well as I did.

Before I could react, Reuel the Leopard came from the east side of the hotel right toward me. I wondered how that animal had made it to Adrian so fast—it had been at my side during the hearing with the konseho of Kammbi, but unlike the Copperwiths and I, it didn't have access to an airplane. The members of the konseho had been astonished by the leopard's appearance and knew what it signified.

"You are a friend of the leopard," the shortest employee said. Both men had astonished look on their faces. They bowed to Reuel. The leopard growled in acknowledgement.

The Copperwiths stood to the left, seeming unfazed by the interaction between the men and Reuel. They had gotten used to Reuel appearing suddenly on this journey.

The employees remained erect as Reuel stopped growling. Both men stared at the leopard like they were waiting for the animal to communicate with them. Could human beings and animals talk to each other?

"Are you going to take us inside the hotel?" Mrs. Copperwith asked sharply.

Reuel growled softly at the employees as the leopard stood next to me. The men nodded at the growl and seemed to understand what Reuel was communicating.

"We have been commanded to take Mr. Azur with us." the shortest employee said after Reuel growled softly again.

"He is not going anywhere!" Mr. Copperwith interjected. "We just arrived here from Issabella. We all need to get some food and rest.

"My husband is correct," Mrs. Copperwith added. "Take us inside, please!"

The hotel employees looked down at Reuel, who started growling at the Copperwiths, and then they glanced up at me. "He must come with us," the shortest one continued. "The leopard is connected to him, and he looks like one of us."

"We just arrived from Issabella with my husband," Mrs. Copperwith retorted and shot a sharp look at Reuel. "We have come together on this journey, and we will remain together."

Reuel left my side and stood next to the hotel employees. The leopard growled back at me and I had sensed that it wanted to go with these men.

"I will go with them," I said.

"Diondray!" Mrs. Copperwith replied.

"Reuel will protect me." I said softly.

The tallest employee grabbed my luggage. Reuel and I followed the employees away from the hotel in the direction the leopard had come from.

Chapter 2

I did not look back at the Copperwiths as I followed the two men into the woods on the east side of the hotel. I had made another decision without their guidance, and I did not want to see their disappointment. Especially from Mrs. Copperwith. However, Reuel was at my side, and I sensed that going with these men would be okay.

We walked onto a paved path inside the woods. Did these men use this path all the time? I wondered. The taller of the two men carried my suitcase, while the shorter one spoke to him in a dialect I had not heard before. He spoke in rapid bursts, while his companion kept glancing back at Reuel. It seemed like the taller man was still surprised that the leopard would be so comfortable traveling next to me.

I adjusted my travel bag on my right shoulder as the path turned left. The men stopped abruptly, causing me to bump into the taller one. He reached back with his left arm to keep me from falling over him. His grip was firm, and it jerked me into place.

As I watched, the shorter man left the path, heading toward a huge tree. Seconds later, he climbed the tree as fast as I had ever seen a human being do so. Reuel growled his approval. The man scampered back down the tree just as fast as he had climbed it—but now he was holding a black leather bag.

The taller man placed my suitcase on the ground and walked over to his companion, who opened the bag and pulled out two masks—gold-painted leopard faces that reminded me of Reuel.

The leopard growled again as the men took off their uniforms and placed the masks over their faces. Both were wearing one-piece leopard-print outfits made of the same material as the masks. They approached Reuel, and the leopard stepped away from my side to greet them. The men bowed to Reuel, and the leopard purred his approval.

"Diondray Azur," the shorter man said. "We are Boma-Men. Because you are a friend of the leopard, you have become our friend as well."

I nodded as the taller Boma-Man picked up my suitcase, and we returned to walking on the path. What was a Boma-Man? Did they travel this path every day before working at the hotel? Did they worship Reuel?

The men remained silent as the path went from the woods to a village. As we approached, a high-pitched sound surrounded me. I covered my ears, feeling as though the sound was piercing throughout my entire body—and lowered my hands slowly as the sound faded and people gathered in the village to watch us arrive. They were dressed just like my escorts and stood erect as we passed by. The people stared at the leopard and me, clearly surprised. Their surprise, however, was not greater than my own! I had come to a place where a group of people worshiped and revered Reuel. I had never thought this kind of thing would mark the first part of my journey to the cities south of the Great Forest. How were these people connected to Oscar's prophecy?

The village consisted of large trees where the people had made their homes, carving them out of the thick trunks. They walked in and out of their tree homes as casually as I did my duplex back home. I had never seen a tree home before, and I could not help staring as we walked.

My escorts led us to the center of the village, where a lanky man wearing an oversized silver mask was sitting on a tree trunk. They must have cut that tree recently, because it appeared smooth as skin and did not have a weathered look like most trees did. Two other lanky men accompanied him, and all three acknowledged our arrival.

"Omari," my taller escort said and bowed to the man in a silver mask. "We have brought a friend to the village."

He placed my suitcase down on the ground as the shorter escort walked up to Omari and bowed as well. Omari grinned through the mask as he stared at Reuel. The leopard purred and walked up to the leader of the village. He rubbed Reuel's head and looked at me.

"We do have a friend amongst us," the village leader said. "A friend of the leopard is a friend of the Boma-Men."

"His name is Diondray Azur," the taller escort said and brought my suitcase to Omari. He flipped the name tag over for his leader to read.

Omari read the name tag and asked, "Are you from Adrian?"

"Charlesville," I replied. Reuel returned to my side, and I watched all the Boma-Men stare at the leopard.

The village leader released the name tag and gazed at me. "From the place near the Kammara Sea. Your name comes from there. And you have dark brown skin and treetop hair like us Boma-Men." Omari took off his mask. His complexion and hair were exactly like mine. The only difference was the gray streaks running throughout his hair. I assumed he was the same age as the Copperwiths.

"Welcome to Boma Village, Diondray Azur," he continued. "Because of your arrival, it looks like the circle of history will finally close its loop. Micah, take our friend to the guest quarters, and we will resume our discussion at sundown. The leopard will stay with me."

What did Omari mean about the circle of history finally closing its loop? What was the connection between the Boma-Men and my people back home? Micah picked up my suitcase, and I followed him to the left, away from Omari and the other Boma-Men. Reuel nuzzled my leg and purred as I was leaving. It was the leopard's way of telling me that he would be okay with the leader of the Boma-Men.

I arrived at a tree home north of the center of the village. Micah opened the door to the tree home and placed my suitcase down next to it. In the middle of the guest quarters was an oval-shaped table with a plate of fruit and green leafy vegetables. Mangoes, brownberries, and sliced bananas filled the center of the plate while the leafy vegetables surrounded the fruit. My escort pointed to the large rectangular cushion that acted as a chair at the table.

"I will return with your drink in a few moments," he said as I sat down and placed my travel bag on the floor.

Micah left the guest quarters. I grabbed handfuls of brownberries and sliced bananas to stuff into my mouth. I had not eaten since the plane ride, and my stomach welcomed the fruit. I wondered if the Boma-Men ate meat. I knew from my studies at school that leopards were meat eaters—mostly hunting and eating smaller animals of the forest. If they were a people who worshiped and emulated the leopard, then meat eating would have to be a part of their diet—wouldn't it?

Micah returned with a drink of brownberry juice and placed it on the table. "Eat all the fruits and vegetables. There is plenty, especially for those who are friends of the leopard."

"No meat?"

He frowned. "Boma-Men do not eat meat. Eating meat is forbidden amongst our people. Fruits and vegetables have sustained us for generations."

"I was taught that leopards eat meat. I thought the Boma-Men would do the same."

Micah had walked to the far side of the room, where a bed hung onto the tree-bark wall. Several thick ropes connected the bed to the bark wall, keeping it off the ground. It looked like a longer version of the cushion at the dining table.

Micah tidied up the bed. "We are aware that leopards eat meat," he replied as I arrived next to him. "But Omari and prior leaders of our people believed that eating meat tended to slow humans down and make them gain weight. Even though Boma-Men worship the leopard, eating meat is one leopard practice we will never participate in."

I cracked a smile. "There are no overweight Boma-Men—that I have noticed."

Micah grinned. "You have an awareness like us."

I sat on the bed. It felt firm and sturdy. My own build was lanky like the Boma-Men, and the bed was the right length for my legs. Another thing we had in common.

The surprising contradiction of leopard worshipers who didn't eat meat reminded me of the contradiction with the people of Santa Teresa, who believed that women must marry by the age of twenty-one, even though the disciple Teresa's section of the Book of Kammbi said nothing of the kind. I wondered if all belief systems had such contradictions.

I opened my travel bag to pull out my writing pad and pencil. An idea for a themily had come to mind. I had not written a themily since my arrival in Issabella earlier in the month of Coter. Micah left the guest quarters again, and I lay back on the bed to write.

Contradictions
Will we always be susceptible to contradictions?
Are we capable of believing in something totally?
Or will we always compromise our beliefs for convenience?
For tradition?
For fitting in?
Can a person truly believe in something purely
when we contradict ourselves all the time?
Or do those contradictions make us who we are?

I wrote an unpolished version quickly as Micah returned. If people from both sides of the forest had contradictions in their belief systems, how could this land ever unite as one, as Oscar's prophecy foretold?

"You write?" Micah asked.

I got up from the bed and joined him at the dining table. "I do. I write themilys."

"Themilys?"

I scooped up some more brownberries and banana slices. "Themilys are a collection of thoughts written on a single sheet of paper that are meant to inspire, encourage, or admonish an audience. They are usually delivered aloud by the writer."

"Words can be deceitful and confusing."

"They can be," I replied. "Themilys are not written to deceive or confuse. I don't write that way for my audience. Do the Boma-Men write?"

"Not Boma-Men. We do read. Omari has made sure everyone in Boma Village can read. The words of city people can be deceitful and confusing. Boma-Men will not be taken advantage of by the words of city people."

I grabbed a leafy vegetable and wrapped it around several mango slices. Why would the Boma-Men know how to read but not write? Reading and writing were different skills, but they always went together. I had learned both reading and writing together in my studies back home—taught by my mother to read and my aunt Maxina to write. Learning how to read and write were the most enjoyable activities I had as a kid. Were written words forbidden amongst the Boma-Men?

Micah handed me a tablecloth as juice from the mango slices dripped off my chin. "I will be back just before sundown. Bring your writing with you for Omari."

He exited the guest quarters, and I began wondering how Omari would receive this unpolished themily I had written.

Sundown arrived, and a stiff breeze ripped through the village, making it cooler than I had anticipated. I wore a blue long-sleeved shirt and pants I had received from the konseho of Kammbi just before we left for Adrian. I had explained to Deputy Santiago that I could not wear anything Mr. Cortes had made for me after what happened at the hearing. To my surprise, he understood my position and got me a new wardrobe.

I had seven days of clothing in my suitcase and was grateful for the deputy's gesture.

Micah brought me back to the center of the village, where Omari sat on the same tree trunk from earlier. Dusk had arrived, and I noticed square-shaped lights surrounding the area. Omari's guards were in the same position as they had been earlier. He motioned for me to take a seat on a stump across from Omari and the guards. All three wore masks, and it felt odd not being able to see their faces.

"Micah tells me that you write," Omari said.

I nodded and replied, "Themilys."

Omari grinned through the mask. I could see his pearly white teeth, but I did not feel comforted by his grin. "Themilys. I would like for you to read one of them for me. I want to hear these words of wisdom."

"Before I do, I would like to know . . . where is Reuel?"

Omari's guards turned their heads to their leader. I glanced at Micah, who stood to my right, and stared at Omari as well.

"Reuel comes and goes, as are the ways of a leopard. I'm sure that you are used to his wanderings by now. The leopard is connected to you. It will always come at the right time."

Omari was correct about that. Reuel's timing so far on this journey had always been at the right time. We were connected in ways I did not fully understand. But I knew that in the Copperwiths' eyes, our connection was another indicator that I was the one to fulfill Oscar's prophecy.

"Please share your words of wisdom," Omari said.

I pulled the paper out from my travel bag and took a deep breath. My audience of four people seemed more intimidating than the crowds I had read to at Aliki Park. I read the unpolished version of the themily about contradictions. Omari bobbed his head in approval while the guards and Micah remained motionless.

"Interesting words of wisdom," the Boma-Man leader remarked. "Do you feel conflicted about contradictions? Human beings have always lived with contradictions."

"Then we should not have any belief systems," I replied after placing the themily back into my travel bag.

Omari grinned again. "You will never find anyone who lives out any belief system absolutely. Our nature as human beings is always to add or change things within a belief system to make it more palatable to those who follow it."

"Is that why Boma-Men don't eat meat?" I replied. "Leopards are meat eaters. Since you worship the leopard, eating meat ought to be part of your belief system."

"You have the gift of perception as well. The circle of history may finally close its loop after all these years."

Those words again. They aroused my curiosity once more. "What do you mean by that?"

I shifted my weight to get more comfortable. I had a sense that I was going to be interrogated for a while.

Omari took off his mask. "Who forced you away from home?"

Although the question was direct, I felt no threat from the leader of the Boma-Men. I sensed that he did not want to harm me or keep me as a hostage. In taking off his mask so I could see his dark-brown face and treetop hairstyle, he showed me respect. I decided being truthful was the best route to take.

"My family did. My mother, Olivia Azur, and my uncle, Xavier Azur, forced me to leave Charlesville."

"Why?"

The guards and Micah remained motionless as statues. There was no way I could have stood so long in one position. "My aunt, Maxina Azur, showed me that we had a book, hidden in our city for generations. The book was left by Oscar Ortega, the disciple of Kammbi from north of the Great Forest."

At my words, the guards cut their eyes toward their leader. Micah shifted in place.

"The traveler did leave his sacred book after all." Omari said.

"You know of Oscar Ortega?"

"Of course, Diondray Azur," Omari continued. "We have been taught the story of the traveler from the north throughout the generations. The traveler from the north was the first man to have a leopard as his companion. Years ago, a second man came to this area from the east, also with a leopard. Now, you have arrived in Boma Village with a leopard as your companion. That is why I believe the circle of history may finally have closed its loop."

"The Book of Kammbi is the sacred book," I said. "After finding it, I questioned my mother and uncle about the teachings inside. It revealed that our family's history began with Oscar Ortega and his attempt to reconcile with his son, Charles. I had always been taught that Charles Azur had a different father, another man from north of the Great Forest. My mother and uncle did not believe the words written in the Book of Kammbi and forbade me from talking about it to people of our city. However, I believe the words in the Book of Kammbi to be true. I read a themily declaring that to the people of Charlesville, just like I did for you and the other men here. And because of those words, I had to leave Charlesville."

"Are you here to share the beliefs from the traveler's sacred book?"

I nodded. Yes—although it had taken me some time to accept it, that was exactly why I was here.

Omari waved for Micah to join him and the guards. The leader huddled with his subjects in front of me. Omari spoke in the dialect I heard earlier from one of my escorts on the way here. The other men nodded as their leader continued speaking. His speech had a rhythmic quality like he was singing instead of talking. I looked down at my right foot as it tapped the ground.

I heard a growl in the distance, and I turned to my left and saw a familiar presence coming toward me. The guards broke the huddle first and watched Reuel come to my side.

"He is a relative of Adrian," one of the guards shouted.

Omari waved his guards and Micah back to their position. "He is indeed. Micah, take our kindred back to his guest quarters. We have more to share with him. The leopard will go with him as well."

After breakfast, Micah led Reuel and I across the village for several miles. The Boma-Man remained silent throughout the journey. I wanted to talk to him about Omari's comments regarding the second man who had come here with a leopard. Was that man a relative of mine? However, Micah had a blank expression on his face that signaled he did not want to speak. He glanced frequently at Reuel. The leopard acknowledged the Boma-Man by purring and nuzzling my left leg.

The terrain around the village was flat, with knee-high grass that had lemon-yellow stalks at the top, and huge trees where I saw leopards dashing from limb to limb. I thought Reuel would want to join his brethren and climb trees as well, but the leopard stayed with me and did not even acknowledge the other animals.

We soon reached an area where a group of Boma-Men were pulling the stalks from the grass and handing them to women who stripped the leaves from the stalks and placed them into huge, oval-shaped silver containers.

"Welcome, Diondray," Omari said and reached down to pet Reuel. Micah had brought us to where he was overseeing the villagers' work with his guards. "I want to continue our discussion from sundown and provide more context about what was said."

The villagers were wearing gold, leopard-faced masks just like Omari's guards and leopard-print one-piece outfits that stopped just above the knee. In my lime-green jumpsuit, I felt instantly out of place. I'd chosen it because it was the coolest outfit I had—in anything else I would have found myself sweating profusely in the heat.

Micah grabbed a small jug from one of the guards and handed it to me.

"Drink," Omari continued. "As you can see, our people are working the land. Boma-Men have done so for several generations."

"How come?" I asked after taking a gulp from the jug. It was brownberry juice, and it thoroughly quenched my thirst.

"Pulling these guanna stalks was a gift your ancestor left to our people."

"Oscar Ortega?" I replied. "He made it this far in his travels?"

Omari grinned through his mask. "Not the traveler. Adrian Azur."

"Who was Adrian Azur?" I asked, eager to find answers to some of my questions.

"The second man who came to this area with a leopard. Adrian taught our people how to pull these guanna stalks like you are seeing right now. The technique has worked throughout the generations and helped keep our people relevant."

"What do you mean by relevant?"

Micah left us and joined in with the villagers pulling the guanna stalks. "Adrian Azur was the one who turned these guanna stalks into food and drink when he arrived. He noticed how the leopards ate the guanna stalks for nourishment. How the stalks seemed to give leopards a special energy to survive in this remote place. Adrian believed if the guanna stalks could provide nourishment for the leopards, they could do the same for people. We are forever grateful for his discovery."

Micah and the other Boma-Men moved through the grass rapidly. Led by the guards, they were several feet away from where I was standing with Omari. If they worked this fast everyday, I could see why the Boma-Men were grateful to Adrian Azur.

"You said he came from the east," I said as Reuel left my side and lay down next to the leader.

"Yes, from your city. The city next to the Kammara Sea."

"But I've never heard of him. My family has never mentioned Adrian Azur."

Omari frowned. "Your family has never spoken of Adrian Azur?"

"No."

23

"Why would your family keep that away from you? Adrian Azur was Charles Azur's younger brother."

"Younger brother?" I shot back.

The guards turned away from the workers and started heading back toward us. Omari waved them off. I started pacing away. Reuel did not move from his position.

Omari shook his head. "It is not good for a family to keep its history from its members. You should know everything about where you came from. Your ignorance of these things is probably why you have taken to believing in the traveler's sacred book so easily."

I finished drinking the rest of brownberry juice and looked at Omari. "I never heard that he had a younger brother."

"Instead of sharing those beliefs from the traveler's sacred book, I believe you were brought here to find out where you came from. And that is another reason why I believe the circle of history is finally closing its loop."

Omari smiled after that comment. He began walking toward the workers, who had gone several more feet east. Reuel got up from the ground and waited for me. We followed the Boma-Man, and I realized that he had just made the most credible point I had heard on the journey so far.

We caught up with the workers, who had made their way through a mile of grass. Micah was out in front of the entire group, and they worked in unison, pulling guanna stalks. Omari received a jug from one of the guards and handed it to me. I took another drink, still trying to digest his claim about Adrian Azur. Adrian was not mentioned in the Book of Kammbi. If Oscar Ortega knew Adrian, surely he would have written about him in his section of the book. Oscar had come to reconcile with Charles, and I did not believe he would have had a second tryst with Mother Adrianna. I had been taught she wanted nothing to do with Oscar Ortega after being forced to leave her people, the Mayza tribe. Had Mother Adrianna had a secret child with another man?

"Come," Omari said. "You have good height, posture, and dark brown skin just like us. You will learn how to pull guanna stalks today."

I stood next to the leader of the Boma-Men and felt a surge of energy come over me, like it had left his body and now hovered over me. I wanted to join the workers at that moment and plow through the grass. Omari motioned for a woman at the back of the group to come. She obeyed his request and arrived in front of us with a container.

"Nya will collect the stalks you pulled off the grass," the leader continued. "Watch."

Omari grabbed several blades of grass from the bottom and slid his hands upward until he reached the yellow stalks. He yanked the stalks away with his left hand while holding the grass with his right. Nya brought the container underneath and collected the stalks. "Your turn, Diondray."

I took his place and repeated what he had just taught me to do. The guanna stalks felt sticky in my hands, and I began rubbing the residue off my fingers.

"You will get use to the stickiness," Omari barked. "Keep going."

He waved for another worker to come from the back of the group. As Omari had indicated, the sticky feeling on my hands dissipated after a few moments. I began working at a good pace due to the surge of energy I had received. Nya stayed next to me, and I could see her smile through the mask she was wearing.

"Excellent, Diondray," Omari said. "Pulling guanna stalks is a part of your heritage. The circle of history will finally close its loop."

The worker joined Nya and me. He handed me his gold-painted mask, which was smooth and shiny like it had been recently made. "It's yours," he said.

I stopped working and took the mask. The worker turned me around and placed the mask on my face. I felt a great surge of energy flowing through my body and was ready to get back to work. My vision became keener, and I could see a lot farther than I ever had before. What was happening?

"You are a Boma-Man," Omari proclaimed. "That is why you came here. To reconnect with who you really are. The Boma Essence is compatible with you. You are the descendant of Adrian Azur. The Boma Essence was compatible with him also."

I continued working and moved quickly through the grass. I felt as though I could stay out here and work all day. I had never felt this energized in my life. Was Omari right? Was this the reason I had come to Adrian?

I worked for eight hours and helped pull guanna stalks for about a mile. Omari explained that this was the normal distance the workers reached each day. I did not feel tired at all. Wearing the mask enhanced the energy surge I had received. As a matter of fact, I ran with Reuel back to the village. I had never run so fast in my life—nor had I ever enjoyed running before, even when I was a child racing with my friends.

Micah escorted me that evening to the biggest tree home in Boma Village. It was the size of several trees fused together, and leopard print design adorned the entrance. I wore the mask before entering Omari's home. Even as night approached, my vision was not impaired. Also, I had been asked to bring my themilys with me. I had them in my travel bag over my left shoulder.

"Welcome to my home," Omari said. He was sitting at the head of a long dining table that filled the left side of the tree home. His guards, a woman, and two children were sitting at the table with him. "You are one of us. And the time is appropriate for you to meet my family."

I was seated at the opposite end of the dining table. A plate of fruit and vegetables awaited on the table in front of me. A tall glass of brownberry juice was placed next to it.

"This is my wife, Ayesha, and our children, Naymor and Taikah," the Boma-Man leader continued. His family sat on the left side of him at the table. They all wore silver masks. I assumed only Omari and his family could wear silver-painted masks, because everybody else I had seen wore masks that were gold in color. "To my right are my brothers, Akbar and Joneh. You have already met."

They all smiled through their masks at me. It was the first time I had seen the guards smile. I guessed they felt comfortable enough with me now, since I was in their brother's home. Micah sat between the guards and myself. He seemed relaxed as well. Being in someone's home for dinner tended to lighten the atmosphere.

"Everyone, please close your eyes," Omari said.

I looked over at Micah, who nodded for me to obey their leader's request. I closed my eyes and felt that surge of energy

27

flowing through me again like the current in a river. The energy surge flowed through every area of my body like it had always belonged inside of me. A blue light flashed before me for a few moments. In a flash, I realized that I could read everyone's mind at the table. Omari wanted to do this ritual as a test for me. He wanted to know if I was truly a descendant of Adrian Azur. His wife and children were there to do whatever pleased him. The guards did not trust me, but they were going along with their brother's wishes. Micah believed I was truly a Boma-Man.

My mind continued to reach out, and I sensed the way in which this tree home had been made years ago. Its intricate details had been crafted by the people, making sure their leader had a home worthy of his status.

The energy surge raced faster through my body, and I started getting visions of a man who appeared familiar to me. I knew him. Or I should know him. The man was traveling west with a group of people. It seemed he had been forced to leave his home. The energy surge flowed to my head, and I had to speak, breaking the silence.

"Adrian Azur!" I bellowed. "I saw Adrian Azur leaving Charlesville, coming west to this area."

Everyone opened their eyes. Omari grinned and said, "Correct, Diondray Azur. The Boma Essence revealed it to you. If you were not one of us, the Boma Essence would have never shown you when Adrian Azur left the city by the Kammara Sea."

Everyone rose from their seats and turned toward me. They bowed and said in unison, "Welcome home."

I looked at them as they returned to their seats. I was still missing pieces of information I needed before I could fully accept their belief that I was a Boma-Man. I did not know

Adrian Azur's story or what connection he had to my family. Also, I had come here with the Copperwiths, and they were very much a part of my life. I could not abandon them. We had to finish our journey to the rest of the cities south of the Great Forest.

I took a drink of brownberry juice, trying to gather myself. I still felt the energy surge inside of me.

"Adrian Azur was forced from your city by the Kammara Sea along with fifty people who believed in Mother Adrianna instead of his brother, Charles," Omari said. Everyone else at the table was eating.

"You know about Mother Adrianna?"

"Of course. Boma-Men learned her story from Adrian. We know that she was forced from her tribe because of her relations with the traveler. She traveled through the Great Forest with her son, Charles, and was protected by the leopards. She made it to the land next to the Kammara Sea and was taken in by the native tribe. They raised Charles as their own, and he rose to become their great leader."

I could not believe what I was hearing. Omari knew Mother Adrianna's history exactly. Yet, I had never heard of the Boma-Men before I arrived in the city of Adrian. I felt so sheltered and closed off from the rest of this region at that moment. Did my family know about the Boma-Men? If they did, why keep this part of our history from me?

"Years later, Mother Adrianna had another child—Adrian. He was eight years younger than Charles. Any parent with multiple children knows that your attention can go a little more to the younger child. Mother Adrianna was no exception."

I saw Ayesha nodding at her husband's comments. I glanced at their children. Taikah seemed to be a few years younger than her brother, Naymor. Her braided hair flowed out from behind her mask. I believed she got most of her mother's attention.

But I was still trying to piece together the details of the story I was hearing. "That means Mother Adrianna had a child with Sidney Azur," I said.

"Adrian and Charles were half-brothers, yes."

"But there is no history in Charlesville that says Adrian Azur existed. Our family rules that city, and no one has ever mentioned him. No schooling I attended mentioned Adrian Azur. Not even friends in passing conversation ever said his name. How could my family keep a secret like that for so long?"

Ayesha and the children got up from the table. Their presence was no longer needed, and they seemed to know it was time to leave. They took their plates and left. Omari, his brothers, and Micah remained. The men listened intently to the conversation.

"People can keep things they don't believe in hidden for a long time," Omari remarked. "You mentioned the traveler's sacred book being in your city. How long has it been there?"

"At least two hundred years," I answered. "Oscar Ortega had already traveled through the region north of the Great Forest before coming south. From his writings in the Book of Kammbi, he was in his midforties when he arrived."

"Your family hid the traveler's sacred book for that long. It would not be hard for them to hide the truth about Adrian. But as I have said, the circle of history will always close its loop."

"You are really sure that Adrian Azur is my ancestor?"

"When Adrian Azur arrived in this area, he was greeted by a leopard. The leopard became his companion for the rest of his life. Our people worshiped the leopard for generations before he arrived. When our former leader, Boymani, saw Adrian with the same complexion and hair as Boma-Men and the leopard as his companion, he declared to our people at that time that Adrian Azur was one of us. Generations later, you have arrived in Boma Village in the same manner as Adrian Azur. And the Boma Essence has shown you who he is. The connection is undeniable. He is your ancestor."

I glanced at Omari and the other men at the dining table. I could sense from the surge of energy inside of me that all believed Adrian Azur was my ancestor. I had no choice but to find out more about the connection between Adrian Azur and the Boma-Men.

I spent the next three days working the guanna stalks with Micah and a small group of villagers. We covered about three miles of land in that time period. The Boma magic kept me energized and refreshed after each day of work. And as we labored together, I learned more about the Boma-Men's relationship with Adrian Azur. How he taught the Boma-Men the technique of pulling the guanna stalks faster. Adrian had the Boma Essence, and he used it to pull those stalks in half the time the Boma-Men did before his arrival. The Boma-Men now worked the guanna stalks faster than anyone else because of Adrian's technique. Their speed had kept their place of honor in the eyes of the people in the city of Adrian. Omari explained that without Adrian's technique, his people would not have a place in Adrian society.

From Omari and Micah, I learned the city was controlled by two families: the Azurs and the Gamons. These two families were the biggest producers of javann, a popular liquor, in the entire region south of the Great Forest. They used guanna stalk production from the Boma-Men to make it. Because of the Boma-Men's ability to produce guanna stalks at such a proficient pace, the families made a truce with them and their beliefs. However, they were forced to live outside of the city limits to practice their beliefs. The Azur and Gamon families thought it was strange for human beings to worship a leopard, and they did not want Boma-Man beliefs to influence the citizens of Adrian.

Nevertheless, I pondered, the city was named after Adrian Azur, and he had practiced Boma-Man beliefs when he came to this area. The families chose to ignore that part of their history, instead highlighting later years when Adrian Azur became more civilized and participated in making javann.

By the power of the Boma Essence, I began to see that Omari believed I could help the Boma-Men become more integrated into Adrian society. However, I had not spent any time amongst the people of the city, and I had only forty-six days left in Adrian, as established by the konseho of Kammbi. I did not know what kind of impact I could have in that time frame. Also, I was here because of Oscar's prophecy from the Book of Kammbi—it was important that I not forget that. However, I did feel a connection to the Boma-Men, and I wanted to help them if I could.

"Diondray!"

I had just finished working in the guanna stalks for the day and had strolled into the center of the village when I heard Mrs. Copperwith call my name. I looked up to see her coming toward me. Diakono Copperwith trailed his wife, but I knew he was glad to see me too.

"Take that mask off!" she said and hugged me. "No man's face should hide behind a mask. Especially the one who will fulfill Oscar's prophecy."

I took off the mask and saw her tear-filled eyes. She touched my face in a motherly way, and I could not deny that I felt as much love for Mrs. Copperwith as I did for Aunt Maxina. I looked away from her to her husband and another man standing beside him. The man had a boyish-looking face and oversized eyebrows, but his expression was serious despite his youthful appearance.

"I knew Reuel and the Eternal Comforter would keep you well," Diakono Copperwith said.

Omari, Micah, and Omari's brothers joined us at the center of the village. Omari stared hard at the man next to Diakono Copperwith—the tension between them was right on the surface. The Boma Essence indicated to me that the man next to the diakono was a member of one of the families of the city. I sensed that he wanted to get rid of the Boma-Men, but he could not because of their prowess with the guanna stalks.

"Reuel has kept me well," I replied. The leopard was somewhere around the village, but he did not bother to make an appearance now. "I have learned a lot from the Boma-Men."

"Diondray, meet Eduardo Azur," Omari said.

Eduardo stepped forward and extended his hand to me. "If he's an Azur, then he needs to learn more about his family," he replied while staring at the leader of the Boma-Men.

"We would not have found you without Eduardo's help," Mrs. Copperwith said as she held my arm. Her voice cut through the tension between Omari and Eduardo. "I knew, by the Eternal Comforter, that you would be okay. But I'm still glad to see you."

I smiled at the diakono's wife.

"Diondray has only learned part of the story about Adrian Azur," Eduardo continued. "I will make sure he gets the entire picture of our ancestor."

Omari nodded as his gaze remained on Eduardo. "We will meet again, Diondray. I told you: the circle of history is ready to close."

Chapter 3

Micah retrieved my suitcase and travel bag before we left the village. I kept the mask and placed it in the suitcase. I still felt the Boma Essence flowing through me after the autobus drove away from Boma Village. Was the Boma Essence a gift from Omari because of my connection to Adrian Azur? Would this magic replace the Eternal Comforter that I was supposed to receive when I finally declared my belief in Kammbi?

"Omari has you believing that you are a Boma-Man," Eduardo said. He sat next to me on the autobus while the Copperwiths sat on the other side.

"My last name would give him a reason to believe that," I replied.

Eduardo laughed. It was a deep, guttural laugh that immediately rubbed me the wrong way. "Omari and the Boma-Men have believed for many years that another Azur would come to 'complete their circle of history,' as the chief told you. They believe once the loop has been completed, our city will return to the original state it was in when Adrian Azur first arrived."

I narrowed my eyes. "So your family and the Gamon family want to get rid of the Boma-Men before the circle of history closes its loop."

"Diondray!" Mrs. Copperwith blurted. "Don't speak like that. We are guests of Mr. Azur. We should always respect the hospitality shown to us."

I glanced at the Copperwiths. Their faces both showed disappointment. I had surprised myself with my response to Eduardo's comment. Normally, I would never respond so sharply to someone I had just met. But I sensed that my comment came from the Boma Essence. It was telling me that once the Azurs and Gamons figured out how they could increase javann production without having to rely on the Boma-Men, they would get rid of them for good.

"Omari has told you a lot more than I expected," Eduardo continued. "And it has affected you deeply. I will admit to you that I'm not fond of a group of people who worship leopards and believe that all the people of my city should do the same. Animals should never be worshiped. The Boma-Men can have those beliefs as long as they keep them away from the city. We can coexist peacefully."

At least he was being honest about not liking the Boma-Men. But I knew he was lying about wanting to coexist peacefully. I sensed there was some other reason he wanted to get rid of the Boma-Men, and as we drove, I pondered whether our arrival in Adrian was meant to stop that from happening.

"Driver, don't take us to the hotel. I would like to show my guests a little of the city."

"Yes, Mr. Azur," the driver replied.

"We as believers and followers of Kammbi do not believe that human beings should worship animals either," Diakono

Copperwith remarked. "My wife and I did not know about these practices when those men asked Diondray to go with them. We would have strongly dissuaded him."

"My husband is correct," Mrs. Copperwith followed. "There is nothing in the Book of Kammbi that says human beings should worship animals."

Eduardo laughed again. I began to perspire and wished I could move to a different seat. "No explanation needed, my guests. I will make sure that Diondray knows the entire history of Adrian Azur. Omari has left some gaps."

On that point, I knew Eduardo was speaking the truth. I had become curious about those gaps myself, and I sensed I would soon have a complete picture of Adrian Azur. How was he connected to this city? How was he connected to Oscar's prophecy and me?

A few minutes later, we arrived at the marperia, near the center of the city—the central location for shopping, eating, and people watching. All of the cities north of the Great Forest had a marperia. I was surprised to find one in the south.

Eduardo led us to an area just east of the main square on the marperia. Several Boma-Men were there, selling hand-sized leopard print masks, jewelry, and pottery. The area around them was crowded with people.

The Copperwiths remained across the street from where the Boma-Men were selling their wares. I noticed people staring at the couple as they passed by them. No one in Adrian wore a long shawl like Diakono Copperwith or a full-length dress like Mrs. Copperwith. My companions carried an air of importance that naturally made people curious.

"This area has become the most popular spot in the marperia," Eduardo said as he guided me through the crowd of people waiting to buy from the Boma-Men. "The people of this city as well as people from Walter's Grove and Terrance come here to buy these leopard-inspired trinkets, thinking they are getting a piece of our history. But it's nothing but junk to make money from."

Eduardo led me to the front of line, where the Boma-Men acknowledged his arrival. They bowed to him, and his eyebrows drew tighter. Witnessing his expression combined with the tone from his last comment, I found myself wondering . . . why did he hate the Boma-Men so much?

"So this leopard paraphernalia is not authentic?" I asked.

"Absolutely not! Look at the jewelry and the hand masks. Omari has his people make these trinkets in an hour and creates a story to tell the buyers to make them believe they are generations old."

Through the noises of the crowd, I overheard the Boma-Men explaining that the hand masks they were selling had been made before the city came into existence. The buyers were engrossed by their explanation, and I was still trying to understand why Eduardo was so offended.

"Can you stop them from selling their paraphernalia here in the marperia?" I asked as Eduardo led me back through the crowd and across the street to rejoin the Copperwiths.

"I cannot," Eduardo said with a defeated look on his face. "My father made an agreement years ago with Omari that his people could sell his trinkets as long as they want. As long as they give the Gamon family and us a percentage of what they sell every thirty days, and they continue to provide guanna stalk production, they can remain."

"Have these men broken their agreement?" Mrs. Copperwith asked.

We made it back to the autobus. Before getting on it, Eduardo answered, "No, they have not broken their agreement. But I believe you can all help me get rid of the Boma-Men finally."

I was following the Copperwiths onto the autobus, so I noticed when Mrs. Copperwith's shoulders tensed at Eduardo's comment. Her husband's posture stiffened as well. Both of them sat down with blank looks on their faces.

"What do you mean get rid of the Boma-Men?" I asked.

"Diondray, you are family. Your arrival in Adrian will show people that our family has roots outside of the city. It will counteract the history Omari has told you about Adrian Azur's connection to his people. And your companions want to teach from their sacred book. They can teach it on the marperia, and since you have declared that your beliefs do not include animal worship, I can make sure people begin to heed your teachings."

"We don't agree with how these Boma-Men practice their beliefs," Diakono Copperwith countered. "However, we did not come here to remove anyone from their place in this city. Kammbi believes that all people should put their trust in him."

Eduardo grinned. "Well, you are in Adrian, and I have a lot of influence here. You can either accept my offer to help you share your beliefs—on my terms—or your time in this city will be quite difficult."

Although they did so silently, I knew the Copperwiths were praying for the rest of the drive to the hotel. I stared out the window and did not speak. I did not take well to Eduardo's ultimatum. It reminded me of going back to my family home for my birthday earlier in the year. I had wanted to have a pleasant dinner with my family, a year after I had moved out of their home. Uncle Xavier began badgering me about living on the eastside with the common folk and how I needed to know my place. Mother agreed with him. Dinner was their chance to tell me how much they disagreed with my decision to move.

Aunt Maxina defended my choice, but once Uncle Xavier and Mother went in on me, the dinner became a lost cause. I had decided to leave. Uncle Xavier demanded I return home and respect the family wishes or warned that I would end up like my ne'er-do-well father. But after his ultimatum, I knew I would never return to the family home under any circumstances. I was twenty-three, and I could make my own decisions.

As we drove, Eduardo pulled me out of my memories by explaining some of the city's history. It was named after Adrian Azur, who had saved the people from a major flood in the year 56 A.O.A that almost wiped out the entire area. Three rivers flowed toward the city: the Mayza River from the north, the Issabella River from the northeast, and the Adrian River from the south. The rivers converged a few miles east of the city into an area called Guanna Lake. Back then, the city was only a loose collection of villages west of Guanna Lake. The Boma-Men controlled the entire area west of the lake, and the leader of the time designated the village closest to the water for Adrian and his people. They could not live amongst the Boma-Men because they were considered to be outsiders.

During the month of Nayur, the first month of the year, heavy rains came for several days, causing Guanna Lake to flood. The water levels rose so high that they threatened to wipe out all the villages. Adrian Azur led an evacuation of his village as well as several others that were in the path of the rising water. He was able to negotiate with the Boma-Men on resettling further west, on higher ground away from the lake.

At first, the Boma-Men did not want Adrian Azur and the people of those villages settling in their territory, because it was sacred ground for the leopards. But time was running short before the rising waters of Guanna Lake would eliminate all the villages in its path. Adrian made a bold move by telling his people they were going to settle in the new area with or without the approval of the Boma-Men. As he was leading the villagers to their new home, the Boma-Men threatened to harm the evacuees. However, the leopards came from the Great Forest and protected Adrian and the villagers from the Boma-Men. The Boma-Men had to acknowledge the leopards' protection of the villagers and offered a section of land that would eventually become the city of Adrian.

Omari had not told me this part of their history. The Boma Essence flowed through my body as I listened to Eduardo's story—and to my surprise, I sensed that he was telling the truth. Why had Omari kept it from me?

"Adrian did not flee from the city by the Kammara Sea just to show the Boma-Men how to pull guanna stalks," Eduardo said as the autobus arrived at the hotel. "He saved people's lives and forced those animal-worshiping primitives to give away the land that became this city."

The Copperwiths had already exited the autobus and walked into the hotel. Eduardo grabbed my right arm as I was getting up from my seat.

"Diondray, we have the same last name. You are from the city by the Kammara Sea. I just told you more about our ancestor. Convince your companions to accept my offer. Our heritage depends on it."

I released myself from his grip and got off the autobus. I knew I had to return to Boma Village, and I would convince

41

the Copperwiths to join me. I needed to share the teachings of the Book of Kammbi with the Boma-Men.

But when I shared my plan with my friends in the morning, Diakono Copperwith answered, "Diondray, we cannot go back to Boma Village with you."

We were eating breakfast in the hotel's cafeteria. I had barely slept the night before. I was thinking about Adrian Azur and his connection to the Boma-Men and Eduardo. It seemed that each side had a narrative about Adrian Azur and wanted to share with me only the part of history that was favorable to them. Why? Listening to both men, I got a better picture of this city's history—their explanations were like two sides of a coin. Eduardo hated the Boma-Men and their beliefs. However, I did not think Omari hated Eduardo Azur. What had caused this divide, and how could I possibly bring them together in the remaining days I had in the city?

"Why not?" I replied. "I believe we need to share the teachings of the Book of Kammbi with Boma-Men. They will respond to them, I am sure."

"People who worship leopards will not receive our teachings," Mrs. Copperwith said. "Plus, I don't trust people who have to wear masks. Showing your face means you are trustworthy. Hiding them does not!"

I glanced at Mrs. Copperwith. "Has Eduardo Azur influenced you?"

She took a sip of brownberry juice and glared at me. "We know of his hatred toward those leopard-worshiping people. The diakono and I don't hate them, but worshiping an animal instead of a god goes outside of our boundaries."

Diakono Copperwith nodded and added, "If the konseho of Kammbi knew we were sharing the teachings of the Book of Kammbi with people like the Boma-Men, we would have problems with them funding the rest of our journey to the other cities south of the Great Forest."

I could not believe what I was hearing from my companions. Eduardo Azur's feelings toward the Boma-Men had colored their views. They sounded like Mother and Uncle Xavier telling me why I should not be going to Aliki Park on the eastside back home. The eastsiders were different from the people of the westside of Charlesville, and I should not associate with them.

Why I responded the way I did, I'm not sure. The words were leaving my mouth before I really realized what I was doing:

"Because of your obedience in leaving your homeland to come a new land, I will continue to make your name great. Even though you have lost a child due to your act of passha, you will have a descendant who will UNITE THE ENTIRE LAND. And the people will believe that Kammbi is the Lord of all. Those who always believed in me and those WHO DIDN'T BELIEVE ME will create a new people, establishing peace and sanctification throughout this land."

The Copperwiths had startled looks on their faces, and I felt eyes from everyone else in the hotel cafeteria looking at me. I did not realize how loudly my voice had carried.

"You recited Oscar's prophecy from memory," Diakono Copperwith finally said after a few minutes. "How long did it take you to memorize it?"

"I did not memorize it," I replied. "The words just came out of me."

"My Kammbi," Mrs. Copperwith said. "You see, the Eternal Comforter is inside of you, Diondray. Only the Eternal

Comforter could have given you the ability to recite Oscar's prophecy like that."

I shook my head in disagreement. "Diakono and Mrs. Copperwith, that was not from the Eternal Comforter. I believe the Boma Essence that's inside of me caused it. As I spoke, I felt a surge of energy moving through me with rapid speed, like a river when it floods. I must share the teachings of the Book of Kammbi with the Boma-Men. Whether you both decide to come with me to Boma Village or not."

Chapter 4

A new month had arrived—Veme, the eleventh month of the year. The weather became cooler, the heat of Coter gone. Adrian's weather became cool enough for a thin overcoat. Back home in Charlesville, I only wore an overcoat in the first and second months, Nayur and Beru. Even then, the colder weather lasted for only a few days at a time. With Charlesville resting between the Bay of Charlesville and the Kammara Sea, it always felt colder than we liked.

Micah greeted me upon my return to Boma Village. He smiled and took me to the guest quarters immediately. I had forty-five days left in Adrian, and I knew I would spend most of my time here, attempting to share the teachings from the Book of Kammbi.

The konseho of Kammbi had granted fifty days in each of the three cities we would be traveling to this part of the journey. The fifty days signified how long it took Oscar Ortega when he first arrived North of the Great Forest from Guadharra, as described in his chapters of the Book of Kammbi. And I had spent fifty days in each city north of the Great Forest during the earlier part of my journey. I did not have a lot of time, and I hoped the Copperwiths would be able to make some headway in the city.

The Copperwiths had prayed with me after breakfast yesterday. My admission of having the Boma Essence caught them off guard. I explained how I had received it during my first visit to Boma Village. Neither of them believed it at first. But Reuel showed up to the hotel later in the day, and when I ran as fast as the leopard in the area behind the hotel, they were astonished. I climbed a huge tree just as fast as Reuel, and my companions fell on their knees to pray. Diakono Copperwith had then asked me to join them for a longer session in their hotel room.

Even though I had prayed for the first time in Issabella, I was still unsure about this ritual. Prayer was an essential ritual for all the disciples of Kammbi, as was written in the Book of Kammbi. Each disciple prayed every day, believing that by doing so, they could communicate directly with Kammbi. Still, I found it hard to believe that you could talk to an unseen god just by dropping to your knees.

Now, back in the Boma Village, a plate filled with fruit and vegetables sat on the dining room table inside the guest quarters. I had time to grab a handful of brownberries before leaving with Micah for the center of the village. Omari was eager to see me, and we had a lot to discuss. I had brought my travel bag carrying the Book of Kammbi, some of my themilys, and the mask given me during my first visit.

The Boma-Man leader sat at his usual place in the center of the village, flanked by his brothers as always. I could feel the Boma Essence racing through me and knew Omari was glad to see me again. Micah helped me put on the mask I had received, and he led me to Omari and his brothers. I bowed to the Boma-Man leader.

"You have returned to Boma Village so soon," Omari said. "Eduardo did not influence you as much as I thought he would."

The Boma-Man leader was wearing his mask, which seemed shinier than I remembered. "Eduardo does not like your people. He made that clear to me," I replied.

Omari grinned, and I could see his pearly white teeth through the mask. "You have been introduced to our conflict. Eduardo Azur believes the presence of the Boma-Men impedes progress for the city. Our ways of living are from the past, and we should not share those ways with the people of Adrian."

I sensed truth in Omari's comments. He knew that Eduardo Azur wanted to get rid of their influence on the city and was doing everything he could to marginalize the Boma-Men.

"Why does he feel threatened by the Boma Men?"

"Because of what flows inside of you."

"Boma Essence."

"Correct, Diondray," Omari answered. I noticed his brothers shifting their stance as he spoke. "The Azur and Gamon families do not like the fact that we have the Boma Essence and that its power has kept my people protected for many generations. The Boma Essence is considered superstition, not something that civilized people should be involved in."

"Eduardo believes the Boma-Men are uncivilized?"

Omari tilted his head. Even though I could not see his entire facial expression behind the mask, I knew he did not like the fact that Eduardo believed his people were uncivilized. I did not either.

"Just because we revere the leopard and treat the animal with respect does not mean that Boma-Men are uncivilized.

That we live amongst trees and only eat fruits and vegetables does not make us uncivilized. Our ways are just as good as the ways of the people of Adrian. And we will not change in the name of progress."

The Boma-Man leader tilted his head back around to me. I felt the force of those words and knew he meant every word of it. Getting him and his people to believe in the teachings of the Book of Kammbi was going to be that much more difficult.

"I believe Eduardo is trying to find a way to facilitate guanna stalk production outside of your people's ability to harvest it."

The Boma-Man leader sighed. "Yes, we know. Eduardo has been trying to influence his father and the patriarch of the Gamon family to find another source for guanna stalk production since he came of age."

"Is it because he feels the legacy of Adrian Azur belongs to my family?"

Omari's nostrils flared through the mask. "He has told you how Adrian Azur saved the villagers from the great flood of Guanna Lake."

I nodded. "He did. And how Adrian Azur settled his people farther west into land owned by your people. The Boma-Men were going to harm Adrian and his people, but the leopards protected them. And they traveled west to the land that became the city of Adrian."

"True," Omari said softly.

"I felt that was something you should have explained to me."

"Take your mask off," Omari asked.

I obeyed his request, and as I did, he took his mask off as well. He seemed to have gotten more gray streaks in his hair since my last visit, and his face scrunched up a bit.

"That is a part of our history we are not proud of. My ancestors did want to harm Adrian and his people. At that time, we did not want to be associated with any outsiders. Our people had never met someone who came from the east. We owned this area from here and all the way east to Guanna Lake. And my people did not want to give that up."

"That changed when the leopards protected him and his people."

The Boma-Man leader smiled sadly. "You catch on quickly, Diondray Azur. What else would you like to know about Adrian Azur?"

"Actually, I came back to Boma Village because I wanted to share the teachings from the Book of Kammbi. I believe the Boma-Men need to listen to these teachings."

Omari looked stoically and put his mask back on.

Would he allow me to share the teachings from the Book of Kammbi with his people?

I worked the guanna stalks for the next three days before I could share the teachings from the Book of Kammbi. Each workday was ten hours long, and I still had plenty of energy afterward because of the Boma Essence. I could have worked another ten hours and not tired out.

I wondered if the Copperwiths had shared the teachings of Kammbi in the marperia. I knew Eduardo had wanted me to convince my companions to accept his offer, and I hoped my return to Boma Village had not caused him to withdraw his support. I would rather the Copperwiths share the teachings from the Book of Kammbi despite Eduardo's feelings toward the Boma-Men.

Omari had gathered a group of Boma-Men at the center of the village. There looked to be about fifty people sitting cross-legged on the ground and facing their leader—only a tiny percentage of the villagers. I sensed Omari only wanted a small number of his people to hear these teachings before I could share it with the rest of the village. The group was mostly women, with about ten men. Everyone wore their gold masks and dressed in one-piece leopard-print outfits.

I had rehearsed in my mind for the past three days what I wanted to share with them about the Book of Kammbi, speaking the teachings out loud in the guest quarters after work each day to practice. I wished for Diakono Copperwith's advice each evening. I wanted his guidance to make sure I would be covering the right sections of the sacred book. But I had made the decision to return to Boma Village on my own. I would have to rely on my own judgment.

Judgment that had failed me with Frederic Cortes, something reminded me. I dismissed the thought. I had finally started getting his presence out of my mind. Anyway, I had the Boma Essence. Did I still have the Eternal Comforter? Or did I have both of those things inside of me?

"Hello, my people." Omari said. "We have a special event this evening. As you know, Diondray Azur has arrived in Boma Village. He is a descendant of Adrian Azur and comes from the city by the Kammara Sea. However, he was forced to leave his city and travel to the cities north of the Great Forest. Through his travels, Diondray has learned the teachings of those people.

He will share those teachings with us this evening. I would ask that you give him your undivided attention."

Omari nodded at me. The people sat transfixed at his feet. I walked up to where he was and took a couple of deep breaths. I wore my mask, and the heat it generated warmed my face.

"The people north of the Great Forest believe in a god named Kammbi," I began. "Kammbi lived amongst his followers for forty years before he sacrificed himself in order for all of humanity to have a connection and relationship with him."

I thought someone was going to make a comment, like they would have in Aliki Park. But this group remained silent, with all eyes on me. With their faces hidden behind their masks, I could not tell how they had received that first comment. I hoped they had received it well.

Before I could go on, however, Omari himself spoke up. "Why does a god have to sacrifice himself for his people? A god is above a human being."

I glanced at the Boma-Man leader and noticed his nostrils flaring open. He seemed bothered by my opening comment.

"Kammbi believes every person is born with a nature that will commit an act of passha, meaning that we all have the capacity to do what's wrong. Kammbi is the only one who never committed an act of passha, so he could be the only god and man to sacrifice himself for the rest of humanity."

Omari frowned, trying to understand. "So Kammbi was a god and human at the same time?"

I nodded and replied, "Yes. A divine and human being at the same time. I will admit, that has been one of the hardest concepts for me to grasp. I was taught all of my life that gods and humankind are not interlinked. But the teachings from the Book of Kammbi say their god was both divine and human."

The group remained motionless, but I still had their undivided attention.

"Did Kammbi split himself between being a god and a human during the time he was alive?" Omari asked.

I began to pace. I needed to gather my thoughts and make sure I answered correctly. "He did not split himself between being a god and a man. Kammbi revealed aspects of his humanity when needed and aspects of his divinity when needed."

"Sounds like Kammbi had a split personality to me."

The group laughed at their leader's comment. It was the first reaction I had gotten from them since I started. I didn't mind. I would take laughter over silence at this point.

I returned to my position and continued, "Also, he had a third aspect to his being."

"What was that?"

"He gave his believers and followers an aspect of himself, called the Eternal Comforter. When he sacrificed himself, he made a declaration that all believers and followers in him would receive the Eternal Comforter as a gift upon their declaration of worship."

"Wait a minute!" Omari remarked. The group shifted the gaze to their leader. The tone of his voice seemed like a command for the people to give him their attention. "Kammbi was a god and man at the same time. And he gave a part of himself to his followers. That seems far-fetched."

"It does. But it is written in the Book of Kammbi. Every disciple in their writings wrote about this three-in-one aspect of their god."

The group returned their gaze as Omari waved his hands in my direction. I could tell that Omari found the trinity of Kammbi's nature hard to accept. But before I could continue with the teachings, familiar faces arrived in the center of the village.

"Diondray, we had to come here to get you," Mrs. Copperwith said as she strode toward me.

"We cannot let you continue with the teachings to these people," Diakono Copperwith added.

The Copperwiths walked directly up to me while Eduardo Azur followed behind him. Eduardo smirked as he stared at his rival. I glanced at Omari to see his protruding eyes and teeth bared through the mask.

"Why not?" I asked.

"Because the Boma-Men have a belief in eating human flesh, just like the leopard they worship," Eduardo answered. "We fear for your life if you stay here, Diondray."

"Akbar and Joneh!" Omari yelled. The entire group rose from sitting and faced the Copperwiths and Eduardo Azur. I would not allow anyone to harm my friends, so although I didn't understand what was happening here, I left Omari's side and joined the Copperwiths.

Seconds later, Omari's brothers seemed to come out of nowhere, taking their usual places next to him.

"Remove Mr. Azur from our village," Omari commanded.

"I told you! These people are like the leopards they worship. They would rather be animal than human!" Eduardo said sharply.

I sensed Omari wanted to tear Eduardo from limb to limb after that comment. I knew it was not the first time he'd heard such a thing from the Azur heir.

"These people are not animals," I replied as the brothers came toward Eduardo. "They are highly intelligent and able to comprehend what I was teaching before you arrived."

Omari waved his brothers off just before they grabbed Eduardo. They returned to their place next to their leader.

Omari's voice was tense. "Be grateful, Eduardo. Diondray's words saved you from the correction you have needed for a long time. The hatred you have in your heart for my people is so transparent that it oozes from your skin. I will never allow that kind of hatred to be brought amongst my people. From this point on, you will not be allowed to come to Boma Village again. And I will make sure that both your father and Ignacio Gamon know about this day."

Eduardo frowned. "I'm so glad my relative has arrived, and his friends. We will finally get rid of you and your people. Let's go!"

The Copperwiths had horrified looks on their faces. I stared at Omari, and he nodded. He wanted me to go with my companions and Eduardo. I turned away from his gaze and left the center of the village.

Chapter 5

Ten days passed after I left Boma Village for a second time. We had thirty-two days left in Adrian before we moved onto the next city in our journey. The Copperwiths had been allowed to teach on the marperia, but Eduardo Azur's hatred of Omari and the Boma-Men was still fresh my mind, as well as the Copperwiths'.

Eduardo accused the Boma-Men of eating human flesh. I knew that was not true from spending time at Boma Village twice. Micah made it clear that Boma-Men only ate fruits and vegetables, not meat of any kind. I expressed that viewpoint to Eduardo and he insisted those people were cannibals. I had sensed from the Boma Essence flowing inside of me that he believed the Boma-Men were cannibals from second-hand knowledge and not seeing it himself. And that added into his hatred of the Boma-Men. I shared my thoughts with the Copperwiths the prior evening before they taught on the marperia and they accepted my sentiments at face value.

However, my companions did not want to blow the opportunity they had to speak about the Book of Kammbi to the people of Adrian. They had prayed each night for Eduardo about removing the hatred he had built in his heart toward the Boma-Men. Mrs. Copperwith told me that she believed

Eduardo wanted vengeance against the Boma-Men for something that had happened in the past. I knew only about Adrian Azur's role in helping the people during the flood of Guanna Lake years ago. There were definitely two versions of Adrian's role during the event, but I had to agree with Mrs. Copperwith that Eduardo's hatred of the Boma-Men went far deeper than what had happened generations ago.

During the day I spent time on the marperia with the Copperwiths, and the evenings I spent in my hotel room writing themilys. I had declined several invitations from Eduardo to their family home (a traditional structure called a *hastancia*) and another one to meet the Gamon family. I still had to process what had happened between Omari and Eduardo. I believed that my presence had kept the Boma-Men from harming him. I had felt the hatred in both of their hearts for each other. And I did not want to hear Eduardo talking about the Boma-Men in such a fashion. I had to find out why he thought of these people as animals. That was worse than anything I'd heard Uncle Xavier and Mother say about the eastsiders back home. I hated when Uncle Xavier called the eastsiders "ants," but I'd never gotten the sense that he actually thought of them as insects. It was more that those people were not of the same status as our family. It was different with Eduardo—it seemed he really believed the Boma-Men were animals.

I had started several themilys in an attempt to capture Eduardo's hatred, but I could only write a few sentences each time. Finally, the words flowed out of me one evening after I had declined another invitation to the hastancia. Eduardo knew I was declining his invitations because of the confrontation he'd had with Omari. It was the first time since my arrival in Adrian

that he became angry with me, and he made a comment that
started my themily.

> You have become more fond of people who
> prefer to live in trees and run like animals than
> the family you have just discovered.

> Does your hatred of people who act different from you run so deep?
> What is it about these people you hate so much?
> Is your contempt of these people because they
> have a special connection to leopards?
> Or is it because our ancestor had a connection to them?
> Or is it because I have a connection to them?

> What have these people done to cause such enmity?
> Did they do something to you personally?
> Did they do something to our family?
> Did they do something to the people of this city?
> What caused your hatred to burn so hot
> that you are willing to use my companions
> as well as your newfound relative,
> as means of trying to get rid of a people who
> are natives to this part of the land?

The words spilled out of me. I had to find out where this
hatred of the Boma-Men originated. Somehow, I perceived
it could be the key to uniting this city. I had experienced a
similar type of division in the city of Alicia. The religious
establishment of Alicia had disassociated itself from a section
of citizens who believed in the river god of the Issabella River
instead of Kammbi. Those dismissed citizens were branded as

heretics by the morrims and diakonos of the city. But Kammbi had enabled us to make peace between them. Hopefully, my experience of that kind of citywide division would come into play as I dealt with a much deeper form of hatred in Adrian.

I finally accepted an invitation from Eduardo to the hastancia two nights later. He had threatened to stop letting the Copperwiths teach on the marperia, and I did not want that kind of access to the people of the city to end. My companions were getting people to stop and listen to the teachings in growing numbers. They were also able to pull some of the crowd away from the Boma-Men selling their wares.

Hastancia de Azur was outside the city and close to Boma Village. I had learned that both the Azur and Gamon families, as well as several of the other rich families of Adrian, lived on hastancias, where they produced javann, brown and cream beans, grains, and other crops. Even though the Azur and Gamon families were considered the rulers, other families with hastancias—like the Echeverria, Ibarra, and Royball families— had nearly as much influence on the city as they did.

It was a thirty-minute drive from the hotel to Hastancia de Azur. The autobus driver rode up to a wooden gate with the letter A engraved into it. As the gate opened, I thought of my family home in Charlesville. I had disliked the way we were in a neighborhood by ourselves. I'd always felt so isolated every time I came home from school or a social function. My friends lived in the neighborhood adjacent to our home, and Willar, the butler, had to drive me over to their homes each time I received permission from Mother to go. I wanted to walk, run, or ride my bicycle to my friends' houses. Mother would not allow it. An Azur should never be seen walking or running in our city, she said. Let other people do that. Not our family, she would tell me. Over the years her words became a constant irritant to me. What made our family so special that we should live in an oversized home and in a neighborhood away from the people?

Eduardo greeted me as I got out of the autobus. He had a satisfied look on his face like he'd finally won a game that had beaten him many times before. Instantly, I wanted to get back in the automobile and return to the hotel. I did not care to stomach that look for the entire dinner. However, I had no choice if I wanted to make sure the Copperwiths could keep teaching on the marperia.

"You have finally made it to your relative's home," he said proudly and placed his arm around my shoulders. "Welcome to Hastancia de Azur."

I gripped the travel bag that hung over my left shoulder and took in the sight of the hastancia. It was a massive, two-story building that seemed to stretch out for miles in either direction. A huge tree similar to what I had seen in Boma Village towered up from the back of the hastancia. The main walkway curved through spectacular grounds. Perfectly cut grass with yellow, white, and lavender flowers lined the walkway, as well as small brownberry trees on each side. Looking at the grounds brought a calmness that I needed at the moment.

"Beautiful home," I said as we reached the entrance. "Hastancia de Azur is much larger than my family home in Charlesville."

Eduardo beamed as two men dressed in white uniforms stood at the entrance. They were twins. Same deep-red complexion, height, and build, with thin mustaches. The twin on the left side of the entrance nodded at Eduardo and opened the door, while the twin on the right stood stiffly in position. Eduardo did not even acknowledge them.

"My home is your home," he continued and dropped his arm from my shoulders. "You come from wealth. So nothing in here should be a surprise to you. Let's head to the outside quarters. Everyone is waiting."

He was correct about my background. I looked at the high ceiling with its chandeliers, the plush sofas on each side of the room, and the huge paintings that took up the walls over the sofas. The center painting was a headshot of a man with dark, brooding eyes and a thick mustache. It seemed like the painting was placed there so he could inspect visitors.

"Poppa is looking forward to meeting you," Eduardo remarked.

I nodded and followed him through this section of the hastancia. The walls were made from a deep blue, almost purple, stone that caught my eye. It seemed that the hastancia was built years ago and had been updated throughout its existence. We reached the outside quarters where a few people had gathered. A lanky, red-complected man with long hair approached Eduardo. The man had on the same white uniform as the twins at the entrance. He was speaking rapidly to Eduardo in a language I did not understand. I assumed this language was native to the people of the area.

Eduardo nodded as the man kept speaking without pausing for a breath. Eduardo pointed back to the front part of the hastancia, and the man left.

"You will see a lot of him today," Eduardo said softly. "Felipe Baston manages Hastancia de Azur and makes sure the place runs like clockwork."

"Is this our relative from Charlesville?" an elderly man announced as we joined the gathering. The elderly man was sitting in a raised chair as a short, heavyset woman with prominent cheeks stood next to him, adorned with silver and dark blue accessories. The dark blue was the same color as the walls of the hastancia.

"Momma and Poppa, this is Diondray Azur from Charlesville," Eduardo replied and went to embrace his parents. After the embrace, he stood on the left side of his father. "Diondray, my parents: Javier and Samantha Azur."

"Javier Azur III," Eduardo's father replied sharply. Eduardo smiled thinly at his father's correction. I sensed that happened a lot between the two.

I shook Javier's frail hand. He still had a firm grip, and he pulled me closer to him. He wore a dangling thick silver and dark-blue stone necklace that hit my right cheek. The elder Azur's leathered, wrinkled face revealed aging, but the grip showed his vigor. "I'm so glad to finally get a relative from the other side of the region here at the hastancia."

Javier released my hand, and Samantha extended hers. "He has dark brown skin just like Adrian Azur and those leopard-worshiping people," she commented.

"Momma!" Eduardo interjected. "I do not want to mention those people today. Let's celebrate our relative coming to Adrian for the first time."

Javier's mother smiled as she shook my hand. Her pale brown skin contrasted against my darker complexion. The other people at the gathering, besides the uniformed workers, had the same complexion as Eduardo's mother. I could see why she'd made her comment. But I could also tell that she was not fond of Boma-Men anymore than her son was.

"I will go into the house to make sure Felipe Baston has all the food ready," she said and excused herself.

Eduardo's father gave his wife a hard slap on her wide bottom as she left his side. Samantha smiled mischievously and headed toward the house.

I sat down on a bench next to Eduardo's father and across from an attractive, heavyset woman who looked like a younger version of Eduardo's mother and a heavyset man of the same build who looked just like Javier Azur.

"I'm Maribel, Eduardo's sister," the young woman said and extended her hand to me. Just like her mother. "And my brother, Patricio." Patricio nodded and gave me a warm smile.

After greeting the Azur siblings, I took the travel bag off my shoulder and placed it next to me. Eduardo stood next to his father but seemed like he wanted to be anywhere else at that moment. Like he was playing his prescribed role for the family. In that sense, I could understand his plight. Mother and Uncle Xavier wanted me to play a role in my family, and I had refused. Look where that refusal had gotten me.

"We have been trying for years to get our javann to your city," Javier Azur began.

"Uncle Xavier did not want to bring in any goods from outside of Charlesville," I replied.

Javier frowned. "I have tried for years. Beginning with Xavier's father, Myro. We have the same last name. I told both of them, we are family. The connection to Adrian Azur is real. Myro and Xavier dismissed that claim and refused to allow the best javann in the entire region south of the Great Forest to be sold in your city."

Was I hearing the elder Azur correctly? He had talked to Great-Uncle Myro during his time as ruler of our city? I had never heard of Great-Uncle Myro having dialogue with anyone from the city of Adrian. I knew about his relationship with Syonne, the governor of Terrance, back in the year 175 A.O.A.—he had allowed immigrants from that city to arrive in Charlesville, settling there for thirty years. Xavier hated that arrangement and made sure immigration ended when he became ruler of Charlesville. But now, to learn there had been overtures from Javier Azur of Adrian too—what other attempts at trade or unity had come that I knew nothing about? Were there attempts made by the leaders of Walter's Grove, the other major city south of the Great Forest, to Uncle Xavier? Why did he want to isolate our city? And why dismiss the claim about Adrian Azur and our connection to Javier and his family? I began to realize there was much I did not know about our history, and that was embarrassing.

"Diondray, our side of the family has reached out for years to Xavier and Myro, like Poppa said," Eduardo said. "We have always assured them it would make money for everybody if they would trade with us. Still, they have refused. Now, with you here in our city, we may be able to finally establish a relationship. A true family connection."

Felipe Baston and Javier's mother returned with trays of food and a couple of glass jars containing javann. But it was the aroma and colorful presentation of the food on the trays that got my attention. I noticed mango slices, corn, and strips of meat were laid on a thin, circular piece of white bread.

"Do you eat *tortas* in Charlesville?" Maribel asked excitedly as she put several of them on her plate. "Tortas are a main delicacy here in Adrian. We got to know that your city eats them too."

"We don't eat tortas back home." I replied as Maribel frowned. I put several of them on my plate while Felipe Baston poured a glass of javann for me. "I had never seen mango slices and corn mixed together like this before."

Samantha gasped. "They don't eat tortas in Charlesville? Javy, I believe we have another item to export beside javann."

"I believe we do, honey." Javier Azur said as he planted a kiss on his wife's cheek. "Our relative needs to be eating tortas as well as whether (should "whether" be replaced by "whatever"? they eat in Charlesville. We could make a lot of money together."

I could tell my newfound relatives were about making money. However, I had to acknowledge that tortas would do well back home. We loved eating mangoes, corn, and meat but never thought to put them together on a piece of bread.

"Those people need some Azur javann in their city," Javier continued. "I have tried to bring our javann to Charlesville for years. Both Myro and Xavier have refused it. I don't understand why people with our last name would not want to make a lot of money and bring the greatest drink ever created to your city. It doesn't make sense. "

"Javy...." Samantha interjected after glaring him.

Eduardo smiled thinly after giving his father a sharp look. "Diondray, I have invited you to Hastancia de Azur because we want to establish our relationship with you. We believe you are family, and we want to have connections throughout the entire region."

"I told you that I had to escape from Charlesville," I interjected. "My family had a copy of the Book of Kammbi in my city for generations, and I did not know that it existed.

I discovered it back in Carm, the third month of the year. Because of that discovery, I had to leave home."

"The Book of Kammbi?" Javier said.

Eduardo shot another look at his father. "I know, Diondray. However, I still believe you can return home, and we can reengage discussions with Xavier on getting javann into Charlesville."

I shook my head in disagreement. "Eduardo, I was placed in confinement by my Uncle Xavier because I spoke publicly about the Book of Kammbi being in our city for ages. He did not want knowledge of that book being known to our citizens. My aunt Maxina helped me escape confinement, and I had to go to the cities north of the Great Forest. The people there believe I am the one who will unite the entire land because of a prophecy written in that book. I cannot return to Charlesville."

All my relatives gaped. I knew I had just told them something they had never heard before. Sometimes, the truth could cut deep.

"So you are here in our city with that mixed complexion couple to share words from some ancient book," Javier said sharply.

I nodded.

"Eduardo, it is time to end this dinner," the elder Azur said and rose from his chair.

"Poppa! We have much to discuss with our relative."

Javier looked sternly at his son. "Discussion is over. I know you believe that you can run the family business better than I can at my age. However, I'm still alive and will run the business. There is nothing to discuss with this distant relative. He has made his intentions clear as to why he's here. And I will not allow anyone to convert my family to a strange belief system.

Samantha, Maribel, and Patricio, let's go. Eduardo, please escort him off our property."

With that, they all followed Javier back to the house. Eduardo stood stiffly and stared at his family walking away. Javier was still the unquestioned leader of this family, and Eduardo knew it. And as I watched them go, I realized how much more difficult my task had become of sharing the teachings from the Book of Kammbi with the people of Adrian.

Chapter 6

Eleven days had passed since my visit to Hastancia de Azur. I had not heard from Eduardo since the abrupt ending to our dinner. Moreover, the elder Azur had the Copperwiths removed from the marperia, and they were no longer allowed to share the teachings of the Book of Kammbi in that section of the city.

I spent my time at Boma Village each day. I picked guanna stalks in the morning and shared the teachings of the Book of Kammbi in the evenings. Omari allowed more and more of his people to listen to the words from that sacred book. They asked hard questions. Why does a god need to sacrifice himself? Why does this god believe all people are born with the nature to commit acts of passha? I struggled with that belief myself. The Book of Kammbi seemed to believe that human beings were not born good, but rather that they came into the world with transgressions inside of them. That concept went beyond my knowledge of anything spiritual. Growing up, I had not been taught from the lifecharts of my people that I needed a god who was without transgression to rescue me from myself. Diakono Copperwith and I had discussed this part of the teaching several times since traveling together, and he had given me a logical explanation every time. But I still did not really get it.

Each day, I asked the Copperwiths to join me at Boma Village. I needed their expertise and knowledge to answer the questions I could not. And each time, they refused. I wondered if my relatives' hatred of the Boma-Men still affected my companions' view of them.

On the eleventh day, we were eating breakfast in the hotel's cafeteria. Although we were simply eating quietly together, the Boma Essence started racing through my body. I was still unsure of what made this magic flow through my body. I had not felt anything since accepting the invitation to Hastancia de Azur. Did the Boma Essence only work at certain times?

Whatever the answer to that question, I knew the Copperwiths had something to share before I left for Boma Village. And sure enough, Diakono Copperwith spoke up.

"We have refused to join you at Boma Village," he said solemnly. "Annalisa and I know that what happened at Hastancia de Azur was not your fault."

That was an odd comment. Of course it was not my fault that Javier Azur had abruptly ended the gathering. Why would Diakono Copperwith mention it?

Mrs. Copperwith nodded. "We have been praying nonstop since our removal from the marperia. Praying that Javier Azur would change his heart. Actually, we prayed for your entire family, Diondray. We can tell their hearts toward other people are dark."

At least the Copperwiths could acknowledge my newfound family's hatred of the Boma-Men. I felt hopeful. Maybe they were planning to come with me today.

"We have finally received guidance from the Eternal Comforter," she continued. My companions managed small smiles. I watched both of their faces, waiting for the good news.

"Are you both allowed to return to the marperia?" I asked after a moment of silence.

Their smiles evaporated. "No. But we have been invited to Hastancia de Gamon," Diakono Copperwith answered.

"Hastancia de Gamon?"

Mrs. Copperwith nodded. "Veronica Echeverria-Gamon came to our hotel room two nights ago and offered an invitation to their hastancia. Veronica felt sorry that Javier Azur forced us off the marperia and said the Gamon family wanted to help. Thank the Eternal Comforter for providing us another opportunity to reach the people of this city."

I had not made any contact with the Gamon family since our arrival in Adrian. Were they annoyed with Javier Azur for having the Copperwiths removed from the marperia? If so, how they could help my companions return?

"We are going to Hastancia de Gamon after breakfast," Diakono Copperwith declared.

"So that's why you refused my latest request for you both to join me at Boma Village."

Mrs. Copperwith grabbed my right hand with a motherly touch. "Actually, Mrs. Gamon wants you to come with us."

"But I have guanna stalks to pull with the Boma-Men."

"Mrs. Gamon said she will talk to Omari about letting you join us for today. She really wants to see you."

Diakono Copperwith nodded. I wished I'd known this information last night. I could have told Omari. I wanted to go to Boma Village. I liked being there, and I felt a genuine connection to the Boma-Men.

"The autobus is waiting for us," Diakono Copperwith said.

The Boma Essence started racing through my body. My vision became blurry, and I began to see the Copperwiths as doubles.

"Diondray!"

The blurriness dissipated, and a blue light flashed in front of me. Then I heard a familiar voice.

"Go with your companions. We will see you soon."

I knew that voice. Omari. But how was he speaking inside my head?

"I can talk to you through your mind. It's okay, Diondray."

"How?" I said aloud.

"We are connected to each other. I spoke to Mrs. Gamon. Go with your companions."

The voice faded, and my vision returned. The Copperwiths were standing next to me.

"Diondray, are you okay?" Mrs. Copperwith asked as she handed me a cup of water.

I nodded.

"Whom were you talking to?" she asked.

I sipped the water and looked at my companions. "Omari. He was talking to me in my mind. He has spoken to Mrs. Gamon and told me it was okay to go to Hastancia de Gamon."

The Copperwiths stared at each other. "You do have magic inside of you," Diakono Copperwith remarked softly.

"Not magic. Boma Essence."

Mrs. Copperwith's eyes widened, and her cheeks became red. "The one who fulfills Oscar's prophecy cannot have magic inside of him. Magic is not for believers and followers of Kammbi."

"I have something inside of me. I can feel it flowing through my body. I can read thoughts, and now Omari spoke to me in my mind."

Her tone when she answered was colder than I had ever heard it. "Then you cannot be the one who will fulfill Oscar's prophecy."

Diakono Copperwith shot a surprised look at his wife. Before he could speak, Mrs. Copperwith reached for his hands. "Oscar Ortega said the Mayza tribe believed in magic when he first arrived in the land. He had to convince them that magic is dark power, not meant to use. Magic is evil."

Oscar Ortega's section was the last part of the Book of Kammbi. He wrote about how he came to the land north of the Great Forest and converted all the tribes across the region. The Mayza tribe in the northwest corner of the region were the first people he encountered. They believed in a magic that kept them in tune with nature. For example, the elders got their magic from the sun on the hot days of the year and from the snow on the cold days of the year. Oscar explained to the tribe that this kind of magic could cause evil—that it was part of being born with acts of passha within them. The elders of the tribe eventually acquiesced to not using magic in Oscar's presence. And that led them to becoming Oscar Ortega's first converts to believers and followers in Kammbi. But I couldn't believe the magic he had objected to was the same as the Boma Essence.

"Boma Essence is not evil," I shot back. "It can be used properly for good."

"Do you believe that?" Diakono Copperwith said.

71

"I do. I can sense it. Every time this essence has flown through my body. Besides, the Boma-Men have always used this Boma Essence for good."

"He is getting a dark power that will keep him from becoming a believer and follower in Kammbi," Mrs. Copperwith replied.

I knew I could never convince her the Boma Essence inside of me was not a dark power or evil. Magic went against her beliefs as a believer and follower of Kammbi.

"What are we going to do, Malcolm?" she continued. "We have to tell the konseho of Kammbi about this."

Diakono Copperwith closed his eyes and rocked in his seat. I had not seen him like this before. Was he praying? Was he communicating with the Eternal Comforter?

"Annalisa, we are not going to tell the konseho of Kammbi," he said after opening his eyes. "Oscar did acknowledge that the Mayza tribe maintained their magic after conversion. It did not go away. Kammbi did not keep those people from becoming believers and followers in him."

"Malcolm!"

"If we are going to believe the Book of Kammbi literally, then we cannot say magic can only be used for evil."

It was the first disagreement I had seen between the Copperwiths. They were always lockstep in every decision regarding their beliefs. Mrs. Copperwith had a bright red face, and tears began to water in her eyes.

"You cannot lie to the konseho of Kammbi," she pleaded with her husband. "If they found out we knew the whole time that Diondray had this magic inside of him, we could lose our standing as believers and followers of Kammbi."

"If he is the one who fulfill Oscar's prophecy, everything we have ever known about being believers and followers of Kammbi will be changed forever. We are to keep this knowledge about Diondray to ourselves."

Mrs. Copperwith wiped the tears off her cheeks and nodded.

"Let's go to Hastancia de Gamon," Diakono Copperwith said as he stared at his wife.

Hastancia de Gamon was farther out of Adrian's city limits than Hastancia de Azur. We passed Boma Village along the route. Mrs. Copperwith was still shaken by the disagreement she'd had with her husband. They did not speak to each other for the entire forty-five minute ride. I sensed she still wanted to tell the konscho of Kammbi about me. Lying, or at least hiding the truth, was something Mrs. Copperwith never would become comfortable with. And I believed she was astonished that her husband, Diakono Malcolm Copperwith of the kahall of Santa Sophia, would want to deceive the konseho of Kammbi so easily. Before I arrived in Santa Sophia, Diakono Copperwith was in line to become morrim of the kahall—a status just below that of a member of the konseho of Kammbi. Mrs. Copperwith had known her husband to be the most upstanding man in her life. And just like that, he had compromised his integrity.

As for Diakono Copperwith, he had seemed to know that his life would change ever since he failed to be appointed morrim of the kahall of Santa Sophia. It was the only thing he had truly wanted for himself beside his marriage to Mrs. Copperwith, and everyone had expected it. But he understood once I came into the picture that he needed to trust the Eternal Comforter, no matter what happened, and Kammbi would use his life for whatever this god wanted of him. Diakono Copperwith's own desires would have to take a back seat.

That kind of trust in something unseen was rare, and it had earned my admiration. I was also grateful for the diakono's trust in me. I had not yet become a true believer and follower of Kammbi, and I was still unsure about being the one who would fulfill Oscar's prophecy. Yet Diakono Copperwith did not waver in his support of me.

The main residence of Hastancia de Gamon formed a U shape. We entered the hastancia on the left side and followed a squat, red-skinned servant to the patio. There, sprouting brownberry trees and purple and yellow flowers decorated the landscape.

The servant brought us to the back of the patio, where a couple was sitting at a short, circular table. A short woman with jet back hair and sharp facial features rose from her seat and smiled.

"Annalisa and Diakono Copperwith!" the woman said after the servant bowed to the couple and left. "Welcome to Hastancia de Gamon."

Mrs. Copperwith managed a small smile, the first she had mustered for the day. I hoped she could find some kind of peace about my situation with the Boma Essence. Even though her pious nature had come off too strong when I first met her, I had enjoyed her presence throughout the entire journey, and I did not want her to become distant toward me.

"Veronica and Ignacio," Mrs. Copperwith replied. "Thank you for the invitation to your hastancia."

Ignacio Gamon rose from his seat and greeted us. Mr. Gamon was about the same height as Diakono Copperwith. He had puffed-out cheeks, piercing eyes, and a long, thin nose. He carried himself like a leader.

"I know it's too early for my guests to have a drink of javann," he said in a deliberate tone. "But we will have the freshest brownberry juice brought out shortly."

The Copperwiths would never drink javann. The Book of Kammbi prohibited drinking liquor. All the disciples in the Ryianza section, the first seven books of the Book of Kammbi, had written strongly against it. Gregory wrote that being drunk was one of the worst states a human being could put himself or herself in. The believers and followers of Kammbi were meant to be sober and clear-minded at all times and never fall into the temptation of liquor. I was glad Mr. Gamon did not offer us javann, because he came across as a man who would not like anyone refusing what he had to offer.

"You are Diondray Azur," Veronica said and extended her hand to me. Mrs. Gamon wore silver and indigo jewelry on her neck, ears, and wrists, just like Samantha Azur. "You are just as dark as the people of Boma Village."

Well, she did not waste any time in noticing my skin color. I assumed the Gamon family felt the same way about Boma-Men as my relatives did.

"Should his skin tone matter?" Mrs. Copperwith said.

Veronica Gamon stiffened. "My apologies, Annalisa. Of course, what he looks like on the outside does not matter to us. We Gamons do not feel the same way about the Boma-Men as the Azur family does. Our family has worked with them for generations in guanna stalk production."

"We know how Diondray's relatives feel toward the Boma-Men. And my husband and I will not listen to any more negative comments about them," Mrs. Copperwith replied, smiling at me.

Her smile was genuine. I knew she was still on my side.

Mrs. Gamon looked over to her husband. Mrs. Copperwith's comments caught her off guard. She was probably not used to someone challenging her so quickly. The servant returned with glasses and a pitcher of brownberry juice. He poured everyone a glass and left.

"We would like to have all of you continue with your teachings from your sacred book," Ignacio said. "People in our city have taken to your teachings and made known to us that they want you to continue. They are disappointed that Javier Azur has stopped the teachings from being heard on the marperia."

Mrs. Gamon gave a reassuring smile. "Several of our servants have spoken about your teachings, Annalisa and Diakono Copperwith. They would like to know more about the Book of Kammbi."

Diakono Copperwith nodded. "Where can we continue to share the teachings?"

"Here at Hastancia de Gamon," Ignacio answered. "We have a little building on the other side of the main house. It can accommodate a couple hundred people. We will arrange for transportation from the city. Veronica and I want to know how soon you can begin."

I gulped the brownberry juice as Mr. and Mrs. Gamon smiled at my companions. Their offer was sincere. Through the Boma Essence, I sensed that Veronica Gamon had persuaded her husband about it.

"Thank you for this opportunity, Mr. and Mrs. Gamon" Diakono Copperwith said. "Annalisa and I were beginning to make a connection with the people of the city at the marperia. And having another opportunity to share the teachings of the Book of Kammbi is the reason we are here in Adrian."

"You are welcome, Mr. Copperwith," Veronica Gamon said. "Our servants mean a lot to us. Some of them have worked for the Gamon family for several generations. And when they come to us with a request, we try to honor it."

I surmised that this attitude toward the servants was a recent development. Veronica Gamon had a lot to do with it. I believed it came from a sincere place.

"We will accept your offer under one condition," Mrs. Copperwith asked.

"What is the condition?" Ignacio asked curtly.

The diakono's wife glanced at me and smiled. "Diondray has become like a son to me and my husband. We are here in this region because of him and what we believe he is meant to do. And he has been sharing the teachings from the Book of Kammbi with the Boma-Men. Those people have been receptive. We want them to be allowed here to listen to the teachings with your servants and other people from the city."

I smiled back at Mrs. Copperwith, filled with relief and gratitude.

"I spoke with Omari yesterday," Veronica Gamon said and looked at me. "Ignacio and I know that Diondray has been sharing those teachings with the Boma-Men. We have a good relationship with Omari and his people. They are welcome to come."

Mrs. Gamon gave me a smile. It looked like our purpose for coming to Adrian had finally started to take shape.

"We would like to add that the three of you can stay here at Hastancia de Gamon for the rest of your time in the city," Ignacio said. "Can you tell us when you will begin the teachings?"

"Tomorrow." Diakono Copperwith said.

Ignacio rose from his seat and gave each of us a handshake. That sealed the deal in his mind. I could not help but wonder how Eduardo would take the news when he found out.

Chapter 7

O mari had brought about fifty Boma-Men to Hastancia de Gamon for the past several days, and the Gamon family allowed all their servants to sit in on the teachings. But the majority of the people present came from the city. Mr. Gamon had arranged for a couple of autobuses to pick up people from the marperia and bring them out here to the hastancia. Of course, they all had to drink his brand of javann on the ride. The Copperwiths did not like that, but they were smart enough not to make it an issue.

We had a cross section of people from the city, and everyone was attentive to Diakono Copperwith's teachings from the Book of Kammbi. I stood off to the far right of a makeshift stage the servants had built. Diakono Copperwith stood in the middle of the stage with his copy of the Book of Kammbi in his right hand. He would glance at the book and then look out at the audience. He was definitely in his element.

"The body is one whole made of many parts," Diakono Copperwith stated. "Each body part, whether it's the brain, hand, or foot, has a role within the body. It is the same way when you are a believer and follower of Kammbi. Kammbi believes everyone has a role, and no one's role is more important than someone's else."

The audience gave Diakono Copperwith their undivided attention. As I looked out at them, I saw light-skinned faces like Mrs. Copperwith and Mrs. Gamon, red and brown faces like my own, and the servants sitting together comfortably. It surprised me how receptively the people of Adrian took to the teachings. My eyes turned to Omari. He had a look on his face like he was ready to challenge this teaching once again. The Boma-Man leader glanced at me and smiled. I acknowledged his smile and knew we had to talk about how he was able to communicate with me in my mind.

Diakono Copperwith read from the book. "The hand would never say because I'm not a foot, I don't belong to the body. Or the foot would never say, because I'm not an eye, I do not belong to the body. Or the stomach would never say that because I'm not the mind, I do not belong to the body."

The audience laughed.

Diakono Copperwith paused and stared at the audience. His stoic look ended the audience's laughter, and he returned to looking at the text.

Before he could go on, though, Omari interrupted. "Kammbi may teach his believers and followers that no one's role is more important than anyone else's, but human nature shows time and again that people will always elevate their own importance. Especially if you are wealthy, highly intelligent, or physically gifted."

The audience murmured in agreement.

"I agree with you, Omari." Diakono Copperwith answered. "People with wealth, people who rule over a city, people who are highly intelligent or educated, and people with physical gifts will believe in their own importance over everyone else's. However, Kammbi did not write these words just as a mere expression. He came amongst the people as one of us. He was born in a hovella. His parents were not wealthy or highly educated. Nor did they have any special physical gifts. Kammbi never raised himself above the people."

"How could Kammbi become a god, then? A god who wants everyone, north and south, to become believers and followers in him."

The audience shifted in their seats each time Omari and Diakono Copperwith spoke, hanging on every word. Diakono Copperwith broke his stoic look and allowed a small smile to appear. I knew he respected Omari's intelligence and was willing to engage in this exchange for the rest of the afternoon if needed.

"Kammbi was both human and divine. Our god became human to have the same experience as his believers and followers. To be tempted as we all are. To think and feel like we all do. To laugh in joy or delight. To anguish in pain or to be embarrassed when something went wrong. To go through the same experiences we all do in life. Kammbi is not a god of the sky or the sea, but a god who lived amongst the people."

Omari nodded in a momentary concession. I could tell he wanted to revisit this subject of Kammbi being human and divine during another teaching. I did too. I still did not get why Kammbi had needed to become human. Why would he want to share our experience? Why would he need to?

Veronica Gamon and Mrs. Copperwith came up to me. The two women had become close over the last few days. They spent a lot of time together, and Mrs. Copperwith held one-on-one prayer sessions with Mrs. Gamon each night. They acted like sisters who had not seen each other in some time.

Mrs. Copperwith finally had someone she could relax with and not have to be just Diakono Copperwith's wife.

As they approached, both women looked concerned. I got up from my seat and followed them away from the covered patio.

"Eduardo Azur has arrived at the hastancia," Mrs. Gamon said. "He wants to see you."

"I told him that his father expressed his feelings clearly about our arrival in this city. We were invited to be here at Hastancia de Gamon and there's nothing he can do about it," Mrs. Copperwith added. "Eduardo apologized and said he wanted to talk to you."

She gave me a motherly touch on my right arm. Mrs. Gamon did the same thing. I managed a smile.

"I will talk to him."

I walked to the main house with both women and wondered what had made Eduardo Azur come to Hastancia de Gamon to speak with me.

Eduardo was sitting with Mr. Gamon in a room near the entrance to the main house. They were speaking to each other in a pleasant tone. I overheard Mr. Gamon ask about Eduardo's father and send his regards. Mrs. Gamon walked over to her husband as we arrived. Both men broke the conversation and looked at me.

"You wanted to speak with me?" I said to Eduardo. He got up from his seat.

"Do you want me to stay?" Mrs. Copperwith asked.

"No," I replied.

Mrs. Copperwith and the Gamons excused themselves from the room. Both women still looked concerned, and I knew they wanted to stay and give their support. I appreciated their concern. But I sensed that Eduardo wanted to speak to me alone.

"I want to apologize for my father and the rest of the family," Eduardo started when they left the room. "He should not have treated you like that. You are an Azur. Family members should always treat each other with respect. Even ones we just met."

"The Copperwiths are like family to me. They were dismissed as well."

Eduardo ran his left hand through his hair and sighed. "Yes. Your companions should not have been dismissed like that. But they are not family. And that matters to me more."

"The Copperwiths deserve to be treated with the same respect as myself. If that will not be the case, then we have nothing else to discuss."

Eduardo ran the other hand through his hair and looked away. I had not seen him so anxious before.

"What is the reason you came here?" I asked.

"My father wants you to come back to Hastancia de Azur. He doesn't like that you are staying here at Hastancia de Gamon. I don't either."

I believed the last part of his comment. His father could not have cared less where I stayed, but Eduardo must have persuaded him that it would be better for me to return to Hastancia de Azur.

"I'm staying here," I replied. "The Gamons have been excellent hosts to me and the Copperwiths. And of course, they have allowed Diakono Copperwith to teach from the Book of Kammbi on their property. Tell your father I reject his offer."

Eduardo became red as he ran his hands through his hair again. "Do you think the people of this city will become believers in this god from the north? The people of this city will only believe what we and the Gamon family tell them to believe. You do not even believe in that book from the north."

"We have nothing else to discuss," I replied. "You have wasted your time coming here."

He grabbed my arm. "I apologized for my father's behavior. Please, Diondray."

I removed his hand from my arm. "I will not be forced into returning to Hastancia de Azur. If that is your goal, then you are mistaken in pursuing it. Your hatred of the Boma-Men angers me. I have been treated well by Omari and his people since our arrival. I will not listen to your contempt anymore. I heard enough hatred from my own immediate family growing up. I will not be around that same kind of talk from newfound relatives."

Eduardo threw his hands up in the air. "Those leopard-worshiping people are not who you think they are. Ask their leader about Elena Diego."

"Elena Diego?"

Eduardo's face had grown dark. "Elena was going to be my wife. She had taken a liking to those leopard-worshiping people and wanted to learn about their ways. However, Elena got sick and died in their leader's arms. Those people killed the woman who would have become my wife. That's why I speak about them in the way that angers you. I hate them. And I will not deny that hatred. They took away someone I loved."

My anger dissipated. Eduardo spoke the truth about why he hated the Boma-Men. Suddenly, the Boma Essence began flowing inside my body. My vision blurred, and a blue light flashed in front of me. I heard Omari's voice again.

"He has told you about Elena Diego."

"Yes."

"Are you okay?" Eduardo asked.

I had dropped to my knees and placed my hands on my head.

"He speaks from anger and has not presented the entire story. I will share with you what happened to Elena Diego."

"I want to know everything," I replied.

"You will."

"Who are you talking to?" Eduardo said.

"Diondray!" Mrs. Copperwith said as she came to my side. "Are you okay?"

The blue light faded. Omari's voice was gone. I looked up at Mrs. Copperwith and Mrs. Gamon as they helped me back to my feet. Mrs. Copperwith had a distant look on her face. She knew that Omari had spoken to me.

"I will make sure he has whatever he needs," Mrs. Gamon said and left the room.

Eduardo stared at me. "I will find out the truth about what happened to Elena Diego," I promised.

Chapter 8

Eduardo's rationale for hating the Boma-Men remained on my mind for the rest of the day. It made me wonder if Uncle Xavier had a reason for his hatred of the people from the eastside back home. The Book of Kammbi made it clear that hatred should never be justified. Kammbi wrote about it directly in his chapter of the book, the last one in the Ryianza section of the Book of Kammbi. This paragraph came to mind: *"Hatred never satisfies. Even if you believe there are proper reasons for hatred, you will always have to drink from that well. And it will consume you for the rest of your days. Give that hatred to me. Let me satisfy that desire with love. And the proper result will always present itself."*

Kammbi's chapter included several paragraphs about the self-destructive nature of hatred and how a person should turn it over to him. But how could you give hatred to someone else? How could you give it to a god? Especially when that hatred came from love?

Using those words from Kammbi as a guide, I spent the next three nights writing a themily in an attempt to express how I felt about Eduardo's hatred of the Boma-Men.

Can love that was taken away from you suddenly cause hatred?
Is that hatred justified?
Does that hatred of the one who took your love satisfy?
Does it fill your need for anger?
Does it fill your need for revenge?
Or could that hatred cloud your judgment?
A judgment that might have overlooked the
reasons love went away suddenly.
Could that hatred blind a person from seeing the truth?
If so, could that hatred end up destroying
something more than what has gone away?

The words felt right as they landed on the paper. I had to find out what had happened to Elena Diego. I sensed that Eduardo's confession was sincere. However, he might have left out some facts about what had really happened. The Boma Essence was suggesting a deeper reason for my relative's hatred.

I went to Boma Village after the day's teachings from Diakono Copperwith at Hastancia de Gamon. Omari wanted to talk at the village, and I agreed to his request. He had seemed calm during the teachings, but I was on edge. It was not only about what had happened to Elena Diego—it was also troubling me that Omari could talk to me through my mind. Were we that connected? If so, could he read all my thoughts? Did having the Boma Essence grant one that ability, or was it caused by something else? My mind was racing with the potential of having the power to read thoughts. But I did not like it.

Micah greeted me at the center of the village. "Welcome back home, Diondray" he said after giving me the customary bow. He believed I was one of them. And I could not deny the connection I felt since my first arrival in Boma Village. "Did you bring the mask?" he asked.

I nodded and pulled the travel bag off my shoulders. "In here."

"Put it on."

I did and placed back on my shoulders. (Placed what back on his shoulders?) I felt an immediate power surge from the Boma Essence. That was interesting. Did wearing the mask automatically trigger the Boma Essence?

Omari and his brothers arrived a few minutes later, wearing their masks. However, the Boma-Man leader did not take his customary seat. He motioned for me to sit down, then sat across from me in a cross-legged position. The brothers stood behind him and did not look at us.

"You have heard a version of what happened to Elena Diego," Omari said. "A version based in anger that left out what actually happened. You will see."

The Boma Essence raced faster through my body, and a blue light appeared. The light began to form into an oval. The oval was blue, and as I watched, it started to change into an image.

"What do you see?"

Omari's voice was in my mind. The oval shape had turned into a picture.

"A woman. Same skin tone as Eduardo Azur. She was in Boma Village and lived amongst the people for a time period."

"Correct. What else?"

"She wanted to be amongst the Boma-Men. The woman saw that Boma-Men had been excluded from the city, and she wanted to create a bridge between the people of the city and the Boma-Men. She felt living amongst the Boma-Men would help with that bridge."

The oval shape created one picture after another, telling a story visually. I had never seen anything like it before.

"Tell me more."

"She is picking guanna stalks with the people. The woman wants to know how the Boma-Men can pick it so quickly and efficiently. I see your face, Omari. You are sharing how your people are able to do it so quickly."

"Correct."

"Two leopards appear out of nowhere. They race toward the woman. She is scared as they advance toward her. You assure the woman they are friendly. The leopards reach the woman and begin to purr. They want her to pet them. The woman becomes calm and obliges the leopards. The leopards nuzzle her legs, one on each side. And then . . ."

"What do you see, Diondray?"

"A blue light appears. Just like the one I saw earlier. Then smoke rises from the leopards and goes into the woman. The woman is in shock. Her body receives the smoke, and she has it."

"Has what?"

"The Boma Essence. It races through her body. She can run and climb like a leopard. She can sense things about people. She has it."

The blue light appeared again, and a new picture comes to my view.

"Tell me more."

"The woman is at a building. Her presence catches everyone's attention in the building. I see Eduardo. He is not happy with the woman, and he believes something is wrong with her. He confronts her, and she does not take it well. She backs away from him to avoid the confrontation. Eduardo pursues her, and she takes off running. Running like a leopard. Eduardo is horrified. He calls out for help, and several men appear."

I received a new picture—a terrible scene unfolding before my eyes.

"What happened next?"

"The men realized they could not catch her. The woman ran circles around them. She began to climb one of the buildings. One of the men had gotten a weapon. He aimed it at the woman as she was climbing. Eduardo joined the men and called out to the woman. She looked back at him, then jumped off the building and headed toward him. As she landed on the ground, the man fired. The weapon gave off a loud sound."

I placed my hands on my head. I grabbed the mask and yanked it off my face. Omari's brothers glared at me but did not move from their position. The Boma-Man leader took off his mask. He had a solemn look on his face.

"She was killed by that man," I replied.

Omari nodded. "I saw that whole thing through my mask just like you did. Elena Diego was a friend of the leopards, and the Boma Essence took to her. However, she was not connected to Adrian Azur like you are, and the Essence made her react like the animal."

"The Boma Essence turned her into a leopard?"

Omari sighed. "No it did not turn her into a leopard. Unfortunately, Eduardo Azur believes so. The Boma Essence manifests differently for each person who receives it. For example, I can communicate with you mentally even when I'm not around. The Boma Essence manifests that ability in you, but it could not do the same with Elena Diego. We offered assistance for healing, but Eduardo Azur refused our help. He blames us for killing Elena Diego. The woman he loved. And he believes if she had never come to Boma Village, she would be alive today."

His brothers helped Omari to his feet. I pondered what I had seen. The man who shot Elena had believed she was going to attack Eduardo. But she was not. She only wanted him to know that she had been changed—changed by the Boma Essence. I could see clearly why Eduardo hated these people. However, it was not their fault.

"The Boma Essence will not turn you into a leopard," Omari said. "Reuel came with you when you arrived in Adrian. The leopard was assigned to protect you. That has not happened since Adrian Azur came here. And when you put on the mask for the first time, the Boma Essence entered your body like it did for Elena Diego. However, I knew it would manifest in you differently because of Reuel's assignment of protecting you.

"I do feel physically stronger since receiving the Boma Essence." I replied softly.

Omari nodded. "Yeah, its power for you does not manifest in physicality. The Boma Essence needed to manifest mentally in you for some reason."

I placed my fingers over my mouth and rocked back and forth on the ground. I was wondering how Eduardo could ever accept this version of what had happened to Elena Diego. She had no reason to be turned into a human version of that animal. But that seemed to have been her fate. Elena Diego had chosen to be amongst the Boma-Men for the right reasons, but her death had created a divide that might never be healed.

"I know you want to help us by inspiring Eduardo Azur to get rid of his hatred for us. However, the hatred in his soul is permanent. He will always believe we are responsible for the death of Elena Diego."

I shook my head. "Eduardo will see that your people were not the cause of her death. He will see that hatred never truly satisfies."

Omari gaped. It was the first time I had seen that kind of look on his face.

"Hatred can be changed to love," I added.

The next evening after dinner, I shared with the Copperwiths what I had seen about Elena Diego. The Copperwiths were still attempting to come to grips with me having the Boma Essence—Mrs. Copperwith especially still had trouble with the whole idea. However, she remained silent during my entire explanation. On the surface, Diakono Copperwith seemed more at peace about it. He asked questions about the oval shape and blue light. However, I sensed that as I explained the images, Diakono Copperwith was just as uneasy about it as his wife.

We had ten days left in Adrian, and while more people from the city were coming to Hastancia de Gamon to hear the teachings, I knew we had to find a way to create a bridge between Eduardo and the Boma-Men. I sensed that was the main reason for our being in Adrian. But how could you change someone's heart toward a group of people? A heart filled with hate, who believed there was a justifiable reason for it.

"It's easy to love those who love you. Most people can do that. But we are called to love those who hate us," Diakono Copperwith began. That sentence came from Kammbi's book in the last chapter of the Ryianza section. "What gain is it to love those who love you? You must love those who don't love you. You must extend love toward those who are unlovable. If you love those who don't love you, then you will learn what it is to be merciful, just like I have done with humankind."

Those words felt wrong to my ears. How could you love someone who didn't love you? I had been taught that love had to be given freely, and it also had to be received. It seemed like Kammbi wanted his believers and followers to give unrequited love to those who hated them. That was wrong.

Mrs. Copperwith gently grabbed my right hand. She was sitting to the right of me at the table. "I know this is a strange concept to you—loving someone who doesn't love you. But Kammbi did it for all humankind. They were many people in Guadharra who hated him as he traveled through that land. Even though he healed people, provided sustenance for those who had nothing, and brought a man back to life, all of those acts were not enough to get everyone's love. The authorities of every city in Gudaharra resented this man of meager means who claimed to be the god of all. But Kammbi loved them anyway. And his sacrifice was the ultimate act of loving those who do not love you."

I nodded and briefly looked away. Mr. and Mrs. Gamon had already left the table for the evening. Felipe Baston (Didn't he manage Hastancia de Azur?) had gone to his quarters for the evening as well. One servant still stood at the entrance, waiting in case we needed him. He was a short, plump man with massive hands and feet. Those hands and feet belonged on a body that was several inches taller, I thought. It seemed like he was listening to our conversation. I was sure he had heard some of Diakono Copperwith's teachings at the little house, so the words we were discussing were not foreign to him.

I too was trying to take in those words from Kammbi's section. I had read about all those acts Mrs. Copperwith mentioned. Feeding thousands of people with only a few loaves of bread and a pound of meat, giving people healthy limbs, restoring eyesight, curing illness, and bringing a man back to life after being dead for a day—I would have thought those things would cause everyone to love Kammbi. Yet they did not. If that was the case for a god, how could he ask people to love those who did not love them? Was he not putting his people in an impossible situation? Moreover, how could I get Eduardo Azur to alleviate his hatred toward the Boma-Men?

"You know what you have to do," Diakono Copperwith said and brought my attention back to our table. "Annalisa and I will pray for you the rest of the evening."

"You will need the guidance of the Eternal Comforter, not that magic you have been given," Mrs. Copperwith added.

"Boma Essence," I replied. "Not magic."

I saw the frown on her face. Even though I knew now that she would not distance herself from me, having the Boma Essence inside of me was going to be an issue for the rest of the journey. I sensed that she still wanted to tell the members of the konseho of Kammbi about it. She did not like that her husband wanted to keep it a secret from the people who were funding our journey. Omission was just as bad as lying, and once you compromised your integrity, there was no turning back from the slide down that slope.

"I will go to Hastancia de Azur," I said. "I have to continue the bridge that Elena Diego started. And it must happen before we have to leave this city."

I sent a message with the help of *Felipe Baston* to Hastancia de Azur. It reached Hastancia de Azur later in the day, and Eduardo responded to it immediately. He was glad I had sent the message and said his father wanted me to come to Hastancia de Azur the following day. Eduardo claimed that Javier wanted to apologize for his behavior last time and extend an olive branch to a relative.

The Copperwiths had prayed nonstop for the past two nights. They prayed through the day's teaching session and got most of the people who came to the teaching session to pray— the Boma-Men were the only ones who wouldn't join in. I was still unsure about the concept of prayer, but I appreciated the gesture. I had felt like the people of the city wanted this bridge to finally happen.

I arrived at Hastancia de Azur around midday. The month of Ceber had gotten colder each day, and I had to borrow a jacket from *Felipe Baston*. He was about my size, and the black jacket I borrowed kept me warm on the drive to the hastancia.

The servant brought me to a room down at the end of the main hallway. Javier and Eduardo were sitting on a plush indigo couch when I entered the room. Javier frowned like he did not want to be there. Eduardo gave me a thin smile and rose from the couch.

"Thank you for coming, Diondray," Eduardo said and pointed me to a chair across from the couch.

I sat down as the servant handed me a glass of javann, and I placed it on the stand next to the chair.

"Have you not had javann during your time in the city?" Javier remarked. "Our brand is the best in Adrian."

"Not for me," I replied.

Eduardo's father sighed. "Son, if he doesn't like our drink, how in the world are we going to convince him to help us sell it in his city?"

Eduardo glared at his father. "It's not the time for that kind of talk," he said in a forceful whisper.

Javier gulped his glass of javann and sighed again.

"Poppa!" Eduardo snapped.

The elder Azur sat up in his seat and stared at me. "I should not have been so rude to a relative. I don't agree with the reasons you are here in our city. However, I could have been more hospitable to you."

I nodded and sensed this was the closest to an apology I would get.

"Thank you, Mr. Azur."

Instead of the huffed response I expected, Javier suddenly grabbed the left side of his chest and had an anguished look on his face.

"Are you okay, Mr. Azur?" I said and got up from my seat. Javier grabbed the couch armrest with his right hand, and I could hear the shortness of his breath.

"We need help!" Eduardo yelled as a servant immediately came into the room. The servant and Eduardo eased Javier up off the sofa. He had a clenched look on his face and was trying to catch his breath.

Javier's legs buckled, and he dropped to his knees on the floor. Eduardo and the servant tried to stand him up again, but Mr. Azur shook his head.

"Javier!" Mrs. Azur entered the room and moved the servant out of the way. "Javier!" she repeated as she grabbed her husband's face.

I felt the Boma Essence stirring inside of me. It flowed through my body faster than it ever had before. I saw the blue light hovering over Javier Azur's body. Eduardo and Mrs. Azur laid his head back on the floor. Javier was still clutching the left side of his chest, and he moaned in pain.

"Javier!" Mrs. Azur screamed again, "You cannot leave me!"

The blue light spun into an oval. I saw an image. It was a familiar face.

"Place your hands on his chest."

"Omari," I replied.

"You are the one who will complete the circle of history. The Boma Essence will respond to you in whatever fashion is needed. Now, place your hands on his chest."

I moved next to Eduardo on the right side of his father. Mrs. Azur kept talking to her husband to keep him from passing out.

"Why did you call out Omari's name?" Eduardo asked.

I did not respond to his question but placed my hands on his father's chest. I moved Javier's hand, and my hands started to glow blue. Mrs. Azur stopped talking to her husband, and I could feel her staring at me.

"What are you doing to him?" she yelled.

"Circle your hands over his chest."

I obeyed the request, and Javier's chest glowed.

"What is happening to my husband?"

The glow faded from Javier's body, and he sat up.

"Samantha," he said and reached out for his wife.

"You are still here, my love!" she replied and kissed his face repeatedly.

"What did you do?" Eduardo asked.

"Omari guided me to save your father's life."

The servant and Mrs. Azur helped Javier off the floor and led him out of the room. I was looking at my hands as Eduardo watched his father leave the room. I had prevented someone from dying. What kind of power did this Boma Essence possess?

"Do you have it?" Eduardo replied sharply.

"Have what?"

Eduardo frowned. "The same thing Elena had. Some kind of magic that made her become a leopard. I know Omari gave her magic. Has he given it to you?"

I sighed. "I saw what happened to Elena Diego. My condolences for your loss."

"You did not answer my question!" Eduardo rose from his seat and looked down at me like I was a child. "Do you have it?"

I straightened up in my seat on the couch. "I do have it, but Omari did not believe it would turn her into a leopard. Nor did he cause it. The Boma Essence chose her."

"Balderdash, Diondray!" Eduardo fired back. "Don't believe that leopard worshiper's version of what happened. My beloved was turned into a leopard by those people!"

The anger in his face revealed how entrenched he was in his position. His eyes had gone red, his nostrils flared and jaw clenched. I could feel his body shaking. His hatred for Omari and the Boma-Men was total.

"I came here to convince you that Elena Diego was not forced into becoming a human version of a leopard," I replied. "What have you gained in your hatred of those people?"

Spit flew from his mouth. "Those people want to turn everybody in our city into a leopard. They lost their land after the flood of Guanna Lake, but they still believe this entire region belongs to them. And the more they can get people in our city to believe they are normal, the more easily they can cause their ways to be accepted."

"But you have not answered my question," I replied.

"Have you ever loved a woman with everything you have?" Eduardo asked. "A woman you know you were meant to be with. A woman you wanted to share everything with?"

I nodded. "Yes. Her name is Maisa Merez."

Eduardo finally sat back down on the couch. "Why is she not with you?"

I sighed. I did not want to relive that episode, especially not with him. "She had to choose between her inheritance of a silver mine or coming with my companions and myself to this region."

Eduardo grinned. "And she chose to keep her inheritance?"

I could hear Deputy Santiago of the konseho of Kammbi speaking at my hearing like it had happened yesterday. *In order for you to get the transfer of ownership of Silver Mine 12, you must*

99

remain in Alicia. If you go with Diondray Azur, the ownership of the mine will go to Mr. Cortes."

"Diondray . . ."

"She was tricked by a businessman from Santa Teresa named Frederic Cortes, who helped her get ownership of the silver mine. However, he wrote into the documents that he would become the owner of it if she came with me to this region."

"And you don't hate this Frederic Cortes? You should feel the same way toward him as I feel toward those leopard-worshiping people. That man separated you from the woman you loved. That is unforgiveable!"

I quoted words that had helped me in my grief and anger over losing Maisa: "Hate harbored can never redeem the love that was lost."

Eduardo looked like he was going to say something else, but that last comment stopped him in his tracks. "Where did you get that from?" he asked slowly with a confused look on his face.

"The Book of Kammbi. Kammbi wrote those words of wisdom in the last chapter of the first section of the book, Ryianza. They just came to my mind."

"Are you becoming a believer in this god Kammbi and that book?"

"I don't know. But those words from his chapter have come to mind. And it has kept me from having hatred toward Frederic Cortes."

"Balderdash!" Eduardo shot back. "Hate is the other side of love. It can be proper when it's justified."

More words from the Book of Kambi came to my lips: "There are people in this land who believe that love and hate are two sides of a coin. That is not true at all. Love is its own coin. Hate is its own coin. While similar attributes can be given to both qualities, it does not mean they are two sides of a whole. Hate can never fill you like love can fill you. Hate can never sacrifice like love can sacrifice. Hate can never build a bridge like love can. Hate is a bridge burner, while love is a bridge builder. That is not two sides of the same coin."

I recited those words as though I had memorized Kammbi's section of the Book of Kammbi, the way Diakono Copperwith would have—but how was this possible? I had read those words a few times since leaving home, but I hadn't tried to memorize them, and I knew I would not be able to do so without a lot of time and study. Yet the words just came out of me.

"I will never build a bridge toward Omari and his people. Those fancy words will not change what happened to my beloved. And I urge you to join me in finally getting rid of them for good."

I rose from my seat and stared for a moment at my relative. "The people of this city are taking words like the ones I just said to heart. They are coming to Hastancia de Gamon to hear words from the Book of Kammbi. I only have a few days in this city before I will be summoned on to the next part of our journey. I truly hope you don't let what happened to Elena Diego consume you for the rest of your life. Otherwise, two people would have died on the day she was shot."

Eduardo frowned. "Maybe one day you will learn that loyalty to family is more than building a bridge. Maybe if you had shown more loyalty to your immediate family, you would not have to journey throughout this land trying to validate a false belief system."

"I'm not trying to validate anything, my relative. This belief system came upon me, and I'm trying to find my own way. I have learned that family will push you out if you don't do exactly what they want. To me, it seems that family should allow for all of its members to become who they are meant to be. And should be on board with things that can exchange hate for love."

Eduardo sneered as his servant entered the room. I followed the servant out and knew I would never see Eduardo again.

The last few days in Adrian went by quickly. The little house at Hastancia de Gamon gained more visitors to hear the teachings from Diakono Copperwith, and word spread throughout the city about it. My relatives remained in opposition to anyone going to hear the teachings. Eduardo spoke at the marperia each day against those who were getting on the autobus to come to Hastancia de Gamon.

However, Eduardo's warnings had the opposite effect from what he intended. For the last few days, the Copperwiths had to move their teachings outside of the little house into an open area. Servants of Hastancia de Gamon built a makeshift covering for the open area in a day to accommodate the growing crowds. *Felipe Baston* reported that about three thousand people came to hear the teachings on our last day in Adrian.

Mrs. Copperwith had begun preparing Veronica Gamon to continue with the teachings after our departure from the city. She began teaching Mrs. Gamon each evening about the core beliefs of being a follower and believer in Kammbi.

Mrs. Copperwith focused on the basic teachings of the Book of Kammbi about how Kammbi was human and divine at the same time, how every person committed acts of passha, and how Kammbi sacrificed himself for all of humanity's acts of passha in order to give them a direct connection with him. She explained that believers and followers of Kammbi received the Eternal Comforter as a gift for their declaration of faith. I still had trouble with those core beliefs and wondered if Mrs. Gamon would be able to teach them without totally grasping them herself.

As our time in Adrian wrapped up, Mrs. Copperwith contacted the konseho of Kammbi to inform them of all we had accomplished. Deputy Santiago would send a morrim, a diakono, and a small staff from a kahall in the city of Issabella to Hastancia de Gamon. They would strengthen Mrs. Gamon's basic knowledge of their belief system and help her teach the people of the city as well. Deputy Santiago was pleased with the reports of how the people of Adrian were taking to the teachings. Diakono Copperwith told him that my connection with the Boma-Men had begun the process of bringing all the people of the city together for the teachings.

Deputy Santiago asked the Copperwiths about my overall interaction in the city of Adrian. The Copperwiths told them their observations—including the fact that I still had not fully embraced becoming a believer and follower in Kammbi. However, I had helped facilitate a path for the Boma-Men to believe. Deputy Santiago believed the Eternal Comforter was at work in me despite my misgivings.

"The Eternal Comforter is working in you," Deputy Santiago said on the other end of the phone. "You have helped faciliate belief in Kammbi to a group of people that worship leopards."

"Boma-men" I replied.

"Boma-men," Deputy Santiago repeated. "I understand you have a connection to these people. That is the power of Eternal Comforter working in you."

Mrs. Copperwith frowned and reached her hand out for the phone. I handed it to her. I knew what she was going to tell Deputy Santiago. She could not keep to herself any longer.

I watched her expression changed from a frown to a blank stare. I hated that I put her in this position. But, what I could do? I did not seek out having the Boma Essence. It chose me like it did for Elena Diego.

Mrs. Copperwith handed the phone back to me.

"I understand that you have received a magic from these Boma-Men," he asked sternly.

"I received the Boma Essence when I visited Boma Village for the first time." I answered.

The phone went silent for a few seconds. Was he going to reprimand me for receiving the Boma Essence?

"Oscar Ortega did not gain magic upon his journey during his travels when he crossed the Omarra Sea coming from Guadharra." Deputy Santiago began. "The Eternal Comforter was the only power he needed."

"The Boma Essence is not magic. Plus, I did not seek out this power. It chose me."

"The ability to see through your mind and communicate with the leader of the Boma-Men is magic to me."

I sighed. "I saved a man's life. The Boma Essence did that through me. This power can be used for good."

Deputy Santiago laughed sharply. "You are still young, Diondray Azur. Power like that you have received can corrupt the one who has gained it."

"Did not Disciples Gregory and Jorge speak with the Volarr people in Guadharra who had magical powers? They could fly through the air like a bird in short distances. All the other peoples of Guadharra shunned the Volarr people because of the magic. But Gregory and Jorge visited them and shared the teachings of Kammbi. Many of the Volarr people became believers and followers of Kammbi.

Deputy Santiago went silent again. I looked over at the Copperwiths and both had blank stares on their faces. I had surprised them with my knowledge about the Volarr People from the Book of Kammbi. They were written about in both disciples Gregory and Jorge's chapters in that book. Again, I surprised myself how those stories came to memory while talking to Deputy Santiago.

"You are correct about the Volarr people of Guadharra." Deputy Santiago replied. " I can tell you have not only read the Baramesa section of the Book of Kammbi, but have read the Ryianza section too. I will speak with the rest of the Konseho about this development. You will hear back from me soon."

Deputy Santiago ended the call. I breathed a sigh of relief. However, I knew it was temporary. They could take away the remaining funds and resources for the journey and summon the Copperwiths back to Issabella. A diakono and his wife were not supposed to be associated with anyone who has magic.

PART 2

Walter's Grove

Chapter 9

"I had to tell Deputy Santiago," Mrs. Copperwith pleaded with her husband. We were on the autobus heading to Walter's Grove, the next city on our journey. But after my rebuke from Deputy Santiago, I did not know if there would be any more journey by the time we arrived.

Diakono Copperwith frowned and looked straight ahead at the road. His cheeks were red, and his blond hair was stiffened like a razor's edge.

"I'm not leaving Diondray if they summon us back to Issabella," he said sharply. "He is the one who will fulfill Oscar's prophecy."

"Malcolm, you know how they are about magic," Mrs. Copperwith said and turned his face to her. "I could not keep that from Deputy Santiago."

"You could have, Annalisa. You did not want to."

Diakono Copperwith removed his wife's hand from his face and continued looking at the road.

"Are we to omit the truth?" she fired back.

"Do you know how many lies have been said for our faith?" Diakono Copperwith replied. "All throughout the Book of Kammbi, every disciple in the Ryianza section: Gregory, Jorge, and Carlos omitted the truth amongst the people in Guadharra to further the faith. Oscar Ortega had relations with a woman who was not his wife."

"Are we to justify those lies and acts of passha?"

I remained silent, feeling this exchange between them was needed.

"It's not a justification. The omission of truth does not hinder belief in Kammbi. Our god uses everything for his purposes. Not just the things approved by the konseho of Kammbi."

Mrs. Copperwith gave her husband a sharp look. "I never knew you thought this way."

"Annalisa, it is not about thinking a new or different way. It is about understanding the situation of life we are in and having the wisdom to adjust to it. Sometimes, as believers and followers of Kammbi we want life to go exactly like it is in the Book of Kammbi, or how the konseho of Kammbi interprets that to be. However, Kammbi understood that life is not always that way. He gave us the gift of the Eternal Comforter and teaches that we must trust its guidance above all else. Well, I'm trusting it, and I'm not leaving Diondray if summoned back to Issabella."

Mrs. Copperwith placed a hand over her mouth and stared at Diakono Copperwith. He did not look at his wife, continuing to stare at the road instead. Nothing else was said for the rest of the trip to Walter's Grove.

Is Loyalty meant to be blind?
Is Loyalty to stay true to everything despite reasons not to?
Should Loyalty to something you believe
have room for interpretation?

*Or would it be disloyal if you left the straight and narrow
path that has been prescribed for your loyalty?*

I wrote that themily during the rest of the journey to
Walter's Grove. It took about five hours to reach the city. Those
words came in response to my last conversation with Eduardo
and to the discussion between the Copperwiths. Was loyalty
meant to be blind? If so, how could you remain loyal when the
truth revealed things you did not expect?

My first thought was about how Uncle Xavier had
preached loyalty amongst the help who worked for us at our
family home and the council members who helped our family
govern Charlesville. I had always thought his remarks rang
false. I had seen how he hired and fired help at the family home
all the time. And he always had a different woman as his latest
interest. So how could someone tell others to be loyal but act
the opposite way in their own life? That inconsistency never
felt right to me.

Eduardo's hatred of the Boma-Men derived from his love
of Elena Diego, but it was misguided. He wanted my loyalty,
as a newfound relative, to garner the same hatred toward
the Boma-Men. But how could I have offered loyalty to my
relatives after my experience with the Boma-Men?

Listening to the Copperwiths' discussion brought home
the fact that loyalty, whether to family or to a belief system,
demanded tunnel vision in order to keep it. And if you decided
to widen the tunnel just a little bit, it would always erode loyalty.
However, it was ironic that Diakono Copperwith was willing
to step outside of that tunnel and trust the Eternal Comforter
because he really believed I was the one who would fulfill
Oscar's prophecy. I had sensed that not becoming morrim

for the kahall of Santa Sophia might have begun to change his convictions about his belief system. But Mrs. Copperwith had not reached the same place as her husband, despite her motherly fondness toward me. Loyalty, I was realizing, was not a two-way street. Either you embraced the truth that was taught to you by your family or a belief system, or your loyalty would always be questioned.

Those thoughts shaped the themily, and it was the best one I had written so far on the journey.

I also thought Eduardo had a point. If I had not questioned Uncle Xavier's attitude toward those who worked for our family or questioned Mother when I found out about the Book of Kammbi being in Charlesville for generations, if I had never asked her to explain why she had never told me about how our family history was connected to Oscar Ortega—if I had accepted what I had been taught all of my life—I might have never been in my current position.

The Copperwiths invited me to their hotel room the next morning. Diakono Copperwith sat at the desk in the room while Mrs. Copperwith sat on the bed. Her eyes were puffy and cheeks red. She had been crying before I came to the room. Mrs. Copperwith patted the bed next to her, wanting me to sit.

"We have been summoned back to Issabella," Mrs. Copperwith said softly after I sat next to her. She grabbed my hands. "There are members of the konseho of Kammbi who believe we should not be with a person who has magic. Magic is evil and corrupting. And the one who is supposed to fulfill Oscar's prophecy should not use magic."

Diakono Copperwith did not look at his wife or myself. He stared blankly at the desk.

"It is not magic," I replied. "I cannot create spells or do things that are magical. The Boma Essence just gives me an awareness I've never had before. It chose me. I did not go looking for it."

"Another human being can speak to you through your mind, Diondray. This essence helped you save a man's life. That is magic to believers and followers of Kammbi. You possess a power only meant for Kammbi. The one who is human and divine at the same time. Not someone who is only human."

I pulled my hands away from Mrs. Copperwith and rose from the bed. That broke Diakono Copperwith from his state, and he turned to look at us.

"I thought you had made peace with the fact that I had the Boma Essence. You spoke up for me when we visited Hastancia de Gamon for the first time. Why do you both have to go back to Issabella?" I started to pace next to the bed.

"Only one of us is going back to Issabella," Diakono Copperwith said.

I stopped pacing and looked at him. "Only one . . ."

"I'm going back," Mrs. Copperwith said. "Malcolm is staying."

I cut my eyes to Mrs. Copperwith and saw the tears had returned.

"It will be the first time that we have been apart since the early days of our marriage," Diakono Copperwith continued. "I never thought our belief in Kammbi would cause separation in our marriage. But it has."

Diakono Copperwith whirled back to the desk. I was stunned.

113

"Why won't you stay with your husband?" I said. "I thought we were together on this journey."

The tears flowed across Mrs. Copperwith's cheeks. "The konseho of Kammbi threatened to take away his title as diakono and his status as someone who can teach from the Book of Kammbi if both of us stayed with you. I agreed to return so my husband could keep his position and status. I do not want to leave his side. Being with him for the last thirty-one years has been the best decision I ever made next to becoming a believer and follower of Kammbi."

I sat back down on the bed next to Mrs. Copperwith. She sobbed on my shoulder, and I placed my arm around her. I felt terrible.

"We believe you are the one who will fulfill Oscar's prophecy," Diakono Copperwith said flatly. "Everything you have done on this journey so far has brought people together. What happened with the Boma-Men in Adrian confirms the guidance we have received from the Eternal Comforter. And we have to trust the Eternal Comforter above everything else. Even over the konseho of Kammbi."

"How can you trust so easily, Diakono Copperwith? You were meant to become morrim for the kahall of Santa Sophia before I came into the picture. That was something you wanted all your life. How can you continue to trust in something so unseen and so unexplainable?"

Diakono Copperwith shifted back around, and there was a glimpse of anger on his face. "I thought my calling in life was to be morrim for the kahall of Santa Sophia. Outside of my marriage to Annalisa, it was the only thing I wanted. I prayed for many years about becoming morrim, and when the opportunity came to finally get the position, you had arrived in Santa Sophia. The Eternal Comforter confirmed from that moment that I would not be a morrim, and that I would help you unite this entire land." He was quiet for a moment and then said, "And being a believer and follower of Kammbi demands you put aside your own desires to serve his wishes."

He had given me that explanation about serving Kammbi above his own desires several times on this journey. At first, I thought it was just religious speak—the thing someone in his position was supposed to say. But now, the explanation felt different. I sensed that he had made peace with not becoming morrim for the kahall of Santa Sophia. But he had believed he would always have Mrs. Copperwith at his side. How would this separation affect his belief?

"I will be leaving tomorrow morning. The konseho of Kammbi will send their airplane," Mrs. Copperwith said and released herself from my embrace. "I do not know how long I will be away from Malcolm." She stopped talking, and tears flowed across her cheeks once more.

Diakono Copperwith got up from his seat at the desk and came over to his wife. They embraced. "The konseho of Kammbi wanted her to leave today," he said sharply. "I had to insist that I get one more day with my wife. It will be a while before we have our alone time again."

Mrs. Copperwith managed a smile. "Our alone time is one of the things I'm going to miss the most with Malcolm."

I understood what they meant. I embraced both of them and left their room.

Our hotel was located on Avenue Javann, the main road in the southwestern district of the city. We were in the business district, and the hotel was one of several high-rise buildings in the area. I looked out my hotel room's window and watched people walking on the sidewalks, some of them stopping at food stands on the street corner, and automobiles speeding by onto their destination. I knew the energy in Walter's Grove was going to be different from Adrian.

However, I did not sleep well that night thinking about Mrs. Copperwith. She would be leaving in a few hours, and I felt responsible for it. I thought if the Boma Essence had not chosen me, I would not have the "magic" the konseho of Kammbi deemed as antithetical to those who were believers and followers of Kammbi. Mrs. Copperwith would never have been compelled to tell the konseho about it. And she would not have to be leaving for Issabella.

But as I thought about this, I realized that it was not my fault the Boma Essence had chosen me. I had not gone looking for its powers, and all throughout our stay in Adrian, it had only responded at the appropriate times. Would that continue for the rest of our journey? I knew the Boma Essence would reappear in its own time, and I had no control over it.

Plus, I reminded myself, the Book of Kammbi was written in part by two disciples, Gregory and Jorge, who wrote about their experiences with people who had magic. Kammbi did not declare that those people could not become believers and followers of his religion. His disciples explained that magical power had to be submitted under Kammbi's authority and used for his purposes. Why would it become an issue for the konseho of Kammbi, when their sacred book had addressed it in this way?

Those competing thoughts kept me awake most of the night, but I did not have the gumption to write a themily about it. I stared at my writing pad several times during the night, but no words came. I read my other themilies in an attempt to jumpstart some writing. No words landed on the paper. My thoughts were consumed with Mrs. Copperwith leaving. She had replaced Aunt Maxina's role in my life, and I was going to miss her.

I managed to get a couple hours of sleep, only to awake to music on the radio. It was on the opposite side of the bed, and the music made me sit up. It began with a heavy drumbeat and had several percussion instruments interspersed throughout the song. Suddenly, my foot was tapping on the floor, and my head bobbed to the rhythm. There were no lyrics to the song, just drums and percussion. I had heard music like this at Aliki Park back home and remembered seeing women dancing instantly when a song in this style came on the radio.

"You are listening to Coltrain Hayes's latest song, 'She Must Move Her Hips for Me,' on Guanamamma Radio One. Coltrain Hayes has decided to go back to his musical roots for this latest song, and this host is glad that one of our greats is playing classic Guanamamma music in the style of Walter Leonardo Fuente. I will be back shortly with another Coltrain Hayes song in the same classic Guanamamma style."

The radio announcement ended as a commercial came on. I had gotten out of the bed and danced across the hotel's room floor. Now I whirled back toward the radio, waiting for the next song. I had felt the Boma Essence flowing through my body in response to the music. Did the Boma Essence have a connection to Guanamamma music? Omari had not mentioned this connection while I was in Adrian. As a matter of fact, I had not heard any music during my time in that city. Would the Boma Essence take on a different power while I was here in Walter's Grove? And would it have anything to do with our purpose for being in this city?

Another Coltrain Hayes song came on the radio, and I began dancing again. I had never been a great dancer, but now I sensed that my arms and legs were moving in synch with the song's rhythm. The Boma Essence guided my movement, and I could tell it was trying to get my mind off Mrs. Copperwith's impeding exit from our journey. It was working.

We dropped Mrs. Copperwith off at the Walter's Grove Airport just before midday. The Copperwiths embraced one last time and kissed. It was the first time I had seen them kiss on the journey. Their passion revealed that the "alone time" mentioned the other night was not an uncommon occurrence.

I embraced Mrs. Copperwith, and they said one last prayer before getting on the airplane. The prayer was for safe travels and guidance from the Eternal Comforter on the rest of our journey throughout this region. It was a short prayer, and I actually wished it was longer. I had not fully embraced the ritual of prayer, but this one felt different. I could have stayed with this prayer for at least another hour.

Diakono Copperwith and I left the airport. He remained silent on the drive back to the hotel. I stared at his face, and he looked blankly out the autobus's window. It was not a good time to tell him about my dancing to Guanamamma music from earlier in the morning. But I knew I had to get his mind on finding our purpose for being in Walter's Grove. I asked the autobus to give us a tour of the city instead of going back to the hotel and hoped that would get Diakono Copperwith's mind away from his wife momentarily.

Our driver was named Abraham, and he had a treetop hairstyle similar to my own. His skin tone was dark brown, and he had a wide forehead that made his face look too large for his body. When Abraham turned around to begin his explanation of Walter's Grove, I was startled by his appearance.

Abraham started explaining as he drove east on Avenue Javann that all the city's main businesses resided in this district. The javann producers, food market suppliers, automobile makers, and so on all had their business in the district. Most of the city's workforce came to this district for employment. Looking out the autobus's window, I could see one business after another. The driver continued his explanation about the founder of the city, Walter Fuente. He did not want to have businesses owning property in every district of the city, so he had relented to having one district for the city's commerce.

"Why would he be forced out of Terrance for having more than one wife? " I asked. "Actually, why would a man have multiple wives?"

I glanced over at Diakono Copperwith. But he still stared out the autobus's window. I did not think he heard any of our conversation.

Abraham laughed. He had a gravelly laugh that seemed like he was coughing. It got Diakono Copperwith's attention, and I saw the normal, stoic look back on his face. Maybe he was starting to make peace with Mrs. Copperwith's exit.

"How many wives did he have?" Diakono Copperwith asked.

"Two," the driver answered. "Roxie and Penelope. We are heading to the district named after them in a few minutes."

Diakono Copperwith frowned. "How could a man marry more than one woman? Having one woman requires so much attention that it could never be divided with someone else. And I don't think any wife should have to share her husband with another woman."

The driver's forehead expanded again as it moved up and down in the mirror. "You sound like one of those officials from Terrance who believe a man should only marry one woman. Walter Fuente was the greatest musician in two cities, and he should have been able to marry as many women as he wanted. I'm surprised he only had two women as wives. He was a musician."

The diakono quoted from the Book of Kammbi by heart: "A man should have only one wife in his lifetime. And a woman should have one husband in her lifetime. The marital bond must remain strong and not let temptation enter in." He cleared his throat. "The people of this city should take heed to those words of wisdom from Kammbi."

Had Diakono Copperwith memorized the entire Book of Kammbi, I wondered? He had recited that paragraph without hesitation. Or did the Eternal Comforter give Kammbi's followers the ability to recall paragraphs from that sacred book when they needed it? I sensed Diakono Copperwith knew the entire Book of Kammbi like the back of his hand—through years of study.

Abraham laughed again. "People don't marry in this city. They go from one partner to another partner. Or have multiple partners at the same time. Walter Fuente wanted his city to reject monogamy, because he lived under it for years in

Terrance. Love and lust should be pursued, and the people of Walter's Grove live by that belief."

Diakono Copperwith clasped his hands together in a prayer position and looked at me. "I know why the Eternal Comforter wanted me to stay on this journey with you, Diondray."

Chapter 10

Abraham continued his explanation of Walter's Grove as we made it to the Roxie and Penelope District. Walter Leonardo Fuente had founded this city in the year 94 A.O.A. after being forced to leave the city of Terrance during his musical heyday. He was declared "King of the Kammarice" in Terrance during the years 83–93 A.O.A with songs like "When You Arrive," "Kammara, Kammara," "Should I Forgive You," and "You're Better than a Glass of Javann." Kammarice was an instrumental style of polished music that wanted listeners to contemplate their listening experience. Kammarice music was meant for dinner parties or concert halls—not dancing. However, Walter Fuente felt Kammarice music had become too bland and stifling. He wanted to make music that got women to dance, and he started to incorporate drums and percussion into his songs. Terrance's rulers and upper-class citizens did not like the "King of the Kammarice" going in a new direction with his music and believed he had started to encourage dancing. Soon they complained to the *konzill*, the city of Terrance's governing body, that the musician had begun parading around the city with two wives, Roxanne Pierponte and Penelope Mentz.

Walter Fuente had secretly married the women shortly after his first wife, Josette Eichenberg, died of illness in Veme, the eleventh month of the year 92 A.O.A. If the konzill allowed the city's greatest musician to have two women as wives, it would encourage men of both the upper and lower classes to adopt the same behavior. So the konzill created a law called the Monogamy Act in Yul, the seventh month of the year 93 A.O.A., to control the lustful behavior of the men in the city. The Monogamy Act declared that no man could marry more than one spouse, and anyone caught breaking the law would have their marriage revoked, be subjected to heavy financial penalties, and face imprisonment up to a year.

Walter Fuente believed the Monogamy Act had been created just for him, and he felt betrayed by the ruling. Also, he had learned that several members of the konzill were going to marry second wives despite the new law. In response, the musician wrote his most infamous song to date, "What You See in the Light Is Not What You Think." The song declared Walter's love for his two wives and explained why the women had consented to this style of marriage. It also exposed those konzill members who were planning to marry multiple wives. "What You See in the Light Is Not What You Think" was played in Walter's new style of Kammarice music, causing people to dance, and it was the first song in that style that had vocals. Walter's wife Roxanne was a great singer and lent her vocals to the song.

The song outraged Terrance's upper-class citizens. They petitioned the konzill to arrest Walter Fuente for breaking the Monogamy Act. Because of his status among the people, only the *regnator*, leader of the konzill, could have the great musician arrested. Benoday was the regnator at that time, and he declared publicly in Coter, the tenth month of the year 93 A.O.A., that Walter Fuente had broken the Monogamy Act and would be arrested.

However, Terrance was also a city where people believed in the gods. The lower-class citizens prayed daily to the goddess of music, Apollonia, to help the great musician. Walter Fuente had negotiated for three months with the regnator on how he would turn himself in to the konzill for breaking the Monogamy Act. In the first month, Nayur of the year 94 A.O.A., members of the konzill came to the musician's home to arrest him—but Walter, his wives, and several musicians had disappeared. Apollonia had used her power to allow them to escape Terrance.

Walter and his small group soon arrived in the region four hours northwest of Terrance, just south of where the Adrian and Kammara Rivers merged. The musician declared his allegiance to Apollonia, and she used her power to build a city that rivaled Terrance. Nearly one hundred sixty years later, Walter's Grove had become that city.

Diakono Copperwith frowned during Abraham's explanation. I sensed he did not like the fact that a man had been forced to leave his birth city because he had married two wives—and he probably didn't like the fact of the marriage either, or that Walter had gotten assistance from a goddess who endorsed the marriage. I understood from the diakono's perspective and beliefs why he would have a problem with that kind of marital arrangement. However, I knew of several wealthy men back home in Charlesville who had multiple wives. Uncle Xavier and Mother never made a big issue of it, and they were certainly not going to create a law forbidding that kind of marriage. They actually preferred that no one get married at all.

"We have arrived at the intersection of Avenue Roxie and Avenue Penelope, the most well-known intersection in the city," Abraham proclaimed. "To your right is the Wall of Walter's Declaration."

Abraham turned right at the intersection and parked the autobus across from the Wall of Walter's Declaration. A crowd was gathered around the attraction. It was a large slab of stone standing several feet high, and it had a life-size painting of a short man with thick hair and a well-groomed beard. His arms were around two women, one on each side of him.

"This painting of Walter Fuente and his wives, Roxie Pierponte on the left and Penelope Mentz on the right, was painted by Felipe Jose Altuve, the city's greatest artist, in the year 144 A.O.A. It was done a year after Walter Fuente's death in honor of our founder," Abraham continued.

I thought we were going to exit the autobus and go across the street to the attraction, but instead, we stayed on board. Abraham opened the side entrance door so we could have a better view of the Wall of Walter's Declaration.

"Roxie has a treetop hairstyle like me, and Penelope has blond hair like Diakono Copperwith," I said.

Abraham laughed. "Walter loved women. Did not matter if they were dark or light-skinned, tall or short, thin or thick. As you can see, Roxie is much taller than Walter, and Penelope is much wider than both of them."

"The crowd is split into two sections. Is there something else next to the painting?" Diakono Copperwith asked.

The driver nodded. "It is the inscription of Walter's Declaration. When he arrived from Terrance, he wrote this declaration for our city: 'If a man wants to marry more than one wife, it will be allowed in this city. I will never create (or allow anyone else to create) a law prohibiting anyone from loving as many people as he or she wants. This will be a city built from the spirit of music, dance, and love. Nothing else. I declare it on this day, the eighth of Nayur, year 94 A.O.A."

Diakono Copperwith shook his head in disgust. "Oh my Kammbi, please give me the guidance to help these people see that marriage beyond one wife is outside of the boundaries you have set for us."

"I don't know what your beliefs are, Mr. Copperwith. But the people here in this city abide by Walter's Declaration. And nothing will change it," Abraham snapped.

Diakono Copperwith returned to his seat as the driver closed the side entrance door. Marriage had come up yet again. I thought back over my journey so far. The people of Santa Teresa had believed a woman should be married at twenty-one, and they tried to justify that belief from the disciple Teresa's section of the Book of Kammbi. Yet Teresa clearly stated in the Book of Kammbi that she chose not to get married because she wanted to have a closer connection to Kammbi. The believers and followers in the city of Santa Teresa took that as a threat to marriage and built a culture around it making sure women got married at twenty-one. I had been glad to help Second Esperah Annika Dorrado keep from getting married by her birthday; instead, she had become a resa—a single woman devoted to Kammbi.

Now in Walter's Grove, we had a culture where men could marry multiple wives and be celebrated by everyone in the city. What was it about marriage that made people from these two cities react so differently? And why did it seem so important for believers and followers of Kammbi, like the Copperwiths and the people in Santa Teresa?

"I'm ready to return to the hotel," Diakono Copperwith said.

Abraham looked through his mirror at us. He had a disappointed look on his face. "We were just getting started in the Roxie and Penelope District. I wanted to show you both everything in this district before I took you back to the hotel."

"No thanks, Abraham. Please take me back to the hotel."

As we drove along, I peered out the window at the people on the sidewalk. I noticed a group of people wearing matching outfits. The men wore skin-tight black V-neck shirts with silver trim and black pants. The women wore silver midthigh dresses with black geometric shapes across the torso. I watched them come out of one building and stand in front of another as we drove by. I wondered why they were dressed like that.

"Those are *dannzas*," Abraham told me. He must have seen me staring at them. "They are the city's best dancers and come each day to practice at the nightclubs before they open for the evening."

I nodded as I watched the group begin dancing on the street. "Do they dance to the Guanamamma music I heard on the radio this morning?"

"They only dance to Guanamamma music. We don't play Kammarice music in this city."

Abraham turned left at an intersection, and I turned around in my seat to continue watching the dannzas. A crowd started to gather around them. I wished the driver would park the autobus so I could go closer to see them dance.

"I'm off duty at six," Abraham said without my asking. "I can bring you back to the district to see the dannzas in action."

"I would like to come back."

"Good! Let's get Mr. Copperwith back to the hotel."

I looked over at Diakono Copperwith, and he frowned. He missed his wife, and I knew it was going to be a challenge for him in this city without Mrs. Copperwith.

Abraham did not come back at six. I received a note from the hotel's front desk. The note said that something came up, and he promised to return the next evening at the same time. I had been playing the radio from the time I got back to the hotel. I was beginning to sense that music and dancing would be one of our main reasons for being in Walter's Grove. I would have to find out about the importance of Guanamamma music and the dannzas to the city.

Music and dancing were not a big deal back home. We listened to Kammarice music from Terrance and followed their beliefs about music being something for serious listening or for background atmosphere. However, my dad would play the guitarist Ruben Davar on tape, and I had become a fan of his music. Ruben Davar played Kammarice music that had a rhythm and got you to tap your feet. I would play the guitarist's music at our family home, and Uncle Xavier would have Willar turn it off immediately. I got scolded each time I played Ruben Davar's music. What was wrong with music that caused physical movement?

I remembered Maisa dancing on the autobus going to the city of Alicia. The driver of the autobus had played some Coltrain Hayes, and I'd liked it. However, Diakono Copperwith had asked me not to dance, as he felt that the one who would fulfill Oscar's prophecy should not partake in dancing. There was nothing in the Book of Kammbi against it, and Maisa had a point when she objected to Diakono Copperwith's instructions. *"I don't believe you were committing an act of passha by dancing,"* she'd told me. I wished she were here.

I spent the rest of the evening writing a themily about this subject and thinking about Maisa at the same time. I needed her company in this city, and I knew she would have wanted to spend most of our time in the Roxie and Penelope District. I hoped after this journey had been completed that I could go back to Alicia to visit her.

After breakfast, Diakono Copperwith and I discussed how we were going to bring the teachings of the Book of Kammbi to this city.

"I'm going to the Roxie and Penelope District this evening." I said.

Diakono Copperwith frowned. "I don't think that would be a wise choice."

"I understand your concern, Diakono Copperwith," I replied. "But, I believe we have to get to know the people of this city on their terms."

"Their terms!" Diakono Copperwith snapped. "This city was founded by a man with two wives and fled his birth city because he could not obey the law."

"Does that mean we can not share the teachings from the Book of Kammbi in this city?"

"Of course, Diondray." Diakono Copperwith replied in a softer tone. "I prefer we share the teachings in another area. Going to a place where drinking, dancing, and pursuing lustful behavior is not the route we should take to reach the people of the city."

"What is it about music and dancing?" I replied. "I remember back on the autobus going from Santa Teresa to Alicia you wanted the driver to stop playing music that Maisa and I were enjoying."

Diakono Copperwith turned red. "Music has the power to make a person lose their inhibitions and do things outside of their normal behavior. Kammbi warned all believers and followers about the power of music."

"So they will not commit acts of passha?" I added.

Diakono Copperwith nodded. "Going to the Roxie and Penelope District will lead you on the path to commit such."

"You have trusted me this entire journey." I snapped. "As a matter of fact, you just told Mrs. Copperwith that you were coming with me for the rest of the journey. You defended me for having the Boma Essence. And now you don't want to go to the Roxie and Penelope District and met the people of this city on their terms. I thought the Eternal Comforter has guided you to trusting me no matter what."

"The Eternal Comforter has guided me to trusting that you are the one who will fulfill Oscar's Prophecy. This is true. But I do not want what happened to Oscar Ortega to happen to you."

"It will not!" I said and finished my breakfast.

We decided to get out of the hotel and walked along Avenue Javann. Traffic was constant as we walked several blocks east of the hotel. I noticed people staring at Diakono Copperwith's shawl as they passed us on the sidewalk. The people of this city had never seen anyone dressed like the diakono. However, he was oblivious to their attention, and he continued discussing with me his strategy to share the teachings of the Book of Kammbi.

"Are you from the konzill?" a dark-skinned man with bloodshot eyes blurted out as he approached. He wore disheveled clothes and stumbled in front of us. I could smell the javann on his body. The man must have been drinking it since last night.

"I asked, are you from the konzill?" He stopped in front of Diakono Copperwith and stood up as best he could.

Diakono Copperwith stopped and replied, "I don't know who you are. But I'm trying to have a discussion with my companion."

"You won't answer my question. I guess people who get drunk on javann are not good enough for people like you."

The man moved aside but frowned at Diakono Copperwith.

"I'm not from the konzill," Diakono Copperwith replied and smiled at the drunken man. "My companion and I would like to pray for you."

"Pray for me," the man said, slurring his words. "Nobody prays in this city. You may not admit to being from the konzill. But you are from Terrance, speaking the way you do."

Diakono Copperwith reached out for the man's left shoulder and bowed his head. I followed suit and closed my eyes.

"Hey man, don't touch me! I moved out of your way!"

The man stumbled just out of the diakono's grasp as I opened my eyes, but I was too late to move aside, and he collided with me.

"Do not drink something that causes you to stumble. Drink in the Eternal Comforter, and he will fill your every need."

I held the man in place as Diakono Copperwith spoke words from the disciple Jorge's section of the Book of Kammbi. I was still amazed at how he could recall paragraphs from the book so easily.

"Eternal Comforter, you said. What is that?" the man replied as he straightened up. "A new kind of javann?"

Diakono Copperwith lifted his head and placed his arm around the man. We started walking with him back toward the hotel. "The Eternal Comforter is not something that will make you inebriated. It will give you life. Would you like to learn more about it?"

The man looked at me for a moment. Then he faced Diakono Copperwith and nodded.

"You have made the best decision of your life. Thank you for wanting to receive it."

We made it back to the hotel, and I noticed a smile on Diakono Copperwith's face. It was the first time he had smiled since Mrs. Copperwith's departure. He believed his strategy of going to the people without embracing their culture would be the right way to take after all. After this encounter, even I thought he might have a point—however, I was still going to use my strategy too.

Abraham came later that evening, dressed sharply in a matching yellow shirt and pants, accented by shiny black shoes. He was ready for the Roxie and Penelope District. I had gotten rid of the clothes I'd received from Frederic Cortes and only had the clothes I received from Deputy Santiago. I did not want to have anything that reminded me of the worst decision I had made so far on this journey. I wore a matching gray shirt and shorts for the evening.

"You cannot wear shorts in the Roxie and Penelope District," Abraham said as soon as he saw me.

"This is my nicest outfit."

Abraham frowned. "It's not good enough, and we will not get into any nightclub with you dressed like that. I will take you shopping on the other side of this district. You will be ready for the evening."

We left my hotel room, and Diakono Copperwith greeted us in the hallway. The smile from earlier was gone, and I could sense he was not pleased with me going to the Roxie and Penelope District. I saw an envelope in his right hand.

"This is for you," he said and handed me the envelope.

"Who is it from?"

"I think you may want to read it before you leave."

I opened the envelope and started reading.

Diondray,

I know you are surprised to get a letter from me. You probably thought that you would never hear from me again after the hearing with the konseho of Kammbi. I have thought about you every day since that fateful decision. I should have known that Frederic Cortes was looking out for his own interests. Bastard. I let him manipulate me into making a choice between Silver Mine 12 and you. And I let pride in my family's heritage override my desire to be with you for the rest of the journey. I feel terrible about that decision. This silver mine has been more trouble than it's worth, and thankfully Jorge Feldman has kept it running smoothly.

I miss you and should be there with you. I have always wanted to go to the cities south of the Great Forest. And I let my foolish pride get in the way. Now, I have learned Annalisa had to leave the journey to keep Diakono Copperwith from losing his status. I may have disagreed with their overly pious manners. But I know those two love each other and are miserable being separated. I feel the same about you, Diondray Azur. Somehow, I know we will be together again. I have been praying every day about us. Even if I have to lose ownership of the silver mine, I will find a way to be at your side. You are the one who will fulfill Oscar's prophecy and bring the entire land together. I love you and miss you a lot.

Sincerely,
Maisa

My right hand, holding the letter, was shaking. I paced the area where we were in the hallway. I was replaying Maisa's words in my mind. She was right. I had thought I would never hear from her again.

"Abraham, I cannot go with you this evening," I said after I stopped pacing.

He frowned. "I know this woman is special to you. But she is not here. You should still come to take your mind off of her absence."

Diakono Copperwith glared at Abraham. "Maisa traveled with us to all the cities north of the Great Forest. She is special to Diondray as well as myself. I don't think it's appropriate for Diondray to be going out this evening."

I heard both of them talking, but I was looking at the letter again. Maisa had already declared her love during our time in Issabella. I felt the same way but wanted to wait until this journey had ended to pursue it. I was surprised that she was willing to give up the silver mine to Frederic Cortes. He had manipulated both of us for his agenda. I knew how much she wanted her family name, Merez, to finally receive the recognition it deserved. She was willing to give that possibility up for me.

"*You are truly inexperienced about love.*" I remembered Maisa telling me that on the way to Alicia. I had expressed what I knew about love from my experience with Mara back home. Maisa laughed and declared I did not know anything about love at all. I sensed that I was receiving my first lesson about it in this moment.

"Abraham, I will go with you," I said and placed the letter in my pocket. "I need to get out for the evening. Get me some new clothes."

Diakono Copperwith looked disappointed. He remained silent as we passed in front of him in the hallway. I was still drawn to my strategy for bringing the message of the Book of Kammbi to the people of Walter's Grove, and I knew I had to see it through. My right hand caressed the letter as we left the hotel.

Chapter 11

At the shopping center near the hotel, Abraham bought me a matching deep blue shirt and pants similar to his own. The clothing felt light and smooth on my skin, and I knew it was made for dancing to Guanamamma music. I had not spoken since leaving the hotel. Abraham tried to get my mind off Maisa's letter with more conversation about the city's history, but I was not listening. My mind kept replaying Maisa's words from the letter. I took it out of my pocket several times on the way to the Roxie and Penelope District, reading a portion of the letter before placing it back into my pants pocket. I needed to soak in every word, because it was my only connection to her until we saw each other again. As we arrived in the district, I wanted nothing more than to abandon our mission here, leave for the city of Alicia, and rescue Maisa from owning that silver mine.

"I have never seen any man be so lovesick," Abraham said as we arrived in the Roxie and Penelope District. "Whoever this woman is, she's got you good."

I remained silent and kept rubbing the letter in my pocket.

"I want you to enjoy the evening. We will have plenty of company to keep your mind off of that woman. You are dressed for the occasion. Let's have some fun."

I pulled my hand out of my pocket during Abraham's pep talk and rolled down the passenger window. People were lined up outside each nightclub as we drove by. Guanamamma music blasted from the street corners. Dusk had arrived, and the people of this city were ready to let loose.

"These nightclubs are considered level two clubs," Abraham explained after we parked. We were a few blocks east of the Wall of Walter's Declaration. I saw it again as we entered the district.

"Level two clubs?"

"Yeah. Level two clubs, because they are the furthest away from the intersection of the main streets. The nightclubs near the intersection are level one clubs, the best in the city."

Everywhere, I noticed men dressed in monochrome outfits, some green, orange, yellow, blue, or even pink. The women wore patterned dresses that stopped just above the knee. Everyone seemed fine with standing in line for the nightclubs they wanted to enter. Several people danced to the music playing in the street.

"Many people go from a level two club to a level one club in the same evening," Abraham continued. "The place to be seen at is a level one club."

"Is that where we're going?" I asked.

He nodded. "We are going to the best club in the city, and we will not have to wait to get in."

We walked for several more blocks until we reached Abraham's destination for the evening. Music blared from the closest intersection. The oversized, glowing pink light above the entrance read *Darcie's*. Two muscle-bound men stood at the doors. I turned my attention to some couples dancing to the left of the nightclub's waiting line. They moved effortlessly to the rhythm of the music. The men led their women in a variety of steps, spins, and twirls. The coordination shown by each couple was fascinating to watch. It was like they spoke an intimate language only they could understand.

"We can see more of the dannzas inside," Abraham claimed and pulled me toward the entrance.

I followed him to the front of the line and felt the stares of the people waiting.

"Who are those two?" I overheard a female voice saying.

"We have been waiting for over an hour," a male voice said.

We reached the doors, and the bouncer on the left looked sternly at us. His rectangular head and shoulders made him look more like a character from the stories my mother read to me as a child than an actual person.

The man raised his left hand in front of Abraham's face.

"We are guests of Darcie," Abraham told him. "Abraham Rivas and Diondray Azur."

The attendant dropped his hand and looked over at his companion. "We got Abraham and Diondray claiming to be on Darcie's list."

The other attendant viewed a clipboard he was holding. He searched it and nodded. "On the list."

"Welcome to Darcie's," the first attendant said and opened the door.

I followed Abraham into the nightclub. As we passed through the door, I reached into my pocket and grabbed Maisa's letter, caressing it like a good luck charm. A glowing pink light lit up the hallway. I could feel Guanamamma music coming through the walls, causing me to place my left hand over my ear.

The hallway led into an open room, with tables and chairs in the middle, a bar on the left, and the dance floor to the right. The dance floor was packed with people. I stopped walking and watched them.

"We are going upstairs," Abraham said and grabbed my arm.

We reached the stairway at the back of the nightclub and headed upstairs. A brunette waitress passed us on the way back to the ground floor. I noticed her smiling at Abraham. She had beautiful white teeth and curvaceous lips. He smiled back and reached for her hand. "Are you coming back to serve us, Krystle?"

The waitress giggled. "Of course."

She released her hand from Abraham and continued downstairs. He watched her walk away for a moment. I sensed they had a connection beyond flirtation.

"Abraham!"

A tall, blonde woman wearing a lemon-yellow dress came toward us. She was almost my height, maybe an inch or so shorter, and had the widest hips I had ever seen.

"Darcie!" Abraham replied and hugged her.

"So glad you came out tonight," Darcie continued after their embrace. "You brought a new friend. New friends are always welcome at Darcie's. I'm Darcie Fendlewiesen."

I took my hand out of the pocket and greeted Darcie. "Diondray Azur."

"Welcome, Diondray. Let's get you a drink of javann. I have the best javann in the city. That should loosen you up."

I followed them into a loft-style room where a long purple couch rested close to the wall. Darcie motioned for me to sit next to her, and Abraham sat on the other side. I could look down over the edge of the loft to the ground floor from my seat. A circle had formed around a couple below—a short, olive-skinned man and a tall, dark-skinned woman with a treetop hairstyle like mine. They were cheek-to-cheek, and the man led the woman in every step of their dancing. I was mesmerized at how in synch the couple was to the music. Every step was in perfect rhythm with the drums and percussion of the song. I began to feel the Boma Essence flowing inside me while I watched.

"Diondray!"

I glanced over at Darcie and Abraham. She pointed to the drink of javann on the table in front of me. Abraham grabbed his drink and threw it back quickly. But I did not want to drink. I returned to watching the couple dance as the Boma Essence flowed faster. I felt the same surge of energy going through my body that I'd felt in Adrian.

I got up from the couch and headed to the stairs. "Where are you going?" Abraham yelled at me. I did not turn around, but kept walking to the stairs. I had to get on the dance floor. The Boma Essence wanted me to dance.

Krystle was coming up the stairs, and she smiled at me. Her gorgeous smile felt welcoming. "Leaving so soon?" she said.

I grabbed her hand. "Do you want to dance?"

"I would like to. But I'm working."

"Please join me."

Krystle's eyebrows rose, and she turned her head toward the nightclub owner. I did not look their way but continued to hold her hand.

"Dance with him," Darcie ordered.

The waitress smiled again, and I led her downstairs to the dance floor. Even though the Boma Essence was flowing rapidly through me, I felt nervous. I had never been so forward with a woman before. I put my opposite hand back in my pants pocket and held Maisa's letter. I caressed it again, and my nerves started to calm.

A new song came on. I held her hand and got into dancing position. I had no idea what I was doing. But I could recall how the couple I'd watched from upstairs had positioned themselves. I saw them dancing again in my mind, and I knew how that image had come to me. I began moving forward, and Krystle stepped back in response. The song was only percussion, and I trusted the Boma Essence to guide my steps. Krystle grinned, and her body moved in synch with my own. She was an experienced dancer but felt comfortable with me leading. I sensed the rhythmic connection between us and could have stayed on the dance floor with her for the rest of the evening.

I noticed a crowd of dancers forming a circle around us. The couple I had been watching earlier entered the circle and danced next to us. The image of how they had danced still remained in my mind, and having them beside me reinforced it. The Essence guided my movements, and it felt like someone had taken control of my body. However, it was not against my will, and I felt calm as I danced. The song ended, and applause roared from the entire nightclub. The couple came up to us and embraced us.

Krystle held my hand and kissed me on the cheek. She had a big smile on her face as she hugged me. "Thank you," she whispered. "I have never danced with anyone like that before. Not even with the dannzas who come here every evening."

I nodded and soaked in her compliment along with the continuous applause. Not even my best themilies at Aliki Park back home had earned me applause like this. It felt good.

Krystle held my left hand and led me back upstairs. Darcie had an excited look on her face, but Abraham was frowning. I knew he had seen how Krystle looked after our dance and was not happy.

"Bravo!" Darcie bellowed as I made it back to my seat. "I have never seen anyone dance Guanamamma like that before. Do they dance Guanamamma in Charlesville?"

I watched Krystle serve Abraham another drink of javann. He still had a frown on his face. "No, we don't dance Guanamamma in Charlesville. We listen to Kammarice music back home."

"Then where did you learn to dance like that? It was not classic Guanamamma dancing, but you and Krystle had a rhythm that was magical."

Darcie handed me a drink, and I placed it down on the table. She was right. The dancing had been magical. I'd had no idea the Boma Essence would react to the music in such a fashion. I had not seen any dancing in Boma Village, and Omari had never mentioned anything like it. Why did the Boma Essence respond to this music?

"At least you are forgetting about that woman," Abraham blurted out. His words slurred . . . he'd clearly had several javann drinks already. I would probably have to call another autobus driver to take me back to the hotel, I thought.

Darcie had a bemused look. "You are trying to forget about someone?"

I placed my hand back in my pocket and felt the letter. I had not forgotten about Maisa one bit.

Abraham rose from his seat and walked toward me. "Some woman from north of the Great Forest left him high and dry. And she sent him a letter trying to make it all better. I brought him here to get his mind off her. If she wanted to be with him, she would have been dancing with him instead of Krystle!"

Abraham's breath stunk. I got up from my seat and stood face-to-face with him. "You have no idea what you are talking about," I replied.

"Gentlemen, there will be no fighting in my club," Darcie said and got between us.

I pulled my hand out of my pocket, and the letter landed on the ground beside Darcie's shoes. She bent down quicker than I could and grabbed it.

"Here's a letter," she said and began to open it.

"I told you," Abraham said.

"Please hand it to me!" I said.

"I did not know that women still wrote letters to the men they claim to love," Darcie continued and took a few steps away from me.

"Hey, that's personal. Give it back!"

Abraham stepped between Darcie and me. I felt my anger rising and was ready to move him out of the way.

But before I could take action, I heard screams coming from below. I walked to the loft edge and looked down to see people running frantically. I heard a growl coming toward us and knew what had arrived.

At the top of the steps was Reuel. I had not seen the leopard since our first few days in Adrian. I knew he was being taken care of by the Boma-Men among his leopard brethren. But I was glad to see him now.

Abraham and other patrons screamed as the leopard approached. Some of them dove behind the couch.

"Where are the door attendants?" Darcie yelled.

Reuel stood at my side, and I reached down to nuzzle his head. The leopard purred, and I knew he was glad to see me.

Darcie went pale. "You know this animal?"

I fixed her with a steady gaze. "Please return my letter."

Darcie folded the letter and handed it to me. I felt her hand shaking when I grabbed it.

"Thank you," I replied and placed the letter back into my pocket.

Darcie stood like a statue as I stroked the leopard. "How did the leopard know you were here?" she asked.

"Reuel has been one of my companions throughout my journey. He always appears at the appropriate time."

The leopard growled, and we headed down the stairs.

Chapter 12

T he leopard appearing at Darcie's remained the talk of the city for five days. I heard about Reuel on the radio in my hotel room. The news anchors and DJs were stunned that a leopard would actually enter the nightclub, a level one club—and of all things, to find and protect a particular person! Darcie Fendlewiesen had been interviewed about the experience, and she did not seem bitter about having a night of business ruined by the leopard. On the contrary, she hoped the leopard would return again in order to gain more publicity for the nightclub,

I heard from Darcie more personally as well. She found out where I was staying and sent phone messages. She wanted me to return to the nightclub and talk. She apologized for taking Maisa's letter and expressed that she wanted to get to know me a little better. I ignored the first couple of messages, but five days after the incident in the club, I received another message right after I woke up. I listened to it and thought about going to the nightclub after breakfast. She had requested that I come by sometime before dusk so we could talk privately.

I heard a knock on my room door and went to open it. Diakono Copperwith entered. He had the usual stoic look on his face. "I have been able to reach some people of this city through my relationship with Fernando. Meeting him the day we walked onto Avenue Javann was a sign from the Eternal Comforter."

I had seen Fernando come to the hotel over the past five days. Diakono Copperwith was sharing the teachings from the Book of Kammbi with him in his hotel room. And I noticed Fernando appeared sober and wore clean clothes as I passed him in the hotel every day. He must have taken the teachings to heart and connected Diakono Copperwith with others he knew.

"I'm going to visit Darcie Fendlewiesen after breakfast," I said.

Diakono Copperwith frowned. "You should stay away from that temptress. I understand your strategy, but I don't think the nightclub scene is the route you should take. There are too many dangers."

"I appreciate your concern, but I believe that connecting with the people of this city in their element is going to help us out. Meeting with Darcie before dusk is a safe bet."

The diakono answered with one of his quotes from the Book of Kammbi: "Be careful of the temptress; she comes on sweet like candy. Once she gets you to taste, you will want it all the time. But if you eat too much of the candy, it will eventually give you a stomachache. The temptress comes in a package meant for deception and entrapment. Attempting to leave her grasp leads to ruin."

"I have read these words from the disciple Jorge's section," I countered. "Jorge led a life of debauchery before becoming a believer and follower of Kammbi. However, I don't think that paragraph you recited is appropriate for my meeting with Darcie. Also, I notice those words seem to blame the woman for tempting a man into committing acts of passha. But I have also read in the disciple Gregory's section that each person has to battle their own nature to keep from committing acts of passha. Kammbi warns us of this through his section as well. Calling a woman 'the temptress' comes off as blaming someone else for our own self-destructive tendencies."

Diakono Copperwith clenched his jaw. I did not think he expected me to use the Book of Kammbi against him in this discussion. However, I had read about the disciples from the Ryianza portion of the sacred book, and I knew they had all lived colorful lifestyles before becoming believers and followers of Kammbi. If their lifestyles prior to conversion was an issue, then why did the book mention them?

"I know what you and Mrs. Copperwith believe about being in this type of environment. I saw that in the city of Alicia when I played Blacks with Big Daddy Red and Bonita Golde. Playing cards and gambling is not the right environment for the one who will fulfill Oscar's prophecy." I continued. "However, we have to meet people on their own playing field if we are going to unite this entire land for Kammbi. Oscar Ortega was willing to do that. And I found out in the city of Adrian, Adrian Azur attempted the same thing. We have to embrace peoples from all walks of life, not just the ones who can or will easily convert."

Diakono Copperwith sighed and nodded slightly. "You make valid points and continue to confirm the Eternal Comforter's decision that I stay on the journey with you instead of returning to Issabella with my wife. But I still believe that woman is a temptress and someone to be wary of. That might seem unfair, but those words are in the Book of Kammbi for a reason. I believe in them. Be mindful of her intentions."

I nodded as he turned to leave my hotel room. I knew that being in the city could not be easy for him.

Darcie had arranged for another driver to come pick me up from the hotel. Abraham probably did not want to be associated with me anymore. Plus, his javann drinking had gone overboard, and I was sure Darcie knew that having him around would not be the right thing in her attempt to get to know me better.

The new autobus driver was a dark-skinned man with a prominent nose. Sidney was his name, and he kept quiet during the drive to Darcie's nightclub. I did not know if Darcie had instructed him not to speak or if he was naturally a silent man. However, the drive to the nightclub was not uncomfortable, and the silence gave me time to reflect on how this meeting would go.

I arrived at Darcie's a few minutes later. She wore a hip-hugging sea-blue dress and silver shoes that added an inch to her height. She was dressed for the evening already, and she certainly got my attention.

"Thank you for accepting my request," she said and reached for my hand. "I apologize for sending you so many messages, but I wanted you to know that I'm sorry for taking something so personal to you and causing a ruckus. I would like to start our relationship off on better footing."

I sensed her comments were genuine, and I followed her to a couch on the left side of the dance floor, near the bar. She handed me a glass of brownberry juice as I sat down.

"I noticed you did not drink javann the other night. And I appreciate that kind of restraint in a man." Darcie smiled and flipped her blonde hair away from her face.

"Why did you invite me here?" I asked.

Darcie maintained her smile and replied, "I want to get to know you better. I know you are from Charlesville, and Abraham told me you came from Adrian before arriving in Walter's Grove. What were you doing there?"

"I have been traveling throughout both regions of this land for the past several months. Adrian was just my prior stop."

"Are you returning to Charlesville after your time here in Walter's Grove?"

"I will visit Terrance after my time in this city," I replied. "Going home is not in the cards for me."

She flipped her hair again and asked, "You can't return to Charlesville?"

I felt at ease in her presence—she was easy to talk to. "I was forced out of Charlesville."

Her cheeks flushed, and she reached for my hand again. Darcie's touch was soft, and I grasped her hand.

"I found a copy of the Book of Kammbi back home," I told her. "My Aunt Maxina showed me where it had been kept for several generations. I did not know this book had ever existed until earlier this year, but once I found it, I learned about a prophecy written by Oscar Ortega declaring a descendant of his would unite this land."

Darcie released her hands from my grasp and placed one over her mouth. "Are you serious? The Book of Kammbi in Charlesville?"

"Do you know about the Book of Kammbi?"

She removed the hand from her mouth and ran it through her hair. "I'm from Santa Teresa. I know all about the Book of Kammbi. I had to read it once every thirty days with my parents as a child. I know about Oscar's prophecy."

I had not drunk the brownberry juice while we talking, but I gulped it down quickly now and rose from my seat. Did Darcie's words mean the teachings from the Book of Kammbi had some influence in Walter's Grove? Was this a sign of the land becoming united?

"I visited Santa Teresa in Aym, the fifth month of the year, and learned about how the people of that city believed women must get married at the age of twenty-one."

"Diondray!" Darcie bellowed. "I was supposed to do the same thing. I was forced to leave my birth city because I did not want to get married. No woman should be forced to marry before she is ready. And it should never be arranged. I can't believe what I'm hearing. Things in life do come full circle."

Her words were surprising in a way, but at the same time, I sensed this was the reason the Boma Essence had been suggesting that I meet with Darcie. Throughout the last few days, I'd been getting images in my mind, similar to what had happened in Boma Village. Her face would appear, as well as the nightclub, each time she left a phone message. I would try to write a themily or listen to Guanamamma music on the radio to get those images out of my mind, but they lingered for a while each time. Now I knew why.

"I wanted to teach you how to dance Guanamamma properly," Darcie said. "But I have learned so much more than I expected. I know we will have a longer discussion in the future. But I would like to show you some dance steps . . . if that's okay with you?"

I nodded. I wanted to dance Guanamamma like the couple I'd seen the other night. Diakono Copperwith had warned me to stay away from this woman. But I knew the Boma Essence wanted me to connect with her and follow this strategy until its conclusion. I had begun to believe the Book of Kammbi might have an influence in this city that was not mentioned in that sacred book or known by Diakono Copperwith.

I spent the next four days with Darcie, learning how to dance Guanamamma. We were a couple of days from the end of the year. It seemed the year was coming to an end more quickly than I had expected. Being on this journey since Lir, the fourth month, had made time go by fast. So much had changed for me over the past eight months.

After three days of lessons, the dance was coming to me more easily, and I felt more confident in my steps. We practiced for four hours each day and had lunch afterward. Our connection was starting to grow, and Darcie began to tell me about her past in Santa Teresa. By the same token, I opened up about my life in Charlesville and being on the journey throughout the two regions.

"Dancing Guanamamma is all about hip and feet movement," Darcie explained as we stood in the middle of the dance floor for today's practice session. Our hands were interlocked, and we stood cheek-to-cheek. Her skin was smooth, and the perfume she wore had an apricot aroma. "Move your right hand to my hip and caress it. You are going to gently rub my hip and move forward at the same time."

"Are we doing this without the music?" I asked.

"Yes. It's best to learn the basic steps and hand placements without music. People get easily lost in the music, like you did with Krystle, and don't dance the basics of the Guanamamma."

"You said I danced magically with Krystle."

Darcie released me from our position and smiled. She did have a nice smile, and I noticed the small freckles on her cheeks.

"You did dance magically. But that was not Guanamamma dancing. You were led by something else. I believe the leopard's arrival had something to do with it."

I nodded as we returned to our position. Reuel had nothing to do with how I'd danced with Krystle. But Darcie was correct about me being led by something else.

"Caress my hip, Diondray." Darcie instructed. "I want you to feel comfortable with me. I feel comfortable with you."

I followed her instruction, and we began to dance. "How did you leave Santa Teresa?" I asked.

"I did not show up for my wedding ceremony at the kahall of Santa Teresa a few days after my twenty-first birthday. My parents had arranged for me to marry a man named Vincent Headwater. He was from one of the most prominent families in the city, and my parents loved him liked a son. Vincent did everything correctly and said all the right things. He was supposed to be the perfect man for me."

We had stopped dancing, and Darcie's cheeks turned red.

"So why didn't you show up for the ceremony?" I asked.

"My parents had forced Vincent to be my suitor. He was a nice and pleasant man. But I had no romantic feelings for him, and I did not like being in his presence."

Darcie grabbed my hand and led to me to the couch by the bar.

"You hated Vincent?" I asked her.

Darcie shook her head. "No, I did not hate him. I had nothing in common with him. Every time we were together, Vincent would talk about his plans of becoming the governor of Santa Teresa. He believed it was his destiny, as preached to him by the morrims of the city. Our conversations were always about his ambition and nothing else. I like a man with ambition, but that cannot be the only thing you talk about with a woman."

She went to the bar and got me another glass of brownberry juice.

"How did you get here?" I asked.

Darcie handed me a new glass of brownberry juice and sat down. She grabbed my right hand and stroked it gently. "I caught an autobus ride to Alicia with a stranger named Feliciano Burns. I knew I could not live in Santa Teresa anymore. I had to leave. Feliciano had found work in the silver mines of Alicia and was moving there because of the opportunity."

"Did you live with him?"

"I did . . ." Darcie replied and paused for a moment.

"Something wrong?"

Darcie sighed and smiled at me again. "No. Feliciano Burns was a good man. He believed in the Book of Kammbi and allowed me to live with him only reluctantly. He believed in the teaching that an unmarried man and woman should not live together."

"From Kammbi's chapters in the first half of the Book of Kammbi, the Ryianza section. 'An unmarried man and woman should not remain in each other's company for a longer than necessary period of time. The temptation and tension between the two could boil over into passion and lead down a road there is no coming back from.'"

I had recalled a section from the Book of Kammbi— again. How did that happen? Would I be able to recall more sections from the sacred book so easily?

"You have read the Book of Kammbi," Darcie replied and released my hand. "I would never have thought someone from this region could have recited from that book. I hope you do not become a believer and follower of that backward religion."

"I have read the Book of Kammbi many times since leaving Charlesville. And I have been traveling with a diakono from Santa Sophia who knows the Book of Kammbi by memory. I have not become a believer and follower of Kammbi but I can not deny its influence throughout my travels."

"Well, you are here with me now," Darcie said and got up from her seat. "Don't believe in that backward religion anymore. I don't want you getting brainwashed like the diakono you have been traveling with. I will do everything in my power to keep you from becoming a believer and follower of Kammbi. The Book of Kammbi has backward teachings. The women in those pages are only meant to be wives and produce children—and meanwhile, the man who wrote the prophecy that is supposed to unite this entire land for Kammbi had an affair with another woman, and she was forced to leave her people. She barely gets mentioned in the entire book. Diondray, you cannot become a believer and follower of anything like that! I believe you are special. You do not need to be associated with anything like that ever again." She shook her head, seeming upset, and reached out for me. "Let's continue practicing."

I was speechless at what she had said. Maybe this was Diakono Copperwith's reason for wanting me to stay away from the nightclub owner. She had renounced being a believer and follower of Kammbi. However, I wanted to know more about her renunciation of the religion. She was the first person I had met on this journey who had reacted to the teachings of the Book of Kammbi in such a fashion. I knew if I told Diakono Copperwith about her intentions, he would try to keep me away from her. But I still sensed that I needed to stick with this strategy, and if the Eternal Comforter truly wanted me to fulfill Oscar's prophecy, it would provide the right guidance for me to do so.

We had reached a new year seven days ago, and I was amazed at how fast the last year had blown by. It was the seventh day in the first month, Nayur, of the year 252 A.OA. I had a birthday coming up in twenty-six days, and if turning twenty-four was anything like turning twenty-three, I had another year of major change ahead. I wondered if most people in their early twenties went through major life changes like I had.

Sidney dropped me off at Darcie's for the day's practice. My dancing had improved, and I felt I had gotten the basic steps of Guanamamma dancing down pat. Darcie had commented more favorably about my dancing in the last couple of practices. I was looking forward to learning advanced dance moves like drops, twirls, and spins today.

While we practiced, I had become a fan of the music and learned more about its history. Darcie added historical background to each song during practice, and that information gave me a better understanding of why people danced to this music.

I entered the nightclub and saw Darcie talking with three couples dressed in silver outfits with black trim. I had not known that dannzas were going to attend practice today. Did Darcie feel my dancing had come far enough for me to learn from the best dancers in the city?

"I want to thank the dannzas for coming this morning as I continue teaching my beloved Diondray from Charlesville how to dance Guanamamma," Darcie announced as she reached for my hand. She had started calling me "beloved" a few days ago, as her comments about my dancing had gotten better. While she was tough on me during practice, her behavior toward me had changed since our initial meeting. She continued to denounce the Book of Kammbi and its teachings, but our time together outside of practice was enjoyable. I knew she was trying to make me forget about Maisa's letter. That did not happen. I read Maisa's letter every day. However, I did appreciate getting to know Darcie Fendlewiesen, and I felt that my strategy of getting to know the people of this city on their terms was working.

I was introduced to the dannzas and recognized the couple from the night I had danced with Krystle. The olive-skinned man with silver hair and his dark-brown skinned companion were striking up close. Ciscoe Maldonado was several inches shorter than his wife, Latisha. He had a thin, angular frame and carried himself in an unassuming manner, while his wife was curvaceous and statuesque. She carried herself like a woman of importance. On the surface, they seemed like an odd couple, but after seeing them dance, I knew the opposite was true.

Darcie clapped her hands as the music came on. Jayden and Rosa Elena, one of the other two couples, led the dance, beginning the dance hand in hand and cheek to cheek. Both were the same height, weight, and olive complexion. Jayden was bald with thick eyebrows, and Rosa Elena had thin brown hair in a ponytail and soft facial features.

"Jayden and Rosa Elena are dancing to Walter Fuente's classic song 'I Like You,'" Darcie explained. "My beloved, notice how Jayden is staying cheek-to-cheek with Rosa Elena. His left hand is intertwined with her right hand, and his right hand is caressing her left hip. That is the position I want you to maintain with me at all times when we are dancing. You tend to release your right hand when we dance, and you don't caress my hip. I want to feel your hand on my hip. Guanamamma is a sensuous dance, and that kind of touch is essential."

I nodded at her explanation as Jayden and Rosa Elena moved gracefully across the dance floor. I guessed my dancing had not improved as much as I'd thought. She was right—I did release my left hand from her right hand, mostly when we moved side to side. And I did not always caress her left hip. I would either move my hand to her waist or to just below her shoulder blade. My hand felt more natural in those areas than on her hip.

"Dancing Guanamamma is about communication with your partner," Ciscoe interjected. "Just because the man gets to touch his partner's hip doesn't make it sensual. Communication about your movement with the music and connections with your partner are the most important. Harrell and Brittany, show my new friend what I mean with the next song."

As the song ended, Ciscoe and Latisha stood next to me and watched Harrell and Brittany as they walked onto the dance floor. Jayden and Rosa Elena stepped to the side and watched their friends get into position. Harrell had night-colored skin with a gangly build. Brittany had short blond hair, pale skin, and a compact frame.

Darcie smirked as she clapped her hands for the next song to come on. "This is 'Move, Move, Move' by Gerardo Oliver Torres. Torres wrote songs for Guanamamma music that emphasized sensuality. He believed that Walter Fuente still had a touch of Kammarice in his style, and he was right. Fuente was from the city of Terrance, and that heritage never left his music.

Torres was a native son to this region and believed his music reflected the true essence of Guanamamma music more than the great Walter Fuente did."

The song was all drums and percussion with a simple chant of 'Move, Move, Move.' I thought it was repetitive and boring. Walter Fuente's 'I Like You' had more variety, including horns and guitar in the song. Harrell and Brittany tried to dance elegantly under the watchful eyes of Ciscoe and Latisha, but I sensed they were not comfortable dancing in this manner. It seemed they wanted to move in harmony with the repetitive song.

"You chose this song on purpose, Darcie," Latisha said. "Ciscoe and I will show you how to dance to an overrated song like this one."

Ciscoe led his wife to the dance floor. Harrell and Brittany stepped back, next to Jayden and Rosa Elena. Darcie frowned like she knew what was coming from the older couple.

"Play that song again," Ciscoe instructed.

The nightclub owner clapped her hands twice, and the song came on again.

Ciscoe and Latisha were in the classic cheek-to-cheek position, but I noticed his right hand was in the middle of his wife's back. His posture was straight as an arrow, and he guided his wife with long strides. Latisha followed her husband's lead without hesitation. She did not move her hips suggestively like Rosa Elena had with Jayden. And she did not look uncomfortable like Brittany did with Harrell. Their footwork and movement to "Move, Move, Move" was a sight to behold.

The song ended, and the other dannzas couples clapped. They knew how a song like that one should be danced.

"Darcie, I hope you have not been teaching our new friend that dancing Guanamamma is about sensuality. If so, then he will never learn the true way to dance it," Ciscoe said.

"I will not argue about dancing philosophy with you, Ciscoe," Darcie snapped. "You and Latisha are dannzas from an earlier generation, and you do not understand that dancing Guanamamma has changed. Plus, you both still believe dannza partners should be married as well."

Latisha glared at the nightclub owner. "We sure do, Darcie. The current generation believes dancing Guanamamma is all about dancing suggestively and being sexual with their partner. They miss the true connection you are supposed to have with your dancing partner. Communication and connection are the essence of dancing Guanamamma. Being married to your partner is the best way to achieve that."

Darcie sighed. "You both make dancing Guanamamma sound like it creates some mystical connection between you and your partner. No one dances like that anymore. There's nothing wrong with shaking our hips and behinds while dancing."

Rosa Elena and Brittany laughed. I saw grins on Jayden and Harrell's faces. I knew how they wanted to dance.

Ciscoe shook his head. "We know our style of dancing is outdated. But my wife and I believe it is the most authentic form of dancing Guanamamma. And we still get invited to dance at the Walter's Grove New Year celebration every Nayur. I guess we older dancers still have something to teach the current generation."

Darcie smiled. "We can agree on that, Ciscoe. Thank you and Latisha for coming, as well as the other couples."

"We would like to invite you both for dinner at our house tomorrow evening," Latisha said. "Ciscoe and I would like to get to know our new friend a little more. Will you accept our invitation, Diondray?"

I nodded, and they seemed pleased.

"See you tomorrow evening."Ciscoe replied,

Chapter 13

O n the street corner outside our hotel, Diakono Copperwith had found a small group of people to share the teachings from the Book of Kammbi with. The hotel would not let him share inside the building, and his attempts to go into the city districts had not borne much fruit. He ended up on the street corner just east of the hotel each morning after breakfast, where he shared the teachings with a small audience, mostly inebriated people.

"Kammbi is both human and divine," Diakono Copperwith started with an explanation that I had already heard several times during the journey. He believed in teaching basic concepts repeatedly until people got a fundamental understanding of the religion. "He came to live amongst humanity for a short time and sacrifice himself so that we can all have a connection with his father, Abbahim."

There were six people sitting on the corner and listening to Diakono Copperwith. They all had bloodshot eyes from a night of drinking, along with disheveled clothes. I noticed the glances of people walking by. Most of them frowned or had looks of disgust at our gathering. I sensed embarrassment from those who passed us. There was no reason for anyone in this city to become so inebriated or disgrace themselves in public.

These men should be able to handle drinking javann like the rest of us, they seemed to think. And listening to some man wearing strange, full-length clothing and talking with a book in his hand was out of the question.

"Why would this God-man sacrifice himself?" a man with bloated cheeks sitting closest to Diakono Copperwith asked. He had a bottle wrapped in a paper bag in his left hand, and he held it tightly.

"First, you have to hand me that bottle," Diakono Copperwith said sternly. "I will not continue teaching to anyone drinking."

"I got this bottle of javann last night," the man replied. "Azur 112 Pure from Adrian. I scraped up enough money to get the best javann in the city." His cheeks seemed to expand as he spoke. "I'm not giving anyone this bottle until I'm finished."

"You better give me some of that Azur 112 Pure!" interjected a man with a treetop hairstyle behind him. He reached out for the bottle of javann, but the one who held the liquor moved out of his reach.

"Then our teaching is done for today," Diakono Copperwith replied and closed the Book of Kammbi.

The other men groaned at Diakono Copperwith's ultimatum. I did not think they understood the basic principles of the Book of Kammbi. But for some reason, they wanted to hear the teachings.

"You said that is Azur 112 Pure?" I asked.

The man with the bottle of javann looked up at me. "Azur 112 Pure, young man. That's what I said. It's not that weak javann from East Walter's Grove District."

All of them laughed at his comment. I could feel Diakono Copperwith's glare on my neck.

"My last name is Azur," I continued. "I'm related to the Azur family from Adrian that makes Azur 112 Pure."

"Balderdash, young man!" another man in the group blurted out. He was to the right of Diakono Copperwith. "You are too dark to be an Azur. The Azur family of Adrian are light-skinned like the teacher here. You don't have to lie to get the bottle away from Lauricio."

"He is not lying," Diakono Copperwith replied before I could. "Diondray Azur is his name, and he is related to the Azur family from Adrian."

I glanced at Diakono Copperwith, but although he was defending me, I sensed he did not want to go down this road with me.

"Are you the one with the leopard in the nightclub?" one of the men asked from the back of the gathering.

I nodded. "Reuel is my companion."

"No kidding, young man," Lauricio said after taking a swig from the bottle. "I bought Azur Pure 112 from that nightclub last night. It cost me 35 Fuente bills. But a woman with those hips could charge me anything she wants. I'll pay it!"

The man laughed again and nodded at Lauricio's comment. Darcie Fendlewiesen was not only known for her nightclub but for the size of her hips, which was a topic of discussion on the city streets.

Diakono Copperwith frowned at Lauricio. "I had one rule for my teachings. No drinking. You have broken that rule, Lauricio. I will ask for the bottle one last time."

"I will give you this bottle on one condition. If your companion is truly related to the Azur family from Adrian, then he has to bring that leopard here to this district."

Diakono Copperwith glanced at me. Reuel had always shown up on his own accord. I did not even know how to call for the leopard.

"If I can get you another bottle tomorrow, will you hand me that one?" I asked.

"We are not going to support his habit, Diondray," Diakono Copperwith retorted.

"Bring the leopard, young man."

The other men nodded at Lauricio's request.

"I will bring Reuel tomorrow morning," I agreed. "However, you must take Diakono Copperwith to the districts where more people can hear his teachings."

Lauricio smiled and gave Diakono Copperwith the bottle. "You can continue, teacher."

Diakono Copperwith opened the Book of Kammbi and continued with his teaching. I had no idea how to make Reuel come to me. But I knew I had better find out, or Diakono Copperwith would not be able to share the teachings of the Book of Kammbi with anyone in this city.

Ciscoe and Latisha Maldonado lived in the East Walter's Grove District. Sidney picked me up from the hotel at dusk. He was more talkative on this drive and explained that this district had the oldest homes in the city. It was the first area Walter Fuente had settled in when he arrived from Terrance.

I nodded at the driver's explanation as he parked in front of a two-story home that looked like it needed a new coat of paint. I got out of the autobus and found Darcie waiting on the sidewalk in front of their home. She looked fantastic. She wore a hip-hugging deep blue dress with gold trim that accented her skin color. She smiled and reached for my hand as I arrived.

"I wore this for you," she said and placed my right arm around her waist. The dress had a silky texture and slid easily underneath my fingers.

"You look wonderful," I replied.

Darcie giggled and moved my hand to her ample behind. I shifted my hand back to her waist quickly as we approached the Maldonados' front door. I had read Maisa's letter again before Sidney came to pick me up and started writing a themily as a reply. Even though I had enjoyed Darcie's company over these past few days, I had no intentions of engaging in anything amorous with her.

Latisha opened the door and we entered the home. The living room was colorful and vibrant. A large orange sofa with blue trim and matching chairs dominated the space. Colorful paintings decorated the walls, and a huge silver radio took up a corner section of the room. I walked over to a painting that depicted a couple dancing as the sun rose in the background.

"I can tell you like colorful things," Latisha said, standing next to me. "Ciscoe had that painting done for our tenth wedding anniversary. It is one of my favorites. Dancing as the sun rises fits us exactly."

"Beautiful painting," Darcie added as she joined us. "Ciscoe always had great taste in all things artistic."

I noticed that Latisha frowned at Darcie's comment, but the frown disappeared quickly as she led us into the dining room. Ciscoe was sitting at the table, and he rose from his seat to greet us.

"Welcome, Diondray! Welcome, Darcie!" Ciscoe announced and motioned us to our seats.

Dinner was already on the table. My plate had several long strips of beef with brown rice, corn, and cauliflower perfectly placed around it. My stomach rumbled at the sight of this feast, and I was ready to eat.

"I will say a prayer to bless the food," Ciscoe continued as Latisha poured brownberry juice into each glass at the table.

"You still pray after all of these years?" Darcie asked.

I glanced at her and saw a look of disappointment on her face.

"Prayer is an essential aspect of our lives. Latisha and I pray as often as we can."

Latisha smiled at her husband's comment. I sensed Ciscoe was genuine about praying. It was the first time I had heard someone in this city mention doing something like that. Personally, even though Diakono Copperwith had done it every day since we started our journey, I still had not fully embraced the concept. Did he actually talk to Kammbi during prayer? I did not believe so. However, I knew how important prayer was to the diakono. Now, I became interested in finding out why the Maldonados prayed.

"Have any of your prayers gotten answered?" Darcie replied. "It seems to be a waste of time to just be talking to yourself and no one responds."

Ciscoe grinned. "You are still challenging our beliefs after all of this time, Darcie. Let's enjoy dinner for now."

Darcie sighed as Ciscoe prayed, letting go of the conversation reluctantly. I could tell that she wanted to continue arguing with Ciscoe about why he prayed. Darcie had not talked with me about the teachings from the Book of Kammbi in the last couple of days. But I knew her feelings about it were always on the surface.

"Ciscoe and I are impressed with your dancing, Diondray," Latisha commented. "We have seen some of your practices with Darcie, and you have a natural rhythm for dancing Guanamamma."

I smiled at her compliment. It was great to hear one of the best dancers in the city recognize my dancing. But I had not realized the Maldonados were watching us practicing. Did they come to the nightclub for each practice session? If so, why had Darcie not mentioned it?

Ciscoe's next statement answered my questions. "Darcie gave us video of your practice sessions. She wanted to show us that you could become a great dancer and participate in the New Year's celebration at the end of Nayur."

"Are you serious?" I replied.

Latisha laughed. "That's one of the reasons we wanted to invite you to dinner tonight. We understand you are only in Walter's Grove for a short time. Ciscoe and I want to make sure that you are really interested in participating in the New Year celebration. If you are, our status as dannzas can get you the opportunity. But there is more practicing that needs to be done by the celebration. We want you to learn how to dance Guanamamma the proper way."

Darcie rolled her eyes and patted my thigh under the table. She had convinced the Maldonados to give me this opportunity. I smiled and squeezed her right hand under the table.

"Do you want to participate in the New Year celebration?" Ciscoe asked.

I nodded.

"Good deal. We will join you and Darcie for practice tomorrow, and you will unlearn everything you have been taught by Ms. Fendlewiesen. You will become one of the best dancers Walter's Grove has ever seen," Ciscoe said.

"I taught him well," Darcie chimed in. "He understands the basics of dancing Guanamamma. Give me some credit."

"You have taught our friend the basics." Ciscoe replied. "But your philosophy is different from ours. And he needs to learn how to dance Guanamamma traditionally."

Darcie waved her hand dismissively at Ciscoe and shook her head.

"Darcie has been a great teacher," I replied. "I have learned a lot from her." She caressed my thigh under the table.

"You have taken well to instruction and can stick up for your teacher. That's a good sign that you can become a better dancer. Also, I have something to show you before we begin practicing with you and Darcie. Come with me." Ciscoe continued.

Ciscoe glanced at Latisha. She had a look of delight on her face. She knew what Ciscoe was going to show me and approved of it.

I got up from the dining room table and followed Ciscoe. We walked through the living room and headed upstairs. Ciscoe opened the first door on the right side of the hallway and made his way to a huge bookshelf at the back of the room. I joined him.

"I believe you are familiar with this book," he said and pulled a book with a plain brown cover off the shelf. Silver lettering adorned the cover, and at the sight of it, I felt a flow of energy surging through my body.

"Where did you get a copy of this book?" I asked.

Ciscoe handed me the book. "I've read the Book of Kammbi every day since I got married to Latisha sixteen years ago. The words in this book have changed my life. It is one of the best gifts I have ever received."

Ciscoe's copy of the Book of Kammbi felt like my copy. Weathered. Brittle. Ready to break apart if not handled carefully. How did a copy of this book get here—especially such an old one? "I did not know a copy of the Book of Kammbi would be here in Walter's Grove," I said and gently flipped the pages.

"Darcie gave it to me," Ciscoe answered as I handed him the book. "We had a fling before I married Latisha. She came to Walter's Grove from the city of Alicia, north of the Great Forest. I met her at a nightclub called Mario's. She watched me dance every night, and one night she asked me to dance with her. We were connected for a while."

"You taught her how to dance Guanamamma?"

Ciscoe laughed after putting the Book of Kammbi back on the bookshelf. "I did. And for about two years, we were inseparable. Darcie is a very attractive and determined woman. When she wants something, she gets it."

I nodded and laughed at that comment.

"I know you have experienced her determination," he continued. "But I saw that Book of Kammbi lying on the table in her apartment one day. I asked her about it. She told me about growing up in Santa Teresa and how she had read from the Book of Kammbi every day."

"But she doesn't believe in its teachings anymore."

"Oh, I know. That's why I had to cut her off at dinner about why Latisha and I pray. She would have argued with me, and I did not want to upset Latisha. My wife knows about my past with Darcie and is respectful toward her. However, Latisha will not tolerate any negativity coming my way from another woman."

Ciscoe continued, "I have learned that you have been traveling through both regions of the land to fulfill Oscar's prophecy. I thought Darcie was joking when she told me about your journey—or playing with my emotions because of her stance against the teachings from the Book of Kammbi. But I was wrong. Latisha knew after meeting you during practice that you are the one to fulfill Oscar's prophecy."

"How could she know that?"

"The Eternal Comforter. *'If anyone declares belief in me in their words and in their heart, I will give them the gift of the Eternal Comforter. And I will always be with them.'*"

"You recited that from memory!" I replied. "That's from Kammbi's section, the first chapter and second paragraph."

Ciscoe smiled. "Correct. I know the words in this book like the back of my hand. I have never read any book like it before. As you know, Guanamamma music and dancing are the religion of the people in the city. Walter Fuente built Walter's Grove on that premise. He did not want his city to become a city of gods like Terrance. So there are no other books in this city about any one god and its connection to humanity—nothing like the Book of Kammbi."

I had numerous questions for Ciscoe. I decided to ask this one. "How did you learn to read the Book of Kammbi? Do other people in Walter's Grove know about this book?"

Ciscoe raised his eyebrows and sighed. "I started asking Darcie questions about the book when we first met. She did not want to talk about it anymore. It had been her childhood and life up to age twenty-one . . ."

"When she would be forced to marry," I interjected.

"Yes. And she believes to this day that the teachings in this book only want women to become wives and produce children."

I nodded.

"Well, I got her to agree to teach me how to read the Book of Kammbi in exchange for learning how to dance Guanamamma."

"And she actually agreed to do it?"

Cisco gave a thin smile. "She did. It was like pulling teeth. But she read the entire Book of Kammbi with me and shared what she learned as a child. Darcie would argue after every reading session. But she has integrity and honored her word. I have always respected that quality in her."

I smiled. I had sensed that same quality in her as well. "Why did you not marry her instead of Latisha?"

He gave me a sharp look, and I knew I might have asked a question too personal. But Ciscoe replied a few moments later. "Because I believe in the Book of Kammbi. I believe in Oscar's prophecy. Darcie would not marry a man who believed in this book and her former religion. She tried to convince me otherwise. But I knew deep down . . . these teachings came into my life for a reason, and I was going to follow them. And after all these years . . . you coming here to Walter's Grove is confirmation I made the right decision."

Ciscoe patted my right shoulder, and I did the same for his left. I could see the emotion on his face and knew it was genuine. We would be connected from this day forward.

"Diondray, the other reason we have invited you to dinner is that after dancing at the New Year celebration, we want you to share the teachings of the Book of Kammbi with everybody at the celebration. If you dance well, the people will listen to these teachings. This city has a seed of connection to Kammbi, although most do not realize it. Are you willing to speak about this book after the dance?"

"I will," I said.

He smiled. "Good. However, we must keep this from Darcie. Only my wife and you and I can know about it. Darcie will not agree to let me teach you to become a better dancer if she finds out. Can you keep it amongst us?"

I shook his hand, and we embraced. It would be difficult to keep this from Darcie, and I didn't like lying. But if more people in this city could hear the teachings of the Book of Kammbi, then the risk to our growing relationship would be worth it.

Chapter 14

Can a connection come from an unlikely place?
Can a connection come from someone you had no idea of?
Can a connection alter the course of one's journey?
Can a connection make you realize that you are not alone after all?

I wrote that short themily the night after dinner with the Maldonados. I'd had no idea that dinner would reveal so much information. I felt an immediate bond with both of them, very much like my bond with the Copperwiths. I could not wait to discuss everything with Diakono Copperwith. However, I could not share what I was going to do after the Walter's Grove New Year Celebration.

In the next few days, Diakono Copperwith got more people to listen to the teachings from the Book of Kammbi on the street corner. Lauricio gathered up other people who lived on the streets to come hear this blond man wearing strange clothing talk about an ancient book. He spoke with sincerity and conviction. Diakono Copperwith became a curiosity not only to people of the streets but to those who passed by too.

Lauricio held up his end of the deal. I did not. I had no idea how to bring Reuel to me. Ten days later, Lauricio stopped coming to the teaching sessions. I was on my way to practice dancing when Diakono Copperwith met me in the hotel lobby.

"You must always act with integrity, Diondray," he began.

I sighed. "You know that Reuel comes of his own accord. I have no idea how to bring the leopard when I want to."

"Then you should have told Lauricio that when you made the deal. He has held up his end of the bargain."

"I know, Diakono Copperwith. I can go find him after practice and apologize."

Diakono Copperwith frowned. "You will not have to do that. He is out on the corner this morning. I was able to convince him to give you one last chance to honor your word."

"I would love to do that, but practice is in twenty minutes. I cannot be late."

"You are willing to keep your integrity for dancing but not to honor your part of the deal with these men."

I was starting to get angry. But Diakono Copperwith was correct. I had offered the leopard to those men who had been listening to the diakono from the beginning. And they deserved to see Reuel. I had to face the truth.

"I will apologize to Lauricio," I replied. "Hopefully he will accept my apology. That's all I can do."

Diakono Copperwith nodded. I followed him out of the hotel. We reached the street corner, and I saw a big smile on Lauricio's face.

"Well, Diakono Copperwith is a man of his word," Lauricio began. "He said you would come this morning. And you are here. I have just one question for you. Where is the leopard?"

I sighed again and threw my hands up in the air. "Lauricio, I have to apologize. Reuel comes on his own. I have no idea

174

when or why he will come to me. He just does. I should have been up front about that."

Lauricio glared. "Young man, your word and how you act toward people are all you have in this land. Even though I'm one who drinks too much javann, I know those things I just mentioned are most important. Don't be a liar, and don't treat people wrongly. Do you understand?"

"Lauricio!" another man sitting on the street corner yelled and pointed. "Look what is coming!"

I heard a familiar growl from the east. My embarrassment dissipated. I was glad to see Reuel.

People on the sidewalks scattered as the leopard made its way toward us. Automobile horns blared as Reuel ran by on the sidewalk. He had caused an uproar on the street, and I smiled at the thought that he sure knew how to make an entrance.

The leopard arrived at my side with an expression on its face that indicated it was glad to see me. I nuzzled its head and sighed in relief.

"You do have a connection to this leopard," Lauricio said. "You are a man of your word after all."

I looked at Diakono Copperwith, and a smile appeared on his face. I could go to dance practice. Reuel growled his approval.

I arrived at practice thinking about Reuel showing up like he did. I had told Lauricio the truth about the leopard coming of his own accord. Reuel had appeared several times during this journey, and I never had any prior knowledge of when he would arrive.

As usual, the leopard disappeared just as quickly as he came. As soon as we left the street corner by the hotel, Reuel took off in the opposite direction and was gone. I had sensed he was only here today to do me a favor. A few lines from Oscar Ortega's section of the Book of Kammbi came to my mind: *"Reuel became my companion. Whenever I needed the leopard, he would be there. It was like we were connected by some kind of spirit or psychic connection."* Reuel had appeared suddenly during Oscar's travels throughout the land, and it seemed history was repeating itself. I was grateful for today's appearance. At the same time, I accepted Lauricio's rebuke. He was right: all you have is your word and how you treat others.

Ciscoe coached our practice session. He watched Darcie and I practice the basic steps without music first. Ciscoe corrected my posture and position several times. I had learned from him that my body needed to be straight as a line and not leaning into the woman. Darcie had taught me to lean into her for positioning. The two argued about that after we went through the basic steps once. Darcie stated that the traditional way made the man, in command position, look too formal—like he had something stuck up his rear end. There could be no connection with any woman dancing with a man in the traditional command position. Ciscoe countered by dancing the basic steps with Latisha, demonstrating how the traditional command position kept the focus on the dance and showcased the woman. It was dancing, not trying to get lucky for the evening.

While I thought about that, Ciscoe reiterated that the man dancing Guanamamma must be in the traditional command position at all times. If he could not remain in the correct position, he would confuse his partner and make her look bad. That was an act of passha in Ciscoe's mind.

Darcie relented from the argument and clapped for music to come on. "My Heart Fell When I Saw You for the First Time" by Diego Washington played through the speakers. It was an up-tempo Guanamamma song with drums and percussion but much more variety in its rhythm than "Move, Move, Move." Diego's song also had a horn section as an ode to the traditional Guanamamma song. I knew this was a selection from the Maldonados.

"Posture straight. Right hand in the small of Darcie's back," Ciscoe instructed. "One, two, three . . . dance!"

"I still want you to caress my hip, Diondray," Darcie whispered as I moved her across the floor. "I need to feel your hands on me so I can dance better."

Ciscoe's voice cut in sharply. "Watch your hand, Diondray. Keep it in the middle of her back."

"I want him to touch me!" Darcie exploded and pulled away from me. "I dance better when his hands are on me. I don't want to feel like I'm dancing Guanamamma with a stranger."

I stood in the middle of the dance floor as Darcie stormed off. Ciscoe walked over to Darcie as she stood next to the bar. Latisha joined them.

"I want his hands on my body," Darcie continued. "I cannot dance the traditional way. You should know that after all these years."

Ciscoe patted Darcie's hand. I knew their relationship was a thing of the past, but I sensed the warmth and fondness in Ciscoe's gesture. "I did not agree to coach you both so we could argue about our differences in dancing philosophies. I don't agree with the new style of dancing Guanamamma. But as a teacher, I must work with what a student does best. I have seen enough of how you dance together to know that it works well for you. I will work with that style."

Darcie's cheeks were red as an apple when Ciscoe released her hand. "Do you still believe only married couples should dance Guanamamma in the new style?"

Latisha frowned. "Yes, we do. The new style leads to things getting out of hand and expectations for something more than dancing."

Ciscoe nodded. "You know I believe the same way, Darcie. We don't dance Guanamamma for sex. We dance Guanamamma for communication and connection. The new style of dancing has taken the people away from that tradition. The music has followed in the same fashion. We believe Guanamamma can create couples who go on to be married, when sex becomes appropriate. It seems the new style of dancing is meant to promote sex without the communication and connection."

Darcie grabbed glasses of water from behind the bar and handed each of us a glass. "You sound just like my father, Feliciano, and all the men I have ever taken an interest in. Marriage should not be the destination for every relationship. People can be together without marriage."

I agreed with Darcie on that point. My mother, Aunt Maxina, and Uncle Xavier had never been married. They'd all had relationships that did not lead to marriage. As a matter of fact, marriage was not common back home. People got together without having to make some kind of public declaration about it. It seemed the people from north of the Great Forest made a big deal about marriage—but of course, that came from their belief in Kammbi and the teachings from the Book of Kammbi.

"Where does that kind of promiscuity lead to?" Ciscoe fired back. "Relationships without communication and connection. Enjoyment for a time, until you get bored with the person. Or even worse . . . children being produced without commitment. I know we live in a city that believes in music and dancing as a religion. But they tend to forget Walter Fuente was married to his first wife until she died. He then married for the second time, and remained married to his wives until his death. He did not go from woman to woman, as many in this city have been led to believe."

"But Walter Fuente married two women. I was taught marriage was supposed to be one man and one woman. That belief was drilled into my head repeatedly. But you must see that his marriage was worthwhile, just because he stayed married to both women. Ciscoe, I should never have given you that Book of Kammbi. You have become just like the people I grew up with in Santa Teresa."

"Watch your tongue, Darcie Fendlewiesen," Latisha snapped. "I know about the past between you two. But I will not have my husband disrespected in any way."

This debate was escalating fast. I could tell that Latisha was ready to snap Darcie into pieces if she kept arguing with her husband.

"Are we going to get back to dancing?" I said. "I want to learn to dance Guanamamma in the correct way. I want to be ready for the Walter's Grove New Year Celebration."

Darcie faced me and said sarcastically, "And what is the 'correct way,' my beloved?"

"You invited Ciscoe and Latisha to teach us. So despite your differences with his philosophy of dance, you still felt I needed to learn from the best—and that he is the best. If the traditional way is the correct way, then we should learn how to dance in that style."

Darcie smirked. "Even my beloved is going the same way. I bet you have told him about the Book of Kammbi I gave you, Ciscoe. Of course, he has traveled throughout this land believing in the myth of Oscar's prophecy."

"He does know about your gift to Ciscoe," Latisha said. "And we invited him to dinner for that reason. I knew when we first met him that he is the one to fulfill Oscar's prophecy. This entire land will be united as one."

Darcie's face flushed with anger. "Get out! I will not have any of that kind of talk in my nightclub. I did want my beloved to learn from the best. But I will not have him converted into becoming a believer and follower of Kammbi."

The Maldonados nodded and began to leave. I saw the disappointed looks on their faces, and I knew they believed their plan for me to share the teachings of the Book of Kammbi after the celebration had likely gone out the window.

"I would still like you both to teach me how to dance Guanamamma," I said.

"I will not allow it, my beloved. Not here."

I turned and faced Darcie. "That is not your decision to make. I want to learn how to dance from the best. I have come this far, and I want to continue."

Darcie threw her glass to the floor. "You will regret that decision, my beloved. I will not allow another man I care about to become a believer and follower of that backward religion."

"I have been placed on a journey that I still don't fully understand. But I have to see it through. I agree with some of the teachings from the Book of Kammbi. And some of the teachings I don't. But I have been allowed throughout this land for reasons connected to those teachings. I have found connections to this book here and in the city of Adrian, both times very unexpectedly."

Darcie walked away from the bar and toward me. "Don't let those coincidences make you a believer and follower, Diondray. You are special, my beloved."

She placed her right hand on my cheek. Her entire face had become red, and I felt her body shaking next to me.

"I have enjoyed your company, Darcie. But my love is for someone else. I may not ever to get see her again—though the letter I received gives me hope. However, I would still like to dance with you for the celebration. It's your decision. But I want to learn how to dance Guanamamma from Ciscoe and Latisha."

Darcie did not consent. I left the nightclub with the Maldonados knowing that might have been my last time in her company.

The Maldonados invited Diakono Copperwith and me for dinner that evening. I had explained to him earlier in the day that Ciscoe had a copy of the Book of Kammbi in his home and had been reading it for several years. It was the first time I had seen Diakono Copperwith surprised. I told him Ciscoe had gotten the copy from Darcie Fendlewiesen and that she had rejected the religion after their brief relationship.

For dinner, we were served roasted chicken, sliced mangoes with a sweet red sauce that I wanted more of, and green beans. Latisha was a fabulous cook, and Ciscoe commented that it was one of the main reasons he had married her. Diakono

Copperwith said it was the best meal he had eaten since arriving in this region. Latisha was pleased at such high praise from a diakono.

Both Maldonados were clearly surprised to have a diakono in their home. I watched them glance at Diakono Copperwith several times during the dinner. After so much opposition from others, seeing their astonished looks was refreshing.

"We are so honored that you came to our home for dinner," Ciscoe began. "Diondray told us he has been traveling with you throughout both regions of the land. And what an influence you have been to him."

Diakono Copperwith smiled warmly. "Diondray has influenced us just as much as we have influenced him. Our lives have been changed by his presence, and thankfully the Eternal Comforter has given us the correct guidance throughout this journey in our attempt to fulfill Oscar's prophecy."

"Us?" Latisha asked.

Diakono Copperwith frowned. "My wife Annalisa was with us until our arrival in Walter's Grove."

I had not told the Maldonados about Mrs. Copperwith. Her influence had been a major part of this journey, more than Diakono Copperwith's in some respects. I wished she could be here with us for dinner. I believed she would have gotten along with Latisha quite well.

"Did she become sick upon arriving in our city?" Latisha asked.

"No sickness, Latisha. She was summoned back to the region north of the Great Forest. We serve under the konseho of Kammbi. They are the governing body for the region north of the Great Forest. We were allowed to travel with Diondray to this region because of their permission. She needed to return."

Diakono Copperwith ended abruptly. I knew he did not want to go into further detail about why Mrs. Copperwith had returned to Issabella. He had received a second letter from Mrs. Copperwith a couple of days ago stating that she was doing well despite their separation and did not know if she would be able to return to us. We still had the city of Terrance to visit. He missed his wife, and bringing her up in conversation pained him.

"Ciscoe and I both hope for a reunion for you," Latisha said. She clearly sensed that Diakono Copperwith did not want to continue with this vein of conversation.

Diakono Copperwith smiled again and grabbed his glass of brownberry juice from the dinner table. The sooner the talk about his wife ended, the better.

After dinner, Ciscoe brought us up to his study, where he pulled out his copy of the Book of Kammbi. I had brought mine as well, and the two books next to each other were a sight to behold.

"When Diondray brought this copy of the Book of Kammbi to me in Santa Sophia, it was the first time in my entire career as a diakono that I felt the reality of Oscar's prophecy being fulfilled. We had read for years that Oscar had attempted reconciliation with his son, Charles, and left a copy of the Book of Kammbi in the area that would become the city of Charlesville. I never thought I would see it. But we were also taught as diakonos that the Charlesville copy of the Book of Kammbi was only one in this region. Now, I see another in your hands. This, after our experience in Adrian, continues to confirm my belief that the time for Oscar's prophecy to be fulfilled is now."

183

I was beginning to agree with Diakono Copperwith's statement. Adrian Azur had taken pages from the Book of Kammbi and carried them with him on his travels across this region. He had wanted to share those teachings with the natives in what became the city of Adrian. The Boma-Men, too, knew about the Book of Kammbi and its teachings before I arrived. It had been a part of their history for generations. Now, in Walter's Grove, I was at the home of someone who had owned a copy of the Book of Kammbi for several years. It seemed all the groundwork for Oscar's prophecy had been prepared for some time now. However, it still seemed odd that I had become a part of linking it all together.

"The time is now," Ciscoe added. "And Latisha and I want to do our part in helping Oscar's prophecy come to pass."

I glanced at Latisha, who was nodding at her husband's comments. "This city needs to have the teachings of the Book of Kammbi shared amongst its people," she added.

"I have learned that beliefs contradicting this city's hedonistic lifestyle are not well received," Diakono Copperwith said. "I have only been able to get an audience of drunks to hear the teachings. It is my duty to share them with anybody who wants to hear. But I had hoped for a larger audience by now."

Ciscoe closed his copy of the Book of Kammbi and placed it back on the shelf. "That's why Diondray must share the teachings of the Book of Kammbi after the Walter's Grove New Year Celebration. That will be the best chance to reach the city."

Diakono Copperwith looked puzzled. "New Year Celebration?"

"It is our annual festival, celebrating a new year for the city. Latisha and I have danced in the festival each year for the past twenty years. We have a special dance honoring our status as dannzas for the festival. Everyone in the city attends the celebration, and it's the perfect place for Diondray to share teachings from the Book of Kammbi."

Diakono Copperwith smiled at me and placed his left hand on my shoulder. "I would like to suggest that Diondray read one of his themilies instead of sharing teachings from the Book of Kammbi."

Now it was the Maldonados' turn to look puzzled. "Themilies?" Ciscoe asked cautiously.

"A themily is a collection of written thoughts that may be encouraging, inspiring, or admonishing for the audience. I have been writing themilies for several years and have written some during this journey throughout the land," I explained.

"Diondray read a themily in Santa Sophia at the glowing of the shimmaro, a light that is lit thirty days before the Festival of Sinquinta. The festival celebrates the arrival of Oscar Ortega in our part of the land. Diondray read words on that night I will never forget. *'Is a stranger always a stranger? Or can a stranger become a friend? Or do people here keep a stranger at arm's distance? Or do people here bring a stranger close enough to be embraced? Is love for a stranger the same as love for a friend or relative?'* Those words from Diondray reminded of Kammbi's greatest statement from the Book of Kammbi: *'Love me as you love yourself. And love others as you love me.'* His themily augments Kammbi's wisdom about loving the stranger just as you love yourself and those close to you."

Latisha blushed and reached for my hand. "That was beautiful. I would love to hear more of your themilies."

I nodded. I knew Diakono Copperwith could memorize paragraphs from the Book of Kammbi like it was second nature, but I'd had no idea he had memorized that themily. I remembered the sweat dropping from my face on the paper I read it from. My hands had shaken so badly I thought I was going to rip the paper. That audience was bowing in front of the shimmaro, and when they lifted their heads and rose to their feet in appreciation of my words, I was so relieved. I appreciated Diakono Copperwith for remembering it.

Ciscoe had a big smile. "I agree with Diakono Copperwith's suggestion. Diondray, you must read a themily at the New Year Celebration. Words like those you read to people of Santa Sophia I hope will have the same effect here in Walter's Grove."

I hoped Ciscoe was right—but I had my doubts. Santa Sophia was naturally receptive to a themily that reminded them of words from the Book of Kammbi. Would people of this city be receptive in the same manner?

Chapter 15

We had ten days left in Walter's Grove. I had spent my time practicing Guanamamma in the mornings and writing my themily for the New Year in the evenings. The days went by quickly, and I felt like I had not gotten to explore the city yet. I remembered Diakono Copperwith taking me to each quadrant in Santa Sophia, giving me a sense of that city. It had seemed like I was rushed through the other cities north of the Great Forest: Santa Teresa, Alicia, and Issabella. That same feeling was happening so far with the cities in the south: Adrian and now Walter's Grove. I wanted more time in this city, and I did not know if I would be coming back anytime soon after our time was up.

Darcie refused to let the Maldonados and I practice at the nightclub. She was still upset at Ciscoe and Latisha for believing in the teachings from the Book of Kammbi and with me for leaving with them that day. I found out she had convinced other nightclub owners in the Roxie and Penelope District to refuse to let us practice at their places either. Darcie told them the Maldonados had become believers and followers of a strange religion from north of the Great Forest. She said they had turned away from Walter's Credo for all citizens of the city and could not be trusted to teach Guanamamma anymore.

The Maldonados were offended and hurt by Darcie's actions. They had never thought she would go so far as to keep them from practicing Guanamamma dancing at the other nightclubs. And they had not realized how much hatred she had for the teachings from the Book of Kammbi and the religion as a whole. Ciscoe believed Darcie would try to stop us from participating in the Walter's Grove New Year Celebration. And he had to come up with a backup plan just in case his suspicions were true.

I practiced at the Maldonados' home. They had a room in the back of the house with a dance floor and a radio where we could dance. It reminded me of the dance floor at Darcie's, and I felt comfortable immediately there.

Latisha found me a new dance partner for practicing, Donya Elena Herrera. She was a short, plump, dark-brown skinned woman with prominent cheeks and a bubbly personality. Donya Elena had become a dannza recently, and Latisha was her mentor. She had grown up in the East Walter's Grove District like the Maldonados and seemed to know everyone.

After our first practice together, Donya Elena helped me adjust to our height difference and did all she could to make me feel comfortable. I had gotten used to dancing with Darcie, who wasn't much shorter than me. I did not like looking down at Donya Elena. It felt like I was above her in status. I did not want to give off that kind of impression to a new dance partner. Also, Donya Elena was curvaceous but not as wide-hipped as Darcie. So moving across the dance floor with her was compact and tight compared to the lengthy, fluid movements I'd had with Darcie.

Ciscoe coached us hard. By the third day of practicing, I had gotten used to his sharp tone. He continued to correct my posture and made sure my guide hand was in the middle of Donya Elena's back. My hand had slipped to her right hip a few times during practice. She laughed each time it happened and gently placed my hand back into position before Ciscoe caught my error.

By the seventh day, Donya Elena and I had settled into a good dance routine. I had learned to shorten my steps and bring our extended arms closer to our bodies. She moved more gracefully with that slight adjustment, and I began to enjoy dancing with her. It was not the same as with Darcie. But I was glad that Latisha had found her.

The Maldonados opened the practice to other people from the district. I thought this might be part of Ciscoe's backup plan. A few couples attended on the first day they opened the practice. Ciscoe created a social atmosphere, but we all practiced the same routine. He snapped at all of us to do it correctly.

The open practice grew in size over the next couple of days. Donya Elena had traveled throughout the entire district after our rehearsal, advertising the open practice at the Maldonados' home. She made sure people of the district understood that this kind of dance instruction from the legendary dannza couple was only for a special occasion. Her efforts brought so many people that we soon had to change the location of the open practice from the Maldonados' home to the Fuente Center a few blocks away.

Our first day at the Fuente Center brought rain. It had not rained the entire time I had been in the city. The rain lasted nearly an hour. I hoped it was not a sign to keep us from practicing. I thought the Maldonados would cancel practice, but they did not, and the employees of the Fuente Center and people who were participating helped move the water off the makeshift dance floor so we could practice. Donya Elena had gotten the Fuente Center employees to build a dance floor the night before our first practice there. It was east of the main building on land reminiscent of Aliki Park back home.

A few hours after the rain had started, the dance floor was ready for the open practice. Ciscoe and Latisha stood on the north end, ready to give instruction. They were dressed like the first night I'd seen them at Darcie's. Ciscoe wore a skin-tight black V-neck shirt with black pants trimmed in silver. I did not know if he was the same age as Diakono Copperwith or older, but his dannza outfit fitted excellently. Latisha wore a silver midthigh dress with black frills at the bottom and silver shoes. She looked beautiful as she smiled at us.

"We will go through the routine once without music," Ciscoe started his instruction. "Dancing Guanamamma is about movement with or without music. Your steps should be natural to you, like walking. On my count . . . one, two, three."

Donya Elena and I were in the front of the group. She had a wide smile on her face as I led her through the routine. I was trying to make sure I got the basic steps down. I had been dancing Guanamamma in this more traditional style for some days now, but I was still thinking through the steps.

"You are doing well," Donya Elena commented.

"Thanks." I replied while trying to concentrate on spinning Donya Elena a couple of times as Ciscoe gave instructions. I wanted to make sure I spun her correctly without the music. Donya Elena understood my concern and spun on time after I guided her into a backward step.

"I'm so glad Mr. and Mrs. Maldonado are doing this open practice for the district," she said as we returned to the basic position of going forward with my left hand interlocked with her right hand. "We are going to have a routine in the Walter's Grove New Year Celebration. That's so incredible for our district."

I looked around at the other couples in the group. They all were following instructions as best as they could. I saw Latisha working with a couple behind us to the right. The man had a frustrated look on his face. Latisha took his position and danced with his partner, showing him how to lead. She placed the man back with his partner and guided him through the steps. I noticed her correcting his posture as he danced.

"We have two days to get this routine ready," Ciscoe announced as he turned on the music. "I want to make sure every couple here dances it correctly. Don't worry about your experience level. I know many of you probably dance Guanamamma in your homes or even go to the nightclubs in the Roxie and Penelope District. However, we are dancing to celebrate our city, and that's completely different from dancing Guanamamma in those other places. I believe our dance routine will be remembered for a long time. And the East Walter's Grove District will be the talk of the city for the entire year."

Donya Elena squeezed my left hand and grinned at Ciscoe's announcement. "It's about time East Walter's Grove gets mentioned citywide!" she yelled out.

"Right on, Donya Elena!" said one of the couples behind us.

"Let's show our city we have the best dancers in the city!" said another couple to the left of us.

The rest of the couples added their appreciation for Donya Elena's comment. Ciscoe waved his hands to calm everyone down.

"We have one more song for practice today. It is a classic by Walter Fuente, 'Longing for Penelope.' It was the first song he wrote for Penelope Mentz after they met. It's an easy song for dancing. Let's end on a good note. I want all the men to lead their partners, going back and forth twice into a left sidestep and then a spin. Remember that your guide hand must be in the middle of her back, not on her hip or behind!"

Donya Elena chuckled and squeezed my hand. "Ciscoe is going to break you from that bad habit you learned from Darcie Fendlewiesen."

I laughed. "For sure."

Before Ciscoe could play the song, I saw a Fuente Center employee running toward us. He had a paper in his hand, and he waved it at Ciscoe. He reached Ciscoe and handed the paper to him. Ciscoe read the paper, and a frown came over his face.

"I'm sorry, Mr. Maldonado." I overheard the employee tell Ciscoe. He spoke with Ciscoe for a couple of minutes. I could not hear the rest of their conversation, but I knew Ciscoe was not happy with what the employee was telling him.

"Everyone, I have something to share with you all," Ciscoe began as the employee stepped to his right. "I have just received a letter stating that my wife and I cannot dance in the New Year's Celebration. The reason given is that they believe we have been under the influence of a strange religion from north of the Great Forest and have broken Walter's Credo. As you know, no resident who has broken Walter's Credo can participate in our city's biggest celebration of the year."

The group became silent. Latisha had joined her husband toward the front of the group.

"We are not allowed to practice here at the Fuente Center anymore. This is city property, and since my wife and I have broken Walter's Credo . . . we cannot use city property to further our beliefs."

"They cannot do this!" Donya Elena erupted. "We will dance at the New Year Celebration."

I glanced at the other couples and saw a few of them nodding at her comment. However, most of the couples simply looked stunned.

"I appreciate your declaration, Donya Elena," Ciscoe replied as his wife stood by his side. "We will continue to practice in our home and prepare our routine. Latisha and I believe something special is meant to happen at the celebration, and we will do our part."

Ciscoe shot a look at me. He pursed his lips, and I sensed that he'd known this action was coming. Darcie Fendlewiesen was behind it. I knew what I had to do.

"You cannot go back to that temptress again," Diakono Copperwith declared that evening in his hotel room. I had told him what happened at the Fuente Center earlier. He admired Ciscoe and Latisha's dedication to continue with the routine. But I had no idea where they were going to have us perform it.

"I have to talk to her," I replied. "She has some integrity."

Diakono Copperwith scoffed. "Integrity! The only integrity she has is in her rejection of her belief in Kammbi and his teachings. She has made that clear to you and the Maldonados."

He was correct. Darcie hated everything about believing and following Kammbi. I knew part of the reason was that she'd had to leave her birth city of Santa Teresa to flee an arranged marriage. However, I believed there were deeper reasons for her rejection of the religion she'd grown up with, and I had to find out what they were.

"She has used her influence to keep the Maldonados from performing at the New Year Celebration. I believe I can convince her to let them perform."

"You are going to get burned again," Diakono Copperwith shot back. "Or maybe that magic inside of you will protect you from her once more."

I had not thought about the Boma Essence since the night at Darcie's when I danced with Krystle. After that encounter at the nightclub, I had not felt any strange sensations or energy flowing through my body. I knew the magic was still inside of me, but I assumed the Boma Essence would come out when I needed it most. I was surprised to hear Diakono Copperwith mention the Essence. I knew he was still struggling with the ramifications of his decision to defend me against the konseho.

"I don't agree with the beliefs of a city that is based on music and dancing. Those things lead to promiscuous behavior and hedonism," Diakono Copperwith said in a soft tone. He ran his left hand through his blond hair and sighed. "But I would not have believed there would be a couple in this city who have a copy of the Book of Kammbi in their possession and have read from it over the past few years. I hope you convince that temptress to let the Maldonados dance."

I smiled and shook his hand. I appreciated his trust in me, and I knew he was relying on the guidance of the Eternal Comforter more than he probably would ever have imagined.

I met Darcie at her nightclub the next morning, one day before the celebration. Decorations lined the streets of the Roxie and Penelope District. Red, green, and gold streamers were flowing from the buildings and traffic lights throughout the district. Replicas of the painting from the Wall of Walter's Declaration were on every street corner. The city was getting ready for its biggest celebration. I hoped that the Maldonados would be a part of it.

Darcie opened the nightclub's main entrance. She had a solemn look but managed a thin smile as I entered. The nightclub owner wore a long, flowing green maxi dress that accentuated her hips. It was a dress for evening, and it seemed out of place at this time of the day.

"I'm pleased you are here, my beloved," she said as we reached the dance floor where we used to practice. I was surprised that she would still call me by that name. *I might have a chance here*, I thought.

"Same here," I replied as I sat next to her at the bar. She handed me a glass of brownberry juice. "Are you keeping Ciscoe and Latisha from dancing in the Walter's Grove New Year Celebration?"

She raised her eyebrows. "Going right into an accusation? I thought we had built a level of trust by now."

"I enjoyed my time with you. And you made up for what happened on the first night we met. However, I need to know if you have used your influence to keep the Maldonados from dancing tomorrow. You should know how much this means to them."

Darcie's cheeks went red, and she moved her blonde hair away from her face. "Ciscoe should have gotten rid of that book I gave him. It has no place in this city. A city about music, dance, and love! I know he has shared with you that he got that book from me."

I nodded after drinking my glass of brownberry juice. "Why did you give it to him? You don't believe in its teachings anymore. And you have rejected being a believer and follower of Kammbi. I'm surprised you would have a copy of that book with you when you came here."

"My beloved, you are perceptive," she replied and reached for my hands. "That Book of Kammbi was a gift from my father. Even though we had our differences, and even though he arranged the marriage to Vincent, I loved my father. He was a good man. He sent me that copy of the Book of Kammbi when I lived in Alicia. He was angry with me for leaving Santa Teresa and refusing to marry Vincent. But he believed if I had the Book of Kammbi with me, I would eventually come back home. If I did, he would have a morrim perform an act of aphemmia for the acts of passha I had committed in not getting married."

I had not heard the word *aphemmia* spoken since leaving Santa Sophia. Diakono Copperwith had explained that aphemmia was an act of contrition performed by a believer and follower of Kammbi in acknowledgement of acts of passha. It was of the greatest importance that believers and followers of Kammbi acknowledge their acts of passha and confess them to the highest-ranking member of the kahall they attended. Each disciple in the Book of Kammbi had performed an aphemmia during his or her journey and written several paragraphs in the book about its importance.

"The Book of Kammbi you gave Ciscoe was your last connection to your past in Santa Teresa and to your father. And you gave it away. Ciscoe must have been special to you."

Darcie pulled me off my seat and embraced me. "I loved Ciscoe. He was the first man I had loved since leaving my birth city. I did not love Vincent. I respected Feliciano. But Ciscoe was different. He taught me how to dance Guanamamma. Even though we have always argued about the style of dancing that is most authentic for the people of this city, Ciscoe is a great teacher. He helped me get this nightclub. When I gave him that book, he changed. He fell under the spell of its teachings. He began to believe the words in that book, just like my father. Like Feliciano. And you are going down that same path."

I released myself from Darcie's embrace and held her hands. Her eyes watered, and she had an exasperated look on her face. "And that's why you have rejected the book. You think the ones you love have become brainwashed by its teachings."

"Yes, my beloved. That's why I had to keep Ciscoe and Latisha from dancing at the New Year Celebration. I know he wants to speak from the Book of Kammbi during the festival. Your arrival in Walter's Grove has given him the confidence to do as such."

I listened carefully. She did not know our plan to have me read a themily after the Maldonados performed their dance. Instead, Darcie believed Ciscoe was going to share the teachings from the Book of Kammbi in some capacity. She knew the power of the words written in that sacred book even as she had rejected it.

"You know I'm here in Walter's Grove because I'm considered to be the one to fulfill Oscar's prophecy. I have traveled throughout both regions, and things have happened I would never have expected. Things that have shown me the connection to Kammbi is not just for the people to the north. Things in this region show me that Oscar's prophecy is meant to be fulfilled."

Darcie jerked away. "Don't say that! It's not true. Oscar had relations outside of his marriage, and he abandoned that woman and child. How can a prophecy be fulfilled when the man who spoke it committed that kind of act of passha?"

"'That woman' was Mother Adrianna, and she will be respected. Oscar attempted reconciliation and performed an aphemmia. It is in his chapter of the Book of Kammbi. You should know that. I have not become a believer and follower of Kammbi yet. But I cannot deny the signs I have seen throughout my journey. And the fact that a man in Walter's Grove received a Book of Kammbi from someone who rejected her religion, and that the man has been reading and living by it for the past few years, is another sign in its favor. There is something here, and I have to follow it to the end."

I began to leave the nightclub.

"Don't leave, my beloved," Darcie pleaded. "I want you to stay here with me. You don't have to fulfill Oscar's prophecy. This land does not need to be united by Kammbi. We simply need to be united."

I whirled around. "Don't you know I love someone else? Remember the letter you took from me."

"She doesn't love you!" Darcie flung back. "If that woman loved you, she would have come with you on this journey. When a woman loves a man, she doesn't leave his side."

I could feel the anger burning inside of me. How could she say that Maisa did not love me? I had a letter that I read every day declaring her love for me. I headed for the exit.

"You have never loved anybody, my beloved," Darcie said as I reached the door. "I got it wrong. That woman may have loved you. But you did not love her. You have always walked away from love."

I stopped and turned my head.

"You can learn to love for the first time, my beloved. Stay here with me."

I left the nightclub for the last time.

Chapter 16

"You have never loved anybody, my beloved. I got it wrong. That woman may have loved you. But you did not love her. You have always walked away from love."

Darcie's last words kept me awake the rest of the evening. I tried to finish the themily I had planned to read for the celebration, but I could not. I telephoned Ciscoe and explained to him that I was having trouble coming up with the words. I told him about my meeting with Darcie and my failed attempt to get her help in letting the Maldonados dance at the celebration. Ciscoe appreciated my effort, but he said his backup plan was coming together. I had to meet him by noon in the parking lot of the Mango Nightclub in the Roxie and Penelope District. That nightclub was across the street from the Josette, the city's largest arena. Donya Elena had spoken with the owner of the Mango, Antonio Henderson, about letting the people of the East Walter's Grove District dance in the nightclub's parking lot. Mr. Henderson agreed to the request. He believed the parking lot would be the best place to catch most of the people going to the New Year Celebration across the street at the Josette.

I had four hours to finish writing my themily before I left for the celebration. I had written the first draft a couple of days ago, and I was glad I'd done that, otherwise I might not have been able to finish it. I kept replaying Darcie's words over and over in my mind. Did I always walk away from love? I remembered Mara telling me that I'd kept her at arm's length during our relationship. She was my first real relationship back home in Charlesville. Mother had arranged for us to be together. Mara came from one of the most prominent families in the city, and Mother felt I needed to have a young lady of the same status as our family. Just before Mara and I began our relationship, I had shown interest in a young lady named Stephani from the eastside of the city. Stephani came to Aliki Park to hear me read my themilys. She was beautiful. However, when I told Mother about Stephani, she forbade me from trying to have a relationship with her. She also demanded that I stop going to Aliki Park at that time, and the nature of our mother-son relationship changed from that moment. While I did not stop going, I did hang out with Mara and tried to get to know her. She was a nice young lady and pleasant to be around. I liked her. But I did not love her. If I had kept her at arm's length, I felt it was justified.

But Maisa had made a similar claim on the autobus when we traveled from Santa Teresa to Issabella. She claimed I was inexperienced about love because of my comments regarding the disciple Alicia's writings in her chapter of the Book of Kammbi, about her husband's sacrifice to the river god for his disobedience toward Oscar Ortega. Alicia wrote glowingly about her husband, but I believed she had overlooked his disobedience. Maisa challenged that assertion and claimed a woman would always protect the man she loved.

Does love cover up faults? Does love push logic to the side?
Does love make it impossible to keep someone at arm's length? Those
three questions started me writing the final draft of my themily.
I wrote everything that came to mind for several minutes.
Finally, I knew what I had to share with the people of this city.

Diakono Copperwith and I made it to the Mango
nightclub parking lot a couple of hours before the celebration
started. We had a good view of the Josette across the street.
It was a large, bowl-shaped arena decorated in red, green, and
purple streamers like the rest of the district. People were already
lined up waiting to get into the Josette.

I stood at the edge of the parking lot people-watching.
Diakono Copperwith walked across the street to let the
festivalgoers know about our performance. It was odd seeing
him not dressed in his usual shawl or carrying a copy of the
Book of Kammbi in his hand. Ciscoe had asked him two
nights ago to dress in a regular jumpsuit for the occasion. To
my surprise, Diakono Copperwith agreed without hesitation. I
thought he would have balked at Ciscoe's request. He did not.
Instead, he mingled in the waiting line with the festivalgoers.

Ciscoe had explained the Walter's Grove New Year
Celebration was one of two major festivals the city celebrated
each year. It lasted one and half days and was less formal than the
Festival of Josette, the city's main festival. The Festival of Josette,
named after Walter Fuente's first wife, Josette Eichenberg, was
celebrated on the twenty-fifth of Yul, the seventh month, and
lasted six days. The city closed down during the Festival of
Josette, and everybody in Walter's Grove participated in some
capacity. Ciscoe believed it was not a coincidence that I had

come to the city around the time of the New Year Celebration instead of the Festival of Josette.

Donya Elena summoned me away from people-watching to another area of the parking lot. There was a makeshift dance floor similar to the one at the Fuente Center. Couples were already standing in place and getting ready to perform. Some smiled tensely as I walked past them with Donya Elena. None of them had ever been asked to perform a dance routine, and nerves were bound to come up at this time.

Donya Elena gave encouragement to each couple we passed on the way to the other side of the parking lot. Whether through a compliment, a pat on the shoulder, or a hug, I sensed that her bubbly personality made everyone feel better. Her energy cut through the tension and anxiety like a stiff breeze on a hot day.

Each couple were dressed like dannzas. The men wore all black with sliver trim on their sleeves and the bottom of their pants. The women wore silver dresses that stopped just above the knee and silver shoes. I found out the Maldonados had provided these outfits for each couple, and everyone looked great.

I made it to the portable bathroom behind the makeshift dance floor. Donya Elena stood next to the bathroom's entrance. She had a big smile on her face.

"There is an outfit for you in here," she said and opened the door.

I nodded and entered the bathroom. There was a leopard-print outfit hanging up. It looked similar to what the Boma-Men wore in Boma Village. I gaped at it. Why would they give me this kind of outfit?

"I've heard about that leopard appearing at Darcie's," Donya Elena said from behind me. "People believe you were the reason for the leopard to come into the nightclub. They say you have a special connection with it. I have been told the leopard has been seen in our district as well. I wanted you to wear an outfit honoring that connection. Ciscoe believes something special is going to happen with you today."

Had Reuel been appearing in the East Walter's Grove District during my time in this city? I wondered if there were woods nearby. That might explain why the leopard had come to the street corner near the hotel so quickly a few days ago.

"I hope you like the outfit," Donya Elena said, breaking me away from my thoughts.

I faced her and smiled. She grinned, and I noticed how her cheeks rose from her face. I closed the portable bathroom door and got dressed quickly. The leopard outfit hugged my body, but I had room to move. However, it was the tightest clothing I had ever worn. I hoped the fabric wouldn't rip or tear while dancing. That would be embarrassing.

I put on the shiny black shoes that came with the outfit. They fitted the same way as the clothing. I stood up straight and took a couple of deep breaths. I looked at myself in the bathroom's mirror and felt a surge of energy flow through my body. It was like the leopard suit facilitated the surge of energy. I felt my body expand in order to receive it.

"We have not communicated since you left Adrian."

I knew that voice. I took another deep breath and focused my mind in order to communicate back to Omari.

"This is true."

"I explained that you are one of us. A Boma-Man. I knew from our first meeting. Micah told me how the leopard responded

to you. Leopards travel their own path. They will choose whom they want to connect to. Reuel has chosen you, like he did Oscar Ortega and Adrian Azur."

I nodded and added, "Are you speaking to me because I'm wearing a leopard outfit?"

"Correct. Anytime you put on anything leopard-oriented, or anytime Reuel is near with you, I will be able to communicate with you. That will be our connection. Also, I will know what is going on with you at that particular time."

"Then you know I'm getting ready to dance."

"I do. And you are going to read words like you did in Boma Village. These people will receive your words as we received them."

"But you should know that I'm to help share the teachings from the Book of Kammbi."

"Let your companion take care of that. Your role is to be yourself for these people, like you were for the people of Adrian. And for us. Dance with the power of the Boma Essence inside of you. You will fulfill Oscar's prophecy if you stay true to that connection."

There was a knock on the door. "Diondray, it's time," came Donya Elena's voice through the door.

"Open your hands."

I obeyed Omari's command, and he continued, *"You don't have the mask we gave you. I'm creating a new mask for you. You will need it."*

Wind circled over my hands for several seconds, and a silver mask appeared suddenly. It was shaped like a leopard's head and gleamed in my hands. Omari had stopped talking to me, but I had received instruction on when I was going to wear it. I was ready.

I stood at the front of the dance floor next to Donya Elena. She smiled but kept glancing curiously at the silver leopard mask I had placed on the floor to the left of us. I knew she wondered where it had come from, but she remained silent. She placed my right hand in position on the small of her back and intertwined her other hand with my left. The Boma Essence was flowing through me, not as powerfully as it had in the portable bathroom but still simmering.

"You are connected to the leopard," Donya Elena whispered.

"More than I could have ever expected," I replied.

The Maldonados stood in the front of the group. Both wore stoic expressions, and I saw them give me a quick glance. Ciscoe clapped his hands, and the band at the edge of the dance floor struck up a song. A huskily built singer with a dark brown complexion and treetop hairstyle started to sing. Behind him were the rest of the band: a guitarist, drummer, and percussionist.

"It's time to celebrate. Celebrate a new year. Celebrate a new beginning. Let the things of the past wash away. Let's move from the past and turn to a new chapter in the book of life. It's time to celebrate."

The singer proclaimed that first verse with conviction, and I was ready to dance. I led Donya Elena into a basic back-and-forth step. Next, we went to several side steps as the singer began the next verse. As we moved with the rhythm of the song, I began to get lost in the music. The percussionist broke into a solo as I spun Donya Elena several times. Her body drew closer to me, but my guide hand stayed in position on her back.

"It's time to celebrate. Celebrate a new year. Celebrate a new beginning. Let the things of the past wash away. Celebration has arrived in Walter's Grove. Celebration in my city . . . the best city

in the region. We know how to celebrate better than anyone else. Am I right?"

"Yes, we do!" Donya Elena erupted. "Sing it, Coltrain!"

I heard the name with interest—so this was Coltrain Hayes. I remembered listening to his music on the autobus when we were traveling from Santa Teresa to Alicia. The autobus driver was originally from Walter's Grove but had moved to Alicia to work in the silver mines before getting hired by Frederic Cortes as a driver. He had played a Coltrain Hayes cassette on the autobus. The driver explained that Hayes wrote about the many women in his life and named his songs after them. "Anna" was the song I remembered from that day. I recognized his voice and was surprised that he was here.

Coltrain began the third verse after a guitar solo. I was able to look out at the other dancers and saw that a huge crowd had surrounded us. Across the street, people in line for the Josette were watching and listening too. Ciscoe's plan was working.

I led Donya Elena into several cross-body moves as the song wound down. She smiled widely as she stared at me. The dance routine came easily. All our practice was paying off. I felt like a real Guanamamma dancer.

The song ended, and Coltrain Hayes took a deep breath. He was a big man, but he carried his size well, especially in the upper body. He snapped his fingers, and the drummer began a drumroll.

"I have a little story to tell everyone before I begin the next song. Stories are good for the spirit, and when you hear a good one, you will remember it. I hope you all will remember this story."

Coltrain paused and stared at the crowd. It seemed like he wanted to make sure everyone paid attention. The singer glanced at me and nodded.

"There is an animal that lives in the forest," he began. "It lives alone and does not travel in a pack. It chooses its prey carefully and takes it up into trees to keep it from other predators. This animal works at night, unlike the other animals in the forest. It sees everything. It hears everything. It sizes up everything. People from the west, near Three Rivers, worship it. Legend has it that this animal chose those people to worship it because those people share its attributes. Now, it has been said that this animal arrived in our city. It appeared inside of a nightclub because of someone it has chosen. Someone who carries the same attributes. Someone who will always stand away from the group. Someone who is a kindred spirit."

As Coltrain told the story, the leopard mask on the ground began to glow. Donya Elena stared at the mask. I grabbed it and felt a surge of energy flow through my hands as I placed it on my face. The flow was similar to what had happened in the portable bathroom earlier. It felt like my body expanded to accommodate the increased surge of energy. I pulled Donya Elena into position, and we began to dance. We started with the basic back and forth of the Guanamamma steps. Then I spun Donya Elena several times in a perfect circular motion. Colors appeared around us: red, green, and purple. Donya Elena kept her eyes on me as we began to dance through the parking lot. The colors streaked in motion with us. The surge of energy continued to radiate from the mask. I could see everyone in the crowd clearly, and I sensed they were all amazed by our performance.

I led Donya Elena back to our original position in the parking lot and released her from my grasp. I danced solo. The colors shot up into the air from my body as I spun several times off one foot. After spinning, I circled Donya Elena. She was transfixed, her gaze on me. I moved away and began running directly toward the crowd. Before I reached them, I did several backflips and returned to my position in the parking lot.

I did not hear any music from Coltrain Hayes and the band. The music was in my mind. I heard every instrument more clearly than I ever had before. I heard Coltrain's voice like he was singing in my mind. Music should be heard like this all the time, I thought. I felt the song travel into my body like it was summoned by the surge of energy flowing through me.

The colors dissipated into the air as I stopped dancing. I had the crowd's undivided attention. And so I began my themily.

The power of the dance
The rhythm of the music
The celebration of a new year
Have come together
For a special time
It's all connected
Connected to what has come before
Connected to what is happening now
Connected to what will happen in the future
And it's time to let that connection come from an unexpected place
A place where it chooses you
A place you did not expect
A place you will never forget
You must embrace that connection

If you want to move forward
Because we have to move on
From the things of the past
In order for a new birth
To come into the world
As it needs to come into the world
And today that birth has come
On the day of a celebration about the new year.
On a day where we forget what happened in the prior year.
This connection comes with a leopard
That has been written about in a book
people of the north consider sacred
That a people to the west of here worship
A leopard that lives in the Great Forest and comes to the city.

After I spoke those words, I heard a familiar growl coming towards me from the east end of the parking lot. It had confirmed the words I spoke to the people of this city.

Chapter 17

Our dance in the Mango nightclub parking lot was the talk of the city for our last couple of days in Walter's Grove. I heard it discussed on the radio in my hotel room. People came up to me in the lobby and asked if I was the one who had danced like a leopard during the celebration. People stared at me as I walked by.

I was still trying to process everything that had happened. Had the Boma Essence guided me to dance like that? I had never felt so powerful in my life. After the dance, the people had gone into the Josette and participated in the New Year Celebration as usual. But I heard from Donya Elena that the traditional Guanamamma dance performed by the dannzas received a lukewarm response from the audience. She knew they were still talking about what they had witnessed in the Mango nightclub parking lot.

I had dinner with Diakono Copperwith at the Maldonados home a few days after my dance in the Mango nightclub parking lot. Our dinner was quiet as well. Everyone was trying to process what had happened in the parking lot. The mask. The colors. My dance. Reuel. All of it.

"I have never seen anyone dance like that," Ciscoe said while staring at me. "Coltrain Hayes's story was perfect for you."

Latisha nodded at her husband's comment. Diakono Copperwith had a stoic look on his face.

"I don't think it was Guanamamma dancing," I replied.

Ciscoe laughed. "No, it was not. But it was magnificent."

"It was. And to see the leopard coming to you like that—it was like your dance called the animal to you," Latisha added.

"What now?" I said.

"Well, we got an audience for Diakono Copperwith's teachings. People are intrigued by the leopard, and it can be shown in the Book of Kammbi that Reuel traveled with Oscar Ortega during his journey," Ciscoe answered.

"It can," Diakono Copperwith finally spoke. "But you are going to need support after Diondray and I leave this city."

Everyone remained silent at that comment. We were leaving in two days.

"The konseho of Kammbi will bring support to this city," Diakono Copperwith continued. "But I have to explain to them what you did, Diondray. That will not be easy."

"Will they call you back to Issabella?" I asked.

Diakono Copperwith shook his head. "Senior Padre Ashland and several of the older members of the konseho may request that I return. However, I will not go. I must finish this journey with you. I will admit that the magic inside of you is deeply concerning to me. I fear it may be used to keep you from connecting to the Eternal Comforter. You may end up responding to the magic instead of the gift that is given to all who believe in and follow Kammbi."

The Maldonados looked blank. I had explained the Boma Essence and what had happened to me in the village to them a few nights ago, and I had told them that it was my receiving the Boma Essence that caused Mrs. Copperwith to return to Issabella.

"You said the Boma-Men knew about the Book of Kammbi?" Latisha asked. "That they were connected to Adrian Azur when he came from the east? Adrian Azur was chosen by the leopard when he traveled to that area, correct?"

I nodded.

"Do you believe having the Boma Essence could keep him from being connected to the Eternal Comforter?" she continued.

"I have been taught to believe that magic could keep someone from being connected to Eternal Comforter." Diakono Copperwith replied. "There are members of the konseho of Kammbi who are adamantly against magic. They believe magic is not from Kammbi and can only be used for evil purposes. In their eyes, the person meant to fulfill the only prophecy in the Book of Kammbi should not be someone who has magic."

Ciscoe frowned. "But if it's used in the right context, then it can be connected to Kammbi. Look at the river god of Issabella River. The tribe in that area believed the river god was the only one to worship until Oscar Ortega arrived. The river god submitted to Oscar Ortega immediately after his arrival and commanded the people of the tribe to do the same. That deity knew Oscar Ortega worshiped a greater authority than itself."

I watched Diakono Copperwith's expression while the Maldonados spoke in my defense. I knew he was surprised at their knowledge of the Book of Kammbi. I felt the same way. They knew the inside of that book just as well as anyone in the cities north of the Great Forest.

"I will use your argument after I get support from the konseho of Kammbi to come to this city. Your wisdom comes from the Eternal Comforter," Diakono Copperwith said.

The Maldonados arranged an autobus for us on our last day in Walter's Grove. An attractive, heavyset woman with dimples greeted Diakono Copperwith and me in the hotel's lobby. She carried our luggage to the autobus parked in front of the hotel's main entrance. I only slept a few hours as I tried to process what had happened during the New Year Celebration. I saw the colors, heard Omari's words in my mind, and felt the Boma Essence flow through my body while I slept. Diakono Copperwith's comments about the konseho of Kammbi's position toward magic awoke me. Would they truly accept me as the one to fulfill Oscar's prophecy? If people in the cities south of the Great Forest became believers and followers of Kammbi, would I get credit for making it happen? Would that be presumptuous on my part? Those thoughts ran across my mind as I wrote a themily before leaving the hotel room.

Can a belief system be absolute?
Can a belief system be totally pure?
If so, where does the purity come from?
Humankind or the one they worship?
Or from the words written in a sacred book?
What if a different perspective comes along
To augment a belief system?
Do those believers and followers reject it?
Do they regard it with suspicion?

Do they accept it?
Or embrace it
With trust that the one they worship
Can use the augmentation for his own purposes?

I reflected on the themily as I got on the autobus. Diakono Copperwith sat across from me and stared out of the window. He had prayed for us earlier and told me that he'd shared everything I did at the New Year Celebration with the konseho of Kammbi. Like he'd predicted at dinner a couple nights ago, the older members of the konseho wanted him to return to Issabella. I had discovered a couple who had been reading the Book of Kammbi for several years and were trying to live their life by its teachings, but that was not enough for some members who believed a person with magic inside of him could not be the one who fulfilled Oscar's prophecy.

During the phone call with the konseho, Diakono Copperwith had used the Maldonado's defense of me. Deputy Santiago had been surprised to hear that the couple were behind it, and it caused him to side with the diakono. He wanted him to remain on the journey with me. Mrs. Copperwith was on the phone call also, and she came to my defense as well. I was surprised by that, especially after our last conversation before she returned to Issabella. Both Mrs. Copperwith and Deputy Santiago encouraged the rest of the konseho to send resources to Walter's Grove and build a kahall in the city. They had done the same thing in the city of Adrian, where they were cultivating believers and followers of Kammbi amongst the people, including the Boma-Men. Deputy Santiago also wanted to honor the Maldonados for their faithfulness to the

Book of Kammbi. Their devotion proved Kammbi could reach anyone throughout the land.

The diakono and I boarded the autobus to leave, but before we pulled away, I heard a knock on the autobus door. The driver waved her hand, signaling the autobus was getting ready to move. But the knocking continued, and someone called my name. I rose from my seat and caught a glimpse of long blonde hair outside.

"She wants to talk to me," I told the driver.

She whirled around. "I don't like people doing that as I'm getting ready to drive. You have five minutes before we leave."

I nodded and left my seat.

"You don't have to talk to that temptress anymore," Diakono Copperwith said. "She made her rejection of Kammbi clear, and she attempted to get you to do the same."

He was correct. A part of me wanted to tell the driver to leave. But I could not do that to Darcie Fendlewiesen.

"You got four minutes!"

"I will talk with her."

Diakono Copperwith frowned as I got off the autobus. I must admit I wanted to hear what she had to say.

Darcie wrapped her arms around me and placed her face on my chest. My body went stiff as a board. I kept my hands at my side and began to wiggle free from her embrace.

"I'm sorry, my beloved," she began. "I cannot stop you from leaving. But I wanted to apologize for our last conversation. I accused you of not being able to love. I was wrong to make that kind of accusation. Please forgive me."

I released myself from her arms and stared at her. "You're forgiven. I hold no ill feelings toward you." I kissed her hand and turned around to get back on the autobus.

"You are the second man I have ever loved. I did not think I would feel this way about any man after Ciscoe. I want you to remember that more than one woman loves you."

I got on the autobus and sat in my seat as the driver took off from the hotel. I looked out the window at Darcie. She waved and blew me a kiss. I waved back, realizing her declaration of love was genuine.

PART 3

Terrance

Chapter 18

I remained silent on the three-hour drive to Terrance.
Diakono Copperwith tried to ask me about Darcie. What
did she say? However, I said nothing. I'd had two women
declare their love to me, but my love was only for one of them.

I had placed Maisa's letter inside of my writing pad where
I kept my themilies. I'd read her letter again this morning
before leaving for Terrance. It gave me comfort in the belief
that I would see her again. However, I wished she were sitting
on the autobus next to me. Her presence would have mitigated
the feelings I was having for Darcie. I knew it was not love I felt
for the nightclub owner. It was desire. I had wanted to take her
in my arms after she declared love for me and become intimate.
Mara was the last woman I had made love to. Darcie brought
out that same desire. Maybe she was a temptress, as Diakono
Copperwith said. And he wanted to keep me away from her. I
could never tell him that I wanted to make love to Darcie.

The drive to Terrance was not scenic—mostly just
farmland and trees. However, the scenery changed once we
reached the city. The autobus driver, Stella Bradenstocke,
explained that we were coming into the city on Avenue Syonne,
the longest street in Terrance. It was named after one of its
greatest regnators, Syonne Lamsdorff.

I knew of Syonne because of his agreement with my Great-Uncle Myro that allowed immigrants from this city to come to Charlesville. The initial twenty-year agreement had started in the year 175 A.O.A. It brought an influx of immigrants to my home city. Uncle Xavier had been angry with his father for making this agreement, because he believed the immigrants from Terrance would overtake Charlesville when he became ruler. Uncle Xavier had always believed Syonne pawned off his outcasts and pariahs for immigration. I was not sure about his claim, but the immigrants did populate the eastside of Charlesville and brought their influence to the city.

We passed one building after another jammed together as the autobus turned from Avenue Syonne onto Avenue Nante. The autobus driver pointed out the city's landmarks, including one called the Stuttgarte, which was to right of us as we turned off Avenue Syonne. The Stuttgarte was the city's oldest landmark and the most distinctive according to the driver. It was a pyramidal building that dominated the skyline. Large murals on each side of the building were a homage to the gods that had founded the city.

"The gods," Diakono Copperwith repeated. "The people of this city believe in more than one god?"

Stella gave Diakono Copperwith a blank stare before she replied, "People used to believe in the gods long ago. They worshiped many, especially Megaro, the sea god. But that ended when Syonne became regnator. He encouraged the citizens of this city to believe in humankind and the government instead of the gods of the past."

"Trust in Kammbi with your heart and mind and not your own faculties for understanding," Diakono Copperwith replied.

"Book seven of the Ryianza section, Kammbi's chapter, the fourteenth paragraph," I said.

Diakono Copperwith cracked a smile. "You have the Eternal Comforter inside of you despite having magic."

I shrugged. I was remembering more of the Book of Kammbi than I would have ever expected. "Why did Syonne encourage the people of this city to stop believing in the gods?" I asked.

Stella glanced at me through the mirror. "I'm not an expert in the history of our city. I'm just a member of the lowerclass trying to make a living and take care of my family. However, I do know that Syonne felt the people of the city became indoctrinated by the gods. He thought they needed to believe in themselves and other people more than the gods."

She pulled into the hotel's parking lot. The hotel had a rustic look, with brown wood enclosing a patterned façade. It was the complete opposite of the hotel we had stayed at in Walter's Grove, or, for that matter, the Hastancia de Gamon in Adrian.

"We may have our biggest challenge yet here, Diondray," Diakono Copperwith said as we exited the autobus. "This city's heritage of multiple gods has not gone away despite the efforts of their leader to move the people away from them entirely. I hope you are able to find a connection with someone here."

I agreed with Diakono Copperwith as we entered the hotel. However, I wanted to learn more about why Syonne believed the people of this city needed to move away from their gods. Did he believe the gods were competing with him for the people's worship and devotion? Did he think it was unhealthy to believe in the gods?

I knew the immigrants who came to Charlesville had spoken reverently about the gods, especially Megaro, the sea god. Many of them would go to Charlesville Bay and pray on the beach to Megaro. Were those immigrants sent to Charlesville because they still believed in the gods? If so, that would make a lot of sense to me.

Many of those immigrants had begun to believe in the lifecharts as well. I grew up having a lifechart that was blessed by the oraki at the top of Ama's Faddar back home. The lifechart was determined by your birth date, and it mapped the entire course of your life. Many of the immigrants wanted to have lifecharts despite not being citizens born in Charlesville. They could not get lifecharts from the oraki, so many of them obtained replicas created by street spiritualists throughout the eastside of Charlesville. Maybe they had too much of a spiritual leaning for Syonne's and the other regnators' liking, and the rulers had wanted to get them out of Terrance.

I hoped that I would not have to bring up my status as a member of the ruling family of Charlesville while we were here. I didn't want it getting back to my family back home. I was not ready to see them yet, and any attention here in Terrance could bring a contingent to the city to secure my return to Charlesville. I had to make a connection with someone in the city like I had in the other cities throughout the journey.

I woke the next morning and realized that my birthday had passed the day before. I had turned twenty-four. The past year seemed like a blur. I could never have expected all the things that happened, from my discovery of Oscar Ortega's copy of the Book of Kammbi in Ama's Faddar to being forced from my birth city to traveling to the cities north of the Great Forest and now doing the same for the cities in the south—and all within one year!

Even at home, I was not a big celebrator of my birthday. I would usually have Willar, our butler, prepare my favorite meal of bluefish, brown rice, and slices of mango bread as a dessert. Of course, that stopped when I left the family home when I turned twenty. Getting older was natural, and I had never understood why people made a big deal about birthdays with gifts, parties, and celebrations. However, I suddenly felt different about it this morning. I missed my customary meal, and I had not even mentioned it to Diakono Copperwith while we were traveling. Oh well, I would make sure to acknowledge it going forward. Especially after the year I'd had.

I wrote a themily after the hotel staff brought breakfast to my hotel room. I had an egg sunny-side up, toasted bread with brownberry jam, and brownberries. It was delicious and gave me energy to write for a couple of hours. I wrote about the past year and how life could change suddenly. I wrote about learning to become prepared for the sudden changes in order to adjust quickly.

Diakono Copperwith came to my hotel room around ten o'clock and got Stella to take us to the Stuttgarte. He wanted to see this building that had the gods of the city painted on it. Like I did, he wanted to know more about why people of this city had moved away from those gods. Even though he did not agree with people worshiping more than one god, he had a bigger problem with people believing in no god at all.

I could understand his perspective after spending nearly a year with him. People always needed to believe in something bigger than themselves, and left to their own whims they would believe in anything that sounded good. Believing in and following Kammbi gave people a solid foundation in how to live and conduct themselves as human beings. However, I wondered about people like the Boma-Men of Adrian or the folks here in this city believing in something that was not Kammbi. Were they wrong? I knew Oscar's prophecy foretold that everyone in the land would worship Kammbi. But what made belief in Kammbi more correct than the beliefs these people already had?

Stella left the hotel a few minutes after ten o'clock and headed west on Avenue Nante. Diakono Copperwith sat next to me on the autobus, and I knew he was in a talkative mood.

"The Stuttgarte will have a crowd of people at each painting kneeling at the gods." she explained.

"This is allowed by the regnator?" Diakono Copperwith asked. "You made it clear on the prior bus ride that Syonne made sure the citizens of the city got away from believing in the gods."

Stella looked at Diakono Copperwith through the driver's mirror and sighed softly before answering. "Yes. It began with Syonne getting the citizens from the upper classes to the lower classes to stop believing in the gods. But the Stuttgarte is our oldest landmark. Even Syonne could not get rid of it."

I nodded at her comment. "So there are people who still believe in the gods despite Syonne's edict?"

She made a left turn onto Avenue Syonne. Stella glanced at me. "Of course. Just because you try to steer people away from the gods doesn't mean everyone will stop believing in them. Syonne tried, as well as every regnator after him. Our current regnator, Jules Raymond, has made declarations about tearing down the Stuttgarte once and for all. However, he has met stiff resistance from the upper classes and lower-class citizens of the city as well as the konzill."

"The konzill?" Diakono Copperwith interjected.

"Yeah. The konzill is the other governing body of Terrance. They enforce the laws that the regnator proposes. Actually, I believe they have more power than the regnator. They control everything from finances to the day-to-day running of the city. As long as they disagree with Jules Raymond, the Stuttgarte will not be torn down."

I stared at the enormous pyramid through the seat window. It had to cover a couple of city blocks. Thick pillars stood on each side of the building, which was grayish-black—the color of ash. I had never seen any building in either region of the land with that kind of color. Had the gods created the color of the pyramid to demonstrate their power? It appeared to be something that went beyond what human beings could have done or imagined.

Stella turned right off Avenue Syonne and onto a one-way street as we got closer to the Stuttgarte. A crowd was walking on the sidewalk toward the landmark.

"The people of this city have not stopped believing in these gods at all," Diakono Copperwith whispered.

I nodded as the crowd began to form a single line. I noticed the variety among them—various skin tones, shapes, and heights were all represented in the line to enter the landmark. Diakono Copperwith was right in his assessment. This kind of crowd would not be here if they had stopped believing in the gods.

Stella parked the vehicle in a parking lot west of the Stuttgarte. She turned to face us and pointed at the landmark.

"The front side of the Stuttgarte features the painting of Megaro, the sea god. Hendric Terrance Goltz, the city's original founder, came across the Kammara Sea from the land of Hamburg about three hundred years ago. He and his crew of sailors made it halfway across the sea until they came across a tropical storm that could have left them at sea forever. However, Hendric Terrance was offered help by Megaro. The sailor only had to pledge his devotion to the sea god in exchange for getting across the Kammara Sea safely."

"Why would anyone try to travel across the Kammara Sea?" Diakono Copperwith asked.

"The only thing I remember being taught at school was that Hendric Terrance and the other sailors coming from the land of Hamburg believed there was silver in this part of the land. Silver was highly valued in Hamburg and in short supply there. Sailors would risk their lives traveling across the Kammara Sea for it. Now, let me get back to my main explanation about the sea god."

I listened with great interest. I had never heard about sailors coming across the Kammara Sea for silver. I'd never even heard about a land called Hamburg on the other side. My history started with Mother Adrianna and their son Charles being forced away from her tribe in the area that became Santa Sophia. It continued with Charles coming into manhood and creating the city of Charlesville. Listening to the driver's explanation made me realize how small my world had become as a member of the ruling family of Charlesville.

"Hendric Terrance agreed to Megaro's request, and the sea god brought his ship safely across the Kammara Sea," Stella continued. "The sailor and his crew encountered the Foncee tribe, the original people of this area. The Foncee knew people with blond hair and white skin would arrive from across the sea, as predicted by Megaro."

"Did the Foncee tribe believe in Megaro?" I asked.

She nodded. "Correct. They had worshiped the sea god for hundreds of years before Hendric Terrance and the other sailors from the land of Hamburg arrived here. Because of Megaro's prediction, the Foncee tribe built the Stuttgarte as an act of devotion to the sea god."

I looked at the painting of Megaro. It covered the entire left side of the landmark. The sea god had a human upper body, muscular like a bodybuilder, but his lower half was fishlike. His penetrating eyes dominated his face. It felt like those eyes could see right through me.

Stella motioned for us to leave the autobus. We followed her off and began walking toward the Stuttgarte. She wobbled as she walked, and I placed my hand in the middle of her back in case she fell.

"Thank you for paying attention," she said and smiled at me. "I walk funny, but I have never fallen in my life. I believe the gods gave me this walk to show evidence that they are still around."

I glanced at Diakono Copperwith, who was on the left side of the driver. He had a thin smile on his face, but he did not speak.

"Did the tribe paint the gods on each side of the Stuttgarte?" I asked.

"All we know is the Foncee tribe built the entire building with some help from Hendric Terrance and the sailors. The Foncee were fishermen and played music. It has never been proven that they had any artistic ability, much less the ability to paint the gods on the Stuttgarte."

"Then who painted the gods?" Diakono Copperwith asked.

"We lower-class folks believe it was Samsic, the god of art and philosophy."

"You have a god of art?" Diakono Copperwith said.

"The gods cover every major aspect of human life. You will see them represented on the Stuttgarte."

We walked several blocks until a group of men dressed in long blue shawls with an overlay of pink covering the chest area met us. They were all bald, with clean-shaven faces. The men were handing out small cups of drink to people as they passed.

"Who are those men?" Diakono Copperwith asked.

"The Dumont Brotherhood," Stella replied as we walked up to the men. "They make the best alhiney in the city."

"Alhiney?" I interjected.

Stella laughed. "You probably drink javann. Only the upper-class folks drink javann in Terrance. Alhiney is our drink. A drink for the common folk. Javann is not even made here in the city. Why would the common folk drink something that comes from elsewhere? Anyway, javann is too sour. Alhiney has a touch of sweetness that keeps you drinking without feeling drunk. A gift from the Foncee tribe. But the Dumont Brotherhood have perfected making it."

One of the Dumont men came up to us and handed each of us a cup of alhiney. I watched the driver drink hers with great satisfaction. The man from the Dumont Brotherhood stood in front of me and stared at my cup.

"Drink it!" Stella commanded.

I tasted the alhiney. It had a sweet taste, like brownberry juice. I drank the rest quickly. It was delicious. It was nothing like javann. I could not drink the javann that Eduardo Azur had given me in Adrian, but I felt like I could drink this all day.

"Thank you for honoring Kammbi by drinking," the Dumont Brotherhood member said and smiled.

"Honoring Kammbi?" Diakono Copperwith said after drinking his cup of alhiney. "I'm a diakono from the kahall of Santa Sophia and have given my life to believing and following Kammbi."

The man from Dumont Brotherhood looked at Diakono Copperwith. "You are from the kahall of Santa Sophia?"

"Yes!"

The man waved the other members over to our area. "Brothers, our prayers about Oscar's prophecy coming true in this season have been answered!"

"You know about Oscar's prophecy?" I said. I could hardly believe what I was hearing.

"We are believers and followers of Kammbi. We have prayed for years about Oscar's prophecy being fulfilled. Having a diakono from the kahall of Santa Sophia arrive here in Terrance unannounced confirms our prayers."

"Well, this young man here is the one who will fulfill Oscar's prophecy. We have traveled throughout this land for nearly a year, and everything he has done proves it will be fulfilled."

The brotherhood members all looked at me. "Praise the Eternal Comforter! Praise Donte and Roger! We would like to invite you to Dumont Abbi," the man who gave us the alhiney said.

Chapter 19

We spent a couple of hours with the Dumont Brotherhood at the Stuttgarte before going to Dumont Abbi in the Samsic District of the city. We learned that only one Dumont Brotherhood member was permitted to speak at a time, while the others remained silent. The brotherhood member who gave me the cup of alhiney was named Diakono Francois du Vann. He was the leader and the main spokesperson for the group. There were four other Dumont Brotherhood members with him: Diakono Arnold Valencia, Diakono Jose Malaga, Diakono Andre Lauer, and Diakono Quinton Neumeier. On the way to the abbi, I learned that Diakono Valencia was from Adrian and Diakono Malaga was from Walter's Grove. I wanted to get a chance to speak with both of them as to how they had become Dumont Brotherhood members.

Diakono Copperwith talked with Diakono du Vann the entire way to Dumont Abbi. Their conversation was like family members being reunited after a long period of separation. Obviously, he wanted to know how a group of diakonos had come to Terrance, and why would they give out liquor to people at the Stuttgarte. If they were true believers and followers of

Kammbi, and especially diakonos, they would have nothing to do with liquor—would they?

"I know you are going to recite Disciple Gregory's words from his chapter," Diakono du Vann said to Diakono Copperwith. Both men sat in the front right seat of the autobus. I sat behind them, and the other brotherhood members were in the seats on the left side.

"He who partakes in liquor will succumb to it. It has the ability to make the partaker treat it like one who commits adultery," Diakono Copperwith recited.

The opening two chapters of the Book of Kammbi in the Ryianza section belonged to Disciple Gregory. The Book of Kammbi was split into two halves: the first half was called Ryianza, and the second half was called Baramesa. *Ryianza* meant "covenant," indicating what Kammbi would always have with his believers and followers. *Baramesa* meant "promise," indicating what Kammbi would establish with anyone in the land who became his believer and follower. Oscar's prophecy was in the last chapter of the Baramesa section and was considered Kammbi's greatest promise to humanity.

Diakono Copperwith had told me after we first met in Santa Sophia that Disciple Gregory was considered the first convert to believe in and follow Kammbi, and he was the only one with Kammbi when the deity sacrificed his blood to cover the acts of passha that humanity had committed and would commit. Disciple Gregory's chapters read more formally, and with a more matter-of-fact tone, than the chapters from the other disciples. He reiterated that being a believer and follower in Kammbi was a black or white proposition. I had to come to believe that Diakono Copperwith identified most with Disciple Gregory.

Diakono du Vann continued, "Disciple Gregory lived in a part of Guadharra that already had devoted believers and followers of Kammbi. Those people were not brought up with other belief systems or traditions like they are here in Terrance. So it was rather easy for Disciple Gregory to make firm statements about being a believer and follower in Kammbi."

"How can a faith survive without firm statements from Kammbi or his oldest disciple?" Diakono Copperwith countered. "Believers and followers need solid teaching on how to live. And keeping away from liquor is sound advice from Disciple Gregory."

We reached a reddish-orange, dome-shaped building that reminded me of the kahall of Santa Sophia, which had a similar dome and color but was several times larger than this building. Dumont Abbi stood only a couple of stories high. It had a patterned façade similar to what I had noticed when we first arrived in Terrance. The autobus driver turned onto the main road for Dumont Abbi, and I noticed an area of immaculately placed vines to the right.

"What do you grow on those vines?" I asked.

Diakono du Vann turned in his seat to look out the window. "We grow the chaysante plant to make alhiney. The chaysante plant has a pink berry that grows inside the leaf, and we plucked it at harvest time to begin the process of making alhiney."

"Is harvest time soon?" I asked.

"We are about ten days away from the first harvest of the year. There are three harvest times for the chaysante plant— Beru, the second month; Aym, the fifth month; and Berm, the ninth month. The first harvest is usually the most plentiful for making alhiney."

I knew Diakono Copperwith wanted to continue his conversation with Diakono du Vann about the Disciple Gregory, but I could sense that Diakono du Vann was glad to talk about the chaysante plant instead.

"How long does each harvest season last?" I asked.

Stella parked the autobus in front of the main entrance, and we got up from our seats to exit. Diakono du Vann allowed the other diakonos to exit the autobus first. Each diakono bowed to him before exiting, and Diakono du Vann returned the gesture while interlocking his hands. I had seen Diakono Copperwith perform the same gesture to the morrim of the kahall of Santa Sophia after I first met him.

"We pluck chaysante for fifty days during each harvest. Fifty is a significant number for us as believers and followers of Kammbi," Diakono du Vann continued as we followed the other diakonos into Dumont Abbi.

"That's how many days Oscar Ortega stayed in each place during his travels north of the Great Forest," I replied.

Diakono du Vann smiled, showing his large teeth. "Correct, Brother Diondray. We adhere to the fifty-day schedule even if there are more berries grown on the chaysante plant afterward."

"We have stayed fifty days in each city during our journey," Diakono Copperwith added.

Diakono Du Vann stopped walking and dropped to his knees. He interlocked his hands again and tilted his head toward his hands. Diakono du Vann remained in that position for several moments silently. Diakono Copperwith and I were gently pulled back from Diakono du Vann by Diakonos Valencia and Malaga. I knew he was performing some kind of prayer, but what was the reason for it?

After a few minutes, the diakono rose to his feet with the assistance of Diakonos Valencia and Malaga. Diakono du Vann bowed to them, and the men walked on ahead of us.

"That was a prayer of acknowledgement. When Diakono Copperwith said you have remained fifty days in each city along your journey, I had to pray to the Eternal Comforter confirming what it said about the one who will fulfill Oscar's prophecy. This person will follow the same timeline as Oscar Ortega."

Diakono Copperwith had a look of awe on his face. I could sense that he had never expected anyone in this part of the land to speak the way Diakono du Vann did about the faith. I knew there were conversations to come about why and how the Dumont Brotherhood had made their way here to Terrance. But I also realized Diakono Copperwith was going to be changed in ways he could never have expected.

Diakono Valencia greeted me when I arrived at Dumont Abbi for breakfast the next day. I had started writing a new themily before Stella brought me to Dumont Abbi. After exiting the autobus, I followed Diakono Valencia to the gathering place of the diakonos. Diakono Valencia did not speak, and it felt weird not to say hello or good morning as a greeting. He did smile, and I took the gesture as his way of saying good morning.

Diakono Valencia was similar in height and size to me. He was tallest of the Dumont Brotherhood I had seen so far. I wanted to ask about him growing up in Adrian. What did he know about the Boma-Men? What did he know of Eduardo

Azur and the rest of the family? How had he become a member of the Dumont Brotherhood?

I arrived at the gathering place where it seemed all the members of Dumont Brotherhood were sitting. There had to be at least twenty-five of them. I noticed Diakono Copperwith sitting across from Diakono du Vann. The head diakono acknowledged my presence, and Diakono Valencia brought me to them. I sat next to Diakono Copperwith. There were two cups in front of me. One cup was filled with alhiney and the other cup was filled with water.

"Good morning, Brother Diondray. I hope you had a restful sleep," Diakono du Vann said.

I nodded.

"Good to know," he continued. "You are getting ready to witness your first Dumont Brotherhood ritual. Grab your cup of water."

I obeyed his request, as did Diakono Copperwith.

"Water represents the Eternal Comforter as the ever-present presence in the life of a believer and follower of Kammbi. Water is the one thing in life that can go anywhere and is something we cannot live without. We as believers and followers cannot live without the Eternal Comforter. It is the gift we have received from Kammbi. We drink in honor of being the recipient of our lord's gift," Diakono du Vann said.

I drank the water and glanced down the table to see all the Dumont Brotherhood members do the same. Diakono du Vann grabbed his cup of alhiney, and everybody else followed suit.

"Alhiney represents the connection we made to this part of the region. Connection means community and an opportunity to share the teachings of the Book of Kammbi. This opportunity was provided by the Dumont Brothers, Donte and Roger. We will never forget the risk they took in attempting to share their belief in Kammbi in this city. Drink, brothers."

I drank the alhiney, and the sweet pink berry taste from the chaysante plant was delicious. I wanted some more of it. All the Dumont Brotherhood members drank their cup at the same time and bowed their heads. I heard a deep baritone voice coming from the other end of the gathering place. It reminded me of Coltrain Hayes, the singer from Walter's Grove. I knew he was not a member of the Dumont Brotherhood. I looked down at the other end and saw a member with a dark brown complexion and prominent cheeks sing with conviction. The rest of his brethren kept their heads bowed.

Bless the day that Kammbi has granted us,
Bless the opportunity to be allowed time in your presence.
Bless the gift you gave us,
A gift that guides us on our path
And brings us as believers and followers closer to you.
Please forgive us for any acts of passha that we will commit.
And may the words you gave to the original
traveler be fulfilled soon.

The diakono stopped singing, and the others began chanting. It was a low-tone chant that had the same melody as the prayer that had just been sung. However, I could not make out the words. I looked at Diakono Copperwith, and his head was bowed. The chanting was beautiful, and I began to feel a surge of energy flow through my body. I knew it was responding to the chant. The energy pulsated throughout my body like it had when I first received the Boma Essence from

Omari. I rose from my seat and started chanting. My voice mimicked the chant of the Dumont Brotherhood. The Essence brought all of its energy to my mouth, and my chant got louder. All the Dumont Brotherhood members had raised their heads and were looking at me with an expression of serenity on their faces, like they had known all along that I was going to chant with them. Like they had accepted me.

My chant ended, and the Boma Essence gave me the words I needed to say to the Dumont Brotherhood. "Because of your obedience in leaving your homeland to come to a new land, I will continue to make your name great," I said, quoting the words to Oscar. "Even though you have lost a child due to your act of passha, you will have a descendant who will unite the entire land. And the people will believe that Kammbi is the Lord of all. Those who always believed in me and those who didn't believe in me will create a new people, establishing peace and sanctification throughout this land."

The Dumont Brotherhood rose from their seats, and all of them faced me and bowed. Diakono du Vann walked up to me and said, "You have just confirmed to us what the Eternal Comforter has said for all of these years. Brother Diondray, you are the one to fulfill Oscar's prophecy. We are glad to be alive for those words you just spoke to come to fruition."

Diakono Valencia became my tour guide for the rest of the day. Diakono du Vann suggested we get acquainted with each other, which I was happy to do. Several hours had passed since breakfast, and I was still trying to comprehend how the Boma Essence had gotten me to chant like the rest of the Dumont

Brotherhood. I thought Diakono Valencia would mention it during our time together. However, he did not say anything about it. As a matter of fact, the other Brotherhood members acted like nothing had happened. I had sensed their acceptance of me right away, and my chant confirmed the connection to Oscar's prophecy.

We arrived in a sanctuary toward the back of Dumont Abbi. There were several members sitting on the floor cross-legged, rocking back and forth. Thick candles burned in each corner of the sanctuary as the only lights in the room, but the dim lights did not make me feel claustrophobic.

"This is the third prayer session of our day," Diakono Valencia began. "It is informal, and not every diakono comes to it. The brothers come in to pray and leave whenever they want."

"How many brotherhood members come to this session each day?" I asked as Diakono Valencia brought me to a pew behind the sitting diakonos.

"Usually three to four. Sometimes only one. Rarely do we all have fifty members come to this session."

"Fifty members. You mean those were not all the members at breakfast?"

Diakono Valencia chuckled and pushed his glasses back on his face. I noticed the deep lines around his mouth. "You are perceptive, Brother Diondray. Since it is harvest time for the chaysante plant, half the members work at the vines during our time of breakfast. They eat breakfast much earlier."

I nodded at his explanation as a couple of the diakonos rose from sitting and exited the sanctuary. "I assume the number fifty is connected to how long Oscar Ortega stayed in each area he traveled to?"

"Not quite, Brother Diondray. Fifty is also significant for how many days it took Donte and Roger Dumont to make it here from Issabella."

I followed Diakono Valencia out of the sanctuary. "The Dumont Brothers traveled by land like Oscar Ortega?"

He shook his head. "They traveled by boat. Roger spent his last finances on a boat. They did not want to travel like Oscar Ortega or Adrian Azur did during their time. However, their travels by boat were probably more hazardous than traveling by land."

"You mentioned Adrian Azur," I interjected. "You know about him?"

The diakono chuckled again as we returned to the main hallway. "I'm from Adrian," he continued. "I know about Adrian Azur and how he was forced to leave the area that is known as Charlesville. How he believed in Mother Adrianna instead of Charles and so was sent away."

"You know my last name is Azur," I added.

We entered a room filled with paintings on the walls. The artwork was excellent, mostly portraits and beach landscapes. "I do. That's why I asked to be your guide while you are here. Brother Copperwith explained to Diakono du Vann that you both spent fifty days in Adrian. I have not been back to my birth city since I became a Brotherhood member five years ago. I want to know how you liked it and what you learned while being there."

I smiled as he brought me to a painting of Donte and Roger Dumont. Donte was tall and rail-thin with blond hair, while Roger had dark hair and a heavyset frame. He was much shorter than his brother. Their sizes were different, but you could tell they were brothers by their facial features. Both had the same prominent nose, and their smiles were alike. But I noticed that both wore weary expressions on their faces, and they seemed a little gaunt.

"This is my favorite painting in Dumont Abbi," Diakono Valencia said. "It captures what the Dumont Brothers actually looked like when they first arrived here."

"Excellent painting," I commented. "It appears the brothers were worn out from the journey."

Diakono Valencia nodded. "They were. Traveling fifty days in a small boat across the Kammara Sea is dangerous."

"Did they get caught in a storm?"

"Yes, they did. But they had the protection of the Eternal Comforter to make it safely to shore."

I looked at the painting again. I saw more clearly the exhausted looks on their faces. The artist had captured how these men would appear after such a voyage.

"Did one of the brotherhood members paint this?"

Diakono Valencia pushed up his glasses again and looked at me. "I painted it."

"You did! That's impressive."

He gave a thin smile. I hoped I had not offended him with my compliment.

"Thank you, Brother Diondray," he replied. "It's my favorite of all the paintings I did in this room."

"You painted all of these?"

"I did," he replied softly. "Diakono du Vann has allowed me to paint since I became a brotherhood member. He believes my art is a gift to the brotherhood. And he has allowed me to paint as much as I want."

I walked over to the left side of the room, where a beach landscape hung on the midsection of the wall. The painting showed a storm in the distance and two men sleeping in a boat just in front of it. A half-human, half-fish figure hovered above the rainstorm. In fact, it looked like the figure was causing it. The blue-green color of the Kammara Sea dominated the rest of the painting, but the dark cloud added an ominous touch.

"Are those the Dumont Brothers sleeping in that boat? And who is that figure above the rainstorm?"

Diakono Valencia joined me at the painting. "You are correct. There are Brothers Donte and Roger sleeping in the boat. They had just come through a dangerous few nights in a storm caused by the sea god, Megaro."

I turned away from the painting and stared at the diakono. "Do the brotherhood members believe in the sea god?"

Diakono Valencia's face went pale. I must have touched a sensitive subject. "As Dumont Brotherhood members, we don't believe in Megaro the sea god. However, I have been told that the sea god did try to stop Donte and Roger from reaching land."

"Do you believe it?"

"I do. That's why I painted it."

I turned away from Diakono Valencia to look at the painting again.

"It is my best selling painting in both the Megaro and Samsic Districts."

I cut my eyes back to him. "You sell your paintings?"

"Yes. All the money I get comes back here to Dumont Abbi. My paintings have brought in a lot of money, and it has helped to keep us self-sufficient. The Eternal Comforter has always provided a way."

I was surprised by what Diakono Valencia had just told me. He was allowed to paint, being a member of the Dumont

Brotherhood. Also, he sold his paintings in two of the city districts for a lot of money. They had carved out a place in the society of Terrance. I wondered if Diakono Copperwith knew about Diakono Valencia's paintings. Did the konseho of Kammbi know about them as well? If so, what would they think about all this?

"I take my latest work, which is in another room, to the districts on the fourth day of every week," Diakono Valencia continued. "I get to spend half a day to sell my work."

I had moved over to another beach landscape to the right. This one showed the sun in the upper right-hand corner and numerous waves coming from the sea to shore. The aqua of the painting was serene and reminded me of back home when I often got away from home by visiting Charlesville Bay.

"You get to leave Dumont Abbi for half a day?" I asked.

"I do. Diakono du Vann believes my gift should be shared with the people of this city."

"Does he expect you to speak about the teachings from the Book of Kammbi?"

"He does not. I'm there to sell my art, not proselytize."

"Wait a minute," I replied and faced Diakono Valencia. "You don't speak about Kammbi or the teachings from the Book of Kammbi to the people of Terrance?"

Diakono Valencia chuckled. "I understand that you and Diakono Copperwith have shared the teachings from the Book of Kammbi throughout your travels. But the Dumont Brotherhood does not function in the same way. Our calling is not to proselytize the people of this city. We are here to show people that the presence of Kammbi can be lived out amongst those who don't believe. Those of us who have chosen to live a spiritual life can function as everyday citizens like those who don't."

"How do you get new members?"

"Well, we are at capacity now with fifty brotherhood members. And I don't want to speak about the death of any brother in the future. However, you would have to be called to become a Dumont Brotherhood member. The Eternal Comforter has always provided the right person at the right time."

I had so many thoughts going through my mind, I did not know what to ask next. But I was fascinated by this conversation. I hoped I would get a chance to spend more time with Diakono Valencia while I was here in Terrance.

"I would like you to join me tomorrow as I sell my paintings," he said. "We still have to talk about your time in Adrian. I would like to hear about my birth city."

I nodded as we left the room.

Chapter 20

Stella brought me to the Megaro District the next morning after breakfast. Diakono Copperwith had already left for Dumont Abbi in order to catch the first prayer service and spend the day with the Dumont Brotherhood. He wanted as much as time as he could get with the diakonos while we were in Terrance. Diakono Copperwith told me that Diakono du Vann wanted to make sure he understood how they operated amongst the people of the city and have it relayed to the konseho of Kammbi in Issabella.

Before he left for Dumont Abbi, Diakono Copperwith told me he had received a letter from Mrs. Copperwith. He did not share details of what she wrote, but I sensed he had needed the letter to know she was doing well and that their love remained on solid ground. I thought about praying as a plea to get the Copperwiths reconnected again. I had not attempted to pray since leaving Santa Teresa, and I was still uncomfortable about this ritual. However, I believed a man should not be away from his wife for a long period of time. I knew this separation hurt him deeply.

As we entered the Megaro District, I noticed a statue of Megaro, the sea god, at the entrance. It stood about fifty feet high, and the familiar half-human and half-fish body projected over Avenue Syonne as we crossed the Kammara River. The sea god's facial expression was menacing, like he was ready to declare war against the citizens of the city. Stella explained that the statue captured the sea god's natural expression. If that were the case, why would any citizens of this city want to worship him?

I was dropped off at the main beach parking lot and was greeted by a Dumont Brotherhood member I did not recognize. He had jet-black skin and an oversized forehead. Like the others, he had the custom-shaved hairstyle and wore a white shawl with a pink overlay across the chest area. However, it looked like he had forced himself into the shawl.

"Hello, Brother Diondray. I'm Diakono Henri Louis Hugo. I was sent by Diakono Valencia to greet you as you arrive and take you to where he has set up his artwork for sale."

I followed Diakono Hugo along the beach for several minutes. It was filled with beachgoers. I saw couples holding hands walking along the shore, families making sandcastles, and people sunbathing. The sun made its appearance, and I felt the humidity rise while we were walking.

We arrived at an area where Diakono Valencia had several paintings displayed on wooden poles that were planted in the sand. The paintings were similar to those I had seen at Dumont Abbi: beautiful, scenic beachscapes capturing the Kammara Sea.

"Welcome, Brother Diondray," Diakono Valencia said and rose from his seat behind the paintings. "The first part of the day is usually slow for sales. It will be a good time to talk about Adrian."

I sat down in a chair next to him while Diakono Hugo stood behind a table with bracelets and necklaces on it.

"You make jewelry too?" I asked Diakono Valencia.

He chuckled. "I do not, Brother Diondray. Diakono Hugo makes the jewelry and sells it here with me on the beach. His jewelry is just as popular as my artwork."

A couple of beachgoers, two women, came up to the table to look at the jewelry. The taller of the two women grabbed a bracelet and placed it on her wrist. It was a circular-patterned silver bracelet with an inlay of blue stone. She began modeling it for the other woman and got her approval.

"Diakono Hugo started making jewelry to sell this past year," Diakono Valencia continued. "He saw that my artwork was bringing good money back to Dumont Abbi, and he wanted to contribute in his own way too."

"You said yesterday that all the money you make from selling artwork goes back to Dumont Abbi? Is it the same for Diakono Hugo's jewelry?"

Diakono Valencia looked over at me. "Yes, it is. Does that bother you, Brother Diondray?"

"No offense," I stammered. "But I would believe you both should be able to keep some of the money you have made from selling your artwork and jewelry. Both of you created these items and should benefit from any money received."

More beachgoers came to the table, and Diakono Hugo began explaining how the jewelry was made. He had the beachgoers' attention. I sensed that he was going to sell all of his jewelry in the next couple of hours.

"Dumont Abbi has given both Diakono Hugo and I the freedom to do our artwork and jewelry without having to worry about how we are going to make a living from it. Selling artwork and jewelry in the city is not an easy way to survive. Our needs for food, clothing, and shelter are taken care of. Our artwork and jewelry are a small sacrifice for the things that have been provided for us as members of the Dumont Brotherhood."

"I can understand that perspective, Diakono Valencia," I replied as I watched more beachgoers come the table and begin looking at his paintings. "But you created those paintings, and Diakono Hugo created that jewelry. You both have a right to keep the money you have made on selling these items."

"Excuse me, Brother Diondray," Diakono Valencia said and got up from his seat. A short, blond-haired man was pointing at one of the paintings. I believed he wanted to know how much it cost. Diakono Valencia told him the price, and the man opened his wallet and handed him several bills. The man continued talking to the brotherhood member, and I gathered from the conversation that he wanted to purchase more paintings. Diakono Valencia bowed, and the man left.

"Otto Daume is one of my best customers," Diakono Valencia said as he returned to his seat. "He buys a painting from me every time I'm here."

"That's great you have a loyal customer like him. Even more reason that you should keep some of the money for yourself."

Diakono Valencia chuckled. "Nonbelievers would believe every word you are saying, Brother Diondray. Otto Daume tells me that every time he buys a painting—like you, he believes I should keep the money. He says I could become wealthy by selling on the beach regularly."

"I guess my argument is old news to you."

Diakono Hugo joined us and added, "Otto Daume is one of Terrance's beach philosophers. He loves to share his philosophy with everyone who comes to beach. Even though we disagree with what he shares, he loves Diakono Valencia's paintings and continues to buy them."

"Beach philosopher?" I replied. "I've never heard that term before."

"It is a self-proclaimed title," Diakono Hugo continued. "Otto Daume and his partner, Barron Roche, share their philosophies just north of us on the beach. They attract quite a crowd of beachgoers, and I have to admit it's quite entertaining."

Diakono Valencia nodded. "I agree. The beach philosophers put on quite a show. They have tried to get me to join their debates. But as members of the Dumont Brotherhood, we don't share our beliefs as a spectacle or for the purpose of entertaining."

The beach philosophers intrigued me. "I would like to see these beach philosophers at work."

"I can take him, Diakono Valencia," Diakono Hugo said. "I have sold my jewelry for today. And I would like to see Brother Diondray's reaction to Otto and Barron's performance."

Diakono Valencia smiled at me. "I will come too."

Both brotherhood members packed up their items and placed them in the autobus provided for them by Dumont Abbi. I helped them with packing their artwork and jewelry (Was the jewelery not all sold according to the earlier statement?). Diakono Valencia finally asked me a question about Adrian as we loaded the autobus.

"What did you learn about my birth city?"

I had to think about how I was going to answer his question. Should I mention receiving the Boma Essence from Omari? Or should I talk about Eduardo Azur's hatred of the Boma-Men because he believed they had killed the woman he was going to marry? Or should I mention staying at Hastancia de Gamon and how the workers of the hastancia had built a kahall on the property so they could listen to the teachings of the Book of Kammbi from Diakono Copperwith?

"I learned about Adrian Azur and his role in founding the city that would become Adrian," I answered. As we talked, we went to pick up the last of the packed items.

"He saved those original settlers from the flood of Guanna Lake," Diakono Valencia replied. "With the help of the leopards, he moved them far enough west to create the city that would be known as Adrian."

"How do you feel about the leopards? And the Boma-Men who worship them?"

Diakono Hugo was a couple of steps ahead of us. It seemed that he knew Diakono Valencia wanted to talk to me about his birth city and did not want to impede on the conversation. I sensed that Diakono Valencia really wanted to discuss this more than anything else we had talked about so far.

"We were taught to view the Boma-Men with suspicion. People are not supposed to worship animals, especially an animal as mysterious as a leopard. That animal does not act like any other animal that comes from the Great Forest."

"What do you mean?" I asked.

"The leopard marches to its own rhythm and has a humanlike quality of deciding how it wants to operate."

"Is that why the people of Adrian are suspicious of the Boma-Men?"

As we finished loading the last of the items, I noticed a huge crowd on the beach nearby. I assumed they were there for the beach philosophers, and I wanted to focus my attention on what they did to draw the attention of so many.

"We will continue our discussion later," Diakono Valencia said. "It's time for you to see Otto and Barron at work."

Diakono Hugo found an opening through the crowd, and we followed him through it. The beachgoers did not look our way. Their attention was on the voices we heard coming from the center of the crowd.

"The Haddoe were greater gods than Megaro," Otto Daume proclaimed as we reached the front of the crowd. He was a short blond man who stood next to a similar sized man with dark-brown skin and a treetop hairstyle. "They kept the sea god in his place when he wanted to kill Hendric Terrance Goltz for naming our beloved city after himself."

I glanced to see some in the crowd murmur and nod in agreement. The crowd were clearly familiar with this type of debate—they knew how to participate.

Barron objected. "Megaro was the only god who helped Hendric Terrance Goltz come across the Kammara Sea from the land of Hamburg. The sea god saved the sailor's life from the treacherous storm. Where were the Haddoe then?" He grinned at the crowd as he finished his contradiction.

The crowd burst out with laughter at Barron's gesture. Some of them called out their agreement with his rebuttal.

Encouraged, Barron continued. "Don't forget, Mr. Otto, that Hendric Terrance Goltz pledged to worship the sea god for saving his life at sea. Megaro was betrayed when the sailor gave his own middle name to the city. If you give your word to a god, especially a god that saved your life, then you can expect retribution when you betray him!"

"Barron wins today's debate!" someone from the crowd yelled out.

Otto frowned in the direction of the outburst. "Not so fast! Barron did not explain the fact that The Haddoe kept Megaro from killing the sailor while he was helping build our city. That surely makes them the greater gods."

"How did Hendric Terrance Goltz die?" Barron asked and crossed his arms. The crowd laughed again at his gesture.

The blond-haired philosopher stared at his counterpart for several moments.

"Answer my question, Mr. Otto! The greatest beach philosopher in our city."

The crowd continued laughing as Barron put his right hand over his ear.

"Hendric Terrance Goltz was killed at sea on his final voyage to the land of Hamburg," Otto said softly.

"What killed him at sea?"

Otto sighed. "Megaro brought a storm as Hendric got halfway across the Kammara Sea. Hendric Terrance Goltz was killed by Megaro, and the Haddoe could not do anything to stop it."

"Thank you, Mr. Otto," Barron declared proudly and grinned at the crowd. "I just won my latest debate on the beach today, ladies and gentlemen. I can finally claim the title of the city's greatest beach philosopher."

"Hold on, Barron," Otto interrupted. "We may have challengers to your title. I see two members from the Dumont Brotherhood here amongst us. Has Diakono Valencia finally agreed to a debate?"

The crowd shifted their attention to us. They seemed eager to have a new beach philosopher to join the debate against Otto and Barron.

"C'mon, Diakono Valencia, and bring us some of the Dumont Brotherhood knowledge," Barron called. "I look forward to defeating you as well."

The crowd laughed at Barron's boast.

"Otto and Barron, you both know that members of the Dumont Brotherhood do not participate in philosophical debates," Diakono Valencia replied. The crowd moaned.

"Well, I thought I would ask," Otto said.

"We brought a visitor to our city to see you both at work," Diakono Valencia continued. "This is Diondray Azur from Charlesville."

The beach philosophers smiled at me, and I shook their hands. "I understand the people of Charlesville believe in the lifechart given by the oraki to determine one's path in life," Barron said.

"Correct," I replied. "Have you spent time in Charlesville?"

"I have indeed, Diondray," Barron continued. "Ladies and gentlemen, I'm giving you another reason why I should have the title of the city's greatest beach philosopher. Not only did I just defeat Otto again today, I provided knowledge about a belief system from another city, south of the Great Forest." He crossed his arms and grinned at the crowd.

The crowd started cheering for Barron as Otto rolled his eyes.

"Actually, Brother Diondray has traveled throughout the land over the past year. He spent time in the cities north of the Great Forest as well as the cities of Adrian and Walter's Grove," Diakono Valencia said.

Barron waved his arms to quiet the crowd. "You've been to the cities north of the Great Forest?"

I nodded.

"Why?" Otto interjected.

"I found a copy of the Book of Kammbi in Charlesville, and there is a prophecy written inside it that declares a descendant of Oscar Ortega will unite the entire land for Kammbi," I answered.

Otto gasped. "The Dumont Brotherhood has talked about the prophecy for years. Do you believe he is the one to fulfill it, Diakono Valencia?"

Before he could answer Otto's question, a downpour came suddenly. The crowd scattered, and I felt Diakono Hugo pull my arm to follow him. It felt odd that heavy rains would come so quickly. I started to run behind Diakono Hugo. But I felt a surge of energy start to flow through me.

"C'mon, Brother Diondray!" Diakono Valencia yelled.

The rain seemed to come down harder as I stopped running. I felt that the surge of energy wanted me to go toward the shore. Huge waves were splashing onto the beach. I began walking to the shore. Even though my clothes were drenched, it seemed I had a covering over me. I noticed a blue light in my peripheral vision. Was the blue light protecting me from the rain? Or was it the Boma Essence protecting me?

I reached the shore as the rain intensified. It seemed like the storm wanted me to confront it. The Boma Essence was racing through my body. I began to hear music. Where would music be coming from? I looked around, but everyone had evacuated the beach. Nobody would be trying to play music in this kind of weather.

As I continued forward, I realized the music was coming from my mind. The Boma Essence was creating it. I knew this music. I had heard all of my life. A guitar lick started it, followed by horns and piano. The instruments began to harmonize. I started moving to the right like I was going to dance. I moved back to the left, and my feet were in synch with the music.

The guitar sound dominated the music. I danced along the shore in rhythm with the music. The rain followed my motion, and the waves harmonized with the music. I kept dancing as the guitar gave way to a horn solo. The horn sound blew harder, as if it were stopping the rest of the storm. I opened my arms wide as a huge wave came toward me. It was like the storm wanted to throw its biggest punch at me. I spun several times as the wave surged straight at me, and a whirlwind of blue light knocked the wave away. The horn solo ended, and the rainstorm was gone.

A nuzzle woke me. I opened my eyes to see Reuel rubbing his head against my right thigh. The leopard growled softly. I knew he was pleased to see me.

I sat up and began brushing off the sand. I needed a bath as soon as I got back to the hotel. I looked up and saw Diakonos Valencia and Hugo staring at me in an uncomfortable fashion. Otto and Barron were standing next to them. I sensed they were not going to come any closer to me because of Reuel.

As I got up, I heard a familiar voice.

"The music you love caused the rainstorm to cease. This is the music that matters most to you."

"You have returned, Omari," I said as Reuel stood next to me. I looked at the leopard and knew he'd come so I could have this conversation.

"I have returned. You sensed correctly that the storm was unnatural. It was meant to show that the power of the gods has not gone away."

"Megaro, the sea god, created the storm?"

"We are at the beach. This is his territory. His power has not gone away, even if the people of this city have been coerced to stop believing in the gods."

Reuel growled as the Dumont Brotherhood members started making their way toward me. The leopard's growl frightened the diakonos, but I could make out that each man was saying prayers as they came closer.

"Your presence in this city will show that the gods still have power. Stay connected to those men who are approaching you. They can help you reach the people here."

Omari ended the conversation and was gone from my mind. Otto and Barron approached behind Diakonos Valencia and Hugo. The beach philosophers stared at Reuel.

"Reuel will not harm you," I said as they arrived. "He has been my companion throughout this journey."

Barron looked away from the leopard to me. "Are you a descendant of Ammaro?"

"Ammaro?"

"He is the god of the animals and brother to Megaro," Otto explained. "Tradition has it that he used to travel throughout this part of the land with a leopard at his side."

"Ammaro controlled every aspect of the land as well. He is the counterpart to his brothers, Megaro, the sea god, and Bomero, god of the underworld," Barron said.

I rubbed Reuel's head as he purred. The leopard took off south along the beach. His visit had come to an end. All of them watched the leopard gallop across the sand until it was gone from sight. Like me, they were trying to digest what had just happened. I had power from the Boma Essence that stopped a rainstorm caused by Megaro.

"You are the one to fulfill Oscar's prophecy," Diakono Valencia said. "I called your name as loudly as I could. But you kept walking toward the storm. We saw a glowing blue light around you. The rain bounced off the blue light. Oh, my Kammbi!"

"There was music. And you danced like I have never seen anyone dance before. The rain moved with you and the music. You were controlling the storm by your dancing. Who are you, Brother Diondray?" Diakono Hugo added.

"I heard the music too," Barron interjected. "It was a rendition of one the most famous Kammarice songs ever recorded."

"'Kammara, Kammara' by Walter Leonardo Fuente," I said softly.

Otto gasped again. "You are a descendant of Ammaro! The gods have returned to Terrance!"

As I danced to the music, the song's name and history had come to me. It was like the Boma Essence wanted me to know everything about the music I danced to. "Kammara, Kammara" was Walter Leonardo Fuente's first major Kammarice song, recorded a few years before he was forced to leave the city of Terrance because of his marriage to Roxie and Penelope. The song expressed Walter's love of the Kammara Sea and his longing to cross it like Hendric Terrance Goltz and others who came from the land of Hamburg. Even though Ruben Davar was my favorite Kammarice musician, I had listened to "Kammara, Kammara" a lot on the beach back home in Charlesville. I liked that song as well.

"If it's okay with Diakono Valencia, Barron and I would like you to come with us for a few days," Otto said. "We would like to show you some information about the gods that you need to know."

"I'm not a god or descendant of Ammaro," I fired back. "My life has turned upside down since I left Charlesville in Carm, the third month last year. I have been trying to come to grips with being a descendant of Oscar Ortega and fulfilling his prophecy. And you are equating me to a god from the past? Right now, I would like to go back to my hotel and just be alone."

I began to walk away from the group, and Diakono Valencia joined me. "We will take you to your hotel, Brother Diondray. Where are you staying?"

"The Strasbourg Hotel."

"Diakono Hugo and I will make sure the entire Dumont Brotherhood prays for you, Brother Diondray. What you did earlier will confirm Diakono du Vann's belief that this is the season for Oscar's prophecy to be fulfilled."

I reached the autobus and turned around to wait for Diakono Hugo. Diakono Valencia had gotten onto the autobus. I noticed the beach philosophers staring at me. They had not moved from where I had left them. It would not be the last time I saw Otto Daume and Barron Roche.

What is the difference between a god and humanity
I have been trying to figure it out this entire journey
I grew up believing a god is higher than humanity
The god-and-humanity relationship was hierarchical

A god from high above can script a person's entire life on a chart
If the human being down below believes and follows the chart
Then a human being's life will already be
determined and favored by the god.
However, if you don't believe and follow the prescribed chart
Then a human being's life would be
worthless and lose the god's favor
Other believers, especially the ones close to you
Would encourage
Would admonish
Or demand you follow that prescribed chart
Otherwise you would lose your connection to
them and the rest of the believers
Why would anyone want to believe in a god
who wants followers to become puppets?

What happens when you learn about another god
Who lived amongst human beings
Like your neighbors on both sides of the street
A god who was flesh and blood
A god who looked like you
But had all the attributes of a god
In essence, god and humankind had merged
And his followers learned about how this
god-human lived from a book
Not just any book
A book that followers believed was the only
book you would ever need to read
A book that was hidden in your birth city for generations
Only to be discovered by someone who
had stopped believing in a god

Who handed out prescribed charts like a teacher
returning a student's test after grading it.
The book had a declaration at the end about how the entire land
Cities north and south of the Great Forest
Would become one and all believe in this god-human
And have a relationship with him like a friendship
Is that better than the god who gives his followers prescribed charts
And has no relationship with them?

What happens when a human being gets a power
That runs through his body at unexpected times
A power that connects to every part of the human being
Physical
Emotional
Spiritual
And allows him to save a person's life
And stop a rainstorm through music and dance?

Then people begin to call you a god
Or claim that you come from a god of the past
How would you receive a claim like that?
Do you reject it
Do you consider it
Or do you have any clue how receive it?
And do you become
Like the god from high above
Or the god-human?

I spent several days writing and rewriting this latest
themily. I had to get on paper everything I felt after what
happened on the beach. I wrote several drafts of the themily

until the words finally flowed enough to produce this one. I was not happy with it. But I felt relief as the words came out and I could begin to digest what had transpired on the shore.

Diakono Copperwith came to my hotel room each night after the beach event and prayed for me. He had learned what had happened from Diakono Valencia and felt sad that he wasn't there. He believed his presence could have helped me after the rainstorm ended. We had spent nearly a year together, and he was my only friend outside of Reuel. Friends needed to be there for each other. I appreciated the sentiment and knew our friendship would remain solid despite my strange new abilities.

In the hotel's cafeteria, I had a fantastic breakfast of corn and sliced mangoes on a dark green leaf with a long, thin piece of toasted bread with a crispy crust. It was called a boissant, and it had a light spread of brownberry jam on it. I could have eaten several more of them if we did not have to leave for Dumont Abbi. I learned from a hotel employee that the Strasbourg Hotel had won the city of Terrance's Best Hotel Award last year, mostly because of its food. The Strasbourg Hotel was known for making the best boissants of all the city's hotels. I did not know if it was the best boissant in the city, but I had never had a piece of bread so delicious before.

Diakono Copperwith and I exited the hotel to get on the autobus to Dumont Abbi. Diakono du Vann wanted to speak with me about the beach event and have the entire brotherhood pray for me. Diakono Copperwith also needed to gather more information about the brotherhood so he could finish writing to the konseho of Kammbi about them. He wanted the members of the konseho to know how the Dumont Brotherhood maintained their belief in Kammbi despite being in a city that did not recognize the deity.

A black, two-door automobile turned into the hotel's parking lot quickly and parked behind the autobus. To my surprise, Barron Roche popped out of the automobile and came toward us as we were getting on the autobus.

"Wait, Diondray!"

Diakono Copperwith placed his left hand on my shoulder. "Do you know him?"

I stopped before getting on the autobus. "I do. He was at the beach and saw everything."

"I would still like to show you about Ammaro," Barron said as he reached us. I was waiting for him to make a joke or act like he did toward the crowd at the beach, but the look on his face was serious.

"I'm heading to Dumont Abbi," I said.

Barron was dressed in a white jumpsuit with black trim on the sleeves and pant legs. He wore shiny black leather shoes, and his treetop hairstyle was perfectly shaped. The beach philosopher's appearance made me realize he was a more serious human being than he portrayed at the beach.

"Otto wanted to respect what you said at the beach, and I understand that being considered a descendant of a god is not something a person gets called everyday. But I spoke with Diakono Valencia a couple days ago, and the entire Dumont Brotherhood believes you are the one to fulfill the prophecy from their sacred book. While I do not believe in their god from north of the Great Forest, I do believe you are something special, Diondray Azur of Charlesville. Not just because you are a member of the ruling family of that city. You are something much bigger than I could have imagined in my lifetime. I want to be a part of it."

Barron looked exhausted, and I could tell he had agonized over coming here to the Strasbourg Hotel to find me. I also sensed that he had a friendship with Diakono Valencia despite having different beliefs.

"Go with him," Diakono Copperwith said.

I looked away from Barron to Diakono Copperwith in surprise. I had thought he would be adamant about me going to Dumont Abbi with him. He had spoken remorsefully about not being at the beach, after all. However, it seemed that Diakono Copperwith knew I had to go with the beach philosopher.

"You have gone out into each city throughout our journey together. If I have finally learned anything through my stubbornness, it is that your role in fulfilling Oscar's prophecy has not been what Annalisa or I expected. Going by our interpretation of the Book of Kammbi is not the route for you. Go with him and begin to connect with the people of Terrance."

I nodded. This was the first time he had mentioned Mrs. Copperwith in a few days. I wondered if her most recent letter had expressed softer feelings about my having the Boma Essence. Was she going to rejoin us soon?

The beach philosopher gave a huge smile and reached out to shake my hand. I shook his hand and began walking to his automobile. I knew I was heading on a path that would be different from any other city I had visited throughout my journey. But if the people of Terrance could connect to the Book of Kammbi and its teachings, then I could start to believe Oscar's prophecy would be fulfilled.

Chapter 21

The Haddoe District was the first place Barron wanted to show me. The beach philosopher lived there, and he wanted to start his tour through this part of the city. While he was explaining the history of the district, I looked out the passenger's window at the homes connected to each other. They were made of stone and had windows with wooden shutters. I got the feeling they were quite old, at least from several generations ago. The stone looked weathered, and I could see cracks in the wooden shutters. Barron stated these duplexes, triplexes, and quadplexes were some of the first homes built in the city after Hendric Terrance Goltz arrived from Hamburg.

People on the streets waved at Barron's automobile as he drove by. I assumed he was quite popular in this part of the city. Barron returned the gesture as he drove past. He turned right off Avenue Pierre to a new street, Avenue Osten, and parked his automobile in front of the second home on the street.

"Otto and I live in this duplex. I own the left unit, and Otto owns the one on the right," Barron said after we got out of the automobile. "We bought this duplex a few years ago after retiring from Heidelberg University."

"You were teachers at the university?" I asked as I followed him to the right unit.

Barron stopped as we reached the front door. "We were. Twenty-six years for me. Twenty-eight years for Otto. We met after my first year and became friends instantly. I taught mathematics, and Otto taught on the city's history. I had a blast teaching the city's best students, but I'm glad I'm retired. University life had gotten boring. I believe teachers should not teach beyond twenty years. Otto feels the same way."

Barron did not look like someone who had taught for twenty-six years at a university. I knew he was older than me, but I had placed him in his mid to late thirties. In reality, he was in the same age range as Diakono Copperwith. The name of the university also called up memories: just before I left the family home, Mother and I had talked a lot about my schooling. She wanted to me to attend Heidelberg University here in Terrance, but Uncle Xavier had believed I should attend Charlesville University back home. He didn't think it would look good to our citizens in Charlesville if the son from the city's ruling family shunned the local university for one in another city. As for me, I'd had no interest in going to university at all. Getting through secondary school as a teenager was enough. I was starting to get noticed for my themilys on the eastside, and I had found a friend in Trayvonne Filleu. That was all I wanted to do. The topic of university was one of the many disagreements we'd had before I left the family home for good.

Barron knocked on the door, and Otto opened it. "Welcome, Diondray!" he said while shaking my hand. "Thank you for accepting Barron's invitation. I can understand how you felt after what happened on the beach."

I nodded and followed them into the living room. Books were everywhere, piled up in every corner of the room. "Have you read all of these books, Otto?" I asked.

"Most of them," Otto answered. "I like collecting books and going through them every chance I get. They come from my days at the university. Plus, I need to keep Barron sharp for our debates at the beach."

Barron laughed. "I'm always sharp, partner and ready to beat you!

Otto grinned as we sat down at the table in the left corner of the living room. Barron continued into another room. I sat on the chair across from Otto. Barron returned to the living room with three glasses and a black, teardrop-shaped bottle.

"Do you drink alhiney in Charlesville?" Otto asked while Barron poured the liquor into the glasses.

"This early in the morning?"

Barron laughed. "Those of us from the lower-class districts like the Haddoe, Samsic, and Megaro drink alhiney any time of the day. Only those folks from the upper-class districts of Apollonia, Anndora, Ammaro, and Bomero drink alhiney for dinner. That's what they see as appropriate, especially while listening to Kammarice music like Einstein and Blackberg or Ruben Davar."

"Ruben Davar is my favorite Kammarice musician!" I replied. "I listen to his music all the time."

Barron smiled and handed me a glass of alhiney. "I did not think someone as young as you would like the old-style Kammarice music."

Otto nodded and added, "I would have believed you would like the new style of Kammarice, from musicians like Kiannah, The Three G's, or Paulie Mulhouse."

"Young people in our city want to dance these days," Barron replied after sitting down and drinking his glass of alhiney. "They have been influenced by the Guanamamma music from Walter's Grove. They have no interest in just listening to music in the traditional style of a Ruben Davar, Einstein and Blackberg, or my favorite, Cassandra Applebaum."

Otto laughed. "I know why you like Cassandra Applebaum. And it's not just for her singing."

Barron laughed and replied, "Cassandra Applebaum is the most beautiful and elegant songstress we have ever produced in our city. 'Do You Belong to Me' is the greatest Kammarice song since 'Kammara, Kammara.'"

"I thought your favorite Walter Leonardo Fuente song was 'You're Better Than a Glass of Javann.'"

"Good one, my partner. I do like that song. Forgot about that one."

I laughed at their bantering and said, "'Mango Surprise' by Ruben Davar is my favorite song. I would listen to it every time I got into an argument with my mother or Uncle Xavier about something I was doing wrong. I would take my radio out to the beach and let it take me away from everything that was going on."

"In that case, you should have had a glass of alhiney with you!" Otto said and raised his glass to drink. "Don't worry, this brand of alhiney has been diluted. It won't have the kick it's known for."

"My mother and Uncle Xavier did not allow me to drink alhiney, or javann for that matter, while I lived in the family home. They felt it would not be appropriate for me to be drinking liquor," I said after taking a drink.

"We are glad to have a friendship with Diakono Valencia. Everyone in the city knows the Dumont Brotherhood make the best alhiney. And we get two kinds of alhiney from Diakono Valencia soon after it's made at Dumont Abbi," Otto continued.

"A bottle with kick, and a bottle like this one, without kick," Barron interjected and poured seconds into our glasses.

I could taste the sweetness of the pinkberries immediately, and it tasted more like brownberry juice than the alhiney I had at Dumont Abbi. That was pure alhiney with a kick, unlike this stripped-down version.

Otto grinned and rose from his chair. "I can tell you like alhiney. It is much better than javann. That drink is too dry for most of us here in the city. As a non-drinker, you have to be careful with this one. Good thing we had the liquor diluted so we can drink it in the morning. Otherwise, it will sneak up on you. Don't let the sweet taste fool you."

I nodded at his warning. He was correct. I could have kept drinking several more glasses of alhiney.

Otto walked over to the other side of the room and pulled a book from one of the piles. "This book is called *The Gods of Terrance: A History . . .*"

"Written by Otto Daume," I said as I peered over at the cover.

Barron replied, "My partner is an author as well. One of his many books."

Otto smiled as he stood next to me. He flipped open the book to the back section. An illustration on the page showed a well-built, dark-skinned man with a stern look. A leopard lingered next to him.

"Ammaro ruled the land with a fierceness that his subjects, the Foncee tribe, never questioned. The god was tall, with night-colored skin, and considered handsome to the women of the tribe. Ammaro always traveled with a leopard at his side. The tribe named the leopard Ami, meaning friend. Man and animal were inseparable. Because of that fact, Ammaro became known as the god of animals as well," Otto read.

I could hardly believe my eyes. "There were leopards in this part of the region as well?"

Barron nodded as Otto glanced over at me. "Of course, leopards have traveled throughout both regions, North and South of the Great Forest for generations. It would make sense for Ammaro to have a leopard with him when the gods were here.

I looked at Otto in surprise. "Reuel has appeared with Diakono Copperwith and myself at every city on this journey. The leopard knew exactly where I would be each time. This animal is much more an essential part of Oscar's Prophecy than just being a traveling companion for Oscar Ortega, Adrian Azur, and myself."

Otto stopped reading and closed the book. "I have studied the gods of our city for my entire teaching career. Even though Jules Raymond, our regnator, preaches the gods are a thing of the past, their influence has not left this city. Seeing that leopard come to you on the beach confirmed and validated what I have studied and written about my entire career. The gods are still with us, and what you did with the rainstorm proves it."

"Leopards are mysterious animals by nature, and they don't just come to human beings and nuzzle them," Barron added.

I grabbed the book from Otto and flipped it back open to the illustration. I stared at the leopard next to Ammaro. Barron was correct. Leopards were mysterious and Reuel displayed that nature on this journey. This animal had been important to people of both regions for different reasons. I understood why each region had a special meaning for the animal.

"There is another reason we wanted to invite you here, Diondray," Otto said after sitting back down in his seat.

I glanced at Barron, who was nodding at his friend's comment.

"I found out two days ago that our university's library owns a copy of a book about what they believe and follow in the cities north of the Great Forest," Otto continued. "It was donated to them."

"The librarian brought it to my attention," Barron added. "I told Otto. We believe it's a copy of the Book of Kammbi."

"Did someone from the cities north of the Great Forest donate the book?" I asked.

Otto and Barron looked at each other like they had a secret to share. "It was brought by a woman from Charlesville," Otto announced. "There was an inscription inside the cover saying 'My nephew will come to Terrance soon. He is the one who will fulfill the prophecy written in the last pages of this book. When he comes to this city, please do not reject him. He is a person who will unite all of us, north and south. If you reject him, you will reject the greatest opportunity for this entire land to become one.'"

I slumped in my chair. How had Aunt Maxina known I would be coming to Terrance? I had not spoken to her since leaving Charlesville—and at the time, I'd had no idea that I would be traveling to both regions of this land. When had she come to Terrance to donate a copy of the Book of Kammbi? And where had she found such a book? I thought I had the only copy left by Oscar Ortega.

271

"The librarian wanted to tell Otto and me first before he reported it to the head of the university. All donations have to be reported for auditing purposes, but if this type of donation got out to the public, it would get the konzill's attention," Barron stated.

"And the attention of Jules Raymond," Otto added.

"I know the person who donated that book," I said softly. "However, I thought I had the only copy of the Book of Kammbi in Charlesville. I do not know where my Aunt Maxina got another copy."

"It was your aunt who donated the book?" Otto asked.

"I believe so. She is the one who let me know the book had been in Charlesville since Oscar Ortega brought it there in his attempt to reconcile with his son. But she gave me that copy of the Book of Kammbi. I did not know there was another one in my birth city."

"Do you have the Book of Kammbi with you?" Barron asked.

"I do. In my hotel room."

"We are meeting with the librarian in two days," Otto said. "Will you come with us and bring your copy of the Book of Kammbi?"

I nodded.

"As you know, the people of the Terrance have been told the gods are no longer with us. And we do not believe in a man-made religion like the people of the north do," Otto continued.

"Kammbi is considered both human and divine," I interjected.

"Understood, Diondray. But we believe something is going on. A change is coming to both regions of the land. We want to know why it's happening and offer our assistance. If the gods are trying to come back, or if this Kammbi has decided to make himself known through you and your companion, Diakono Copperwith, we want to be a part of it."

"Our city needs a balance to offset what has been publicly declared by our regnator and the konzill. If you are bringing the balance our city needs, we welcome it," Barron said.

Barron brought me back to my hotel room around three o'clock. I had spent several hours with the beach philosophers, getting to know them a little better. I told them about writing themilys and reading my words at Aliki Park back home. The immigrants who had come from this city during Great-Uncle Myro's rule had brought their love of themilys with them and influenced us. Otto commented that the reading of themilys had started in the Haddoe District at Bremen Park. Barron mentioned that on day three of every week, Bremen Park held a contest which anyone who had written a themily and wanted to read it could enter. The audience's applause determined the winner, who would receive a cash prize of three hundred Syonne bills. They both suggested that I enter the upcoming contest in six days and thought I might have a good shot of winning. I was not sure about entering the contest, but I did want to go to Bremen Park.

After an excellent lunch of grilled marrone, a brown fish from the Kammara Sea off the coast of this city, with green leaf vegetables, sliced mangoes, and brownberries, Barron drove me through the Haddoe District before returning me to my hotel room. He tried to convince me to enter the contest while showing me the sights of the district.

However, I was distracted thinking about Aunt Maxina and how she had gotten another copy of the Book of Kammbi. She had made it clear that the copy found at Ama's Faddar back in Carm of the year before was the only one in Charlesville. When had she left to come this city? And why? Had she been forced to leave like myself? Had Uncle Xavier and Mother found out it was her who got me out of the holding cell and planned my exit to Santa Sophia?

I was barely listening to Barron as he talked about the game of hoop played at another park we drove by, Munich Park. Hoop was played on a full court with two raised goals with netting attached, one on each end of the court, and the players shot a leather ball through the goal that had netting attached on it. We played hoop back home, but I was not tall or athletic enough to be any good. Trayvonne, on the other hand, was excellent at the game.

I made it back to the hotel room and grabbed my travel bag, which was lying on the desk. I opened the travel bag and pulled out the Book of Kammbi I had received from Aunt Maxina. I reread the letter she had placed inside when I left Charlesville on my way to Santa Sophia. I wanted to see if there were signs that she'd known I was going to be traveling throughout the land and coming here to Terrance.

The letter mentioned that I would have a lot of questions as I escaped. I had. And I still did. She would be all right, it said, even if Uncle Xavier found out I had escaped Charlesville with her help. I read the last paragraph, where she referenced the last themily I'd read publicly in Aliki Park about discovering the truth of our connection to Oscar Ortega and the Book of Kammbi. "Truth is freedom" was the last sentence of her letter.

There was nothing in the letter that indicated she knew what would happen after I went to Santa Sophia. Somebody must have given her the idea that I would arrive in this city—maybe the same somebody who gave her another copy of the Book of Kammbi. I knew whom I had to ask when he returned from Dumont Abbi this evening.

Dinner at the hotel's cafeteria was an oversized grilled sausage wrapped in a boissant with a thick purple and white vegetable called choux and corn. I remembered having choux at Trayonne's duplex back home, when one of his many girlfriends, who came from Terrance, had prepared it for dinner. It was crunchy, but the corn mixed with it softened the sound.

Diakono Copperwith arrived a few minutes later and said a quick prayer over his dinner. I noticed he had a somber look on his face.

"Did something happen at Dumont Abbi?" I asked him after drinking a glass of brownberry juice that was placed at our table.

"I spent most of the day in prayer and song with Diakono du Vann," he replied after taking a bite of his dinner. "One of the diakonos is sick and could be dying soon."

"Who is it?"

"Diakono Abeldorff. I don't think you have met him. He is one of the pinkberry farmers at Dumont Abbi. Actually, he is considered their best pinkberry farmer. He makes sure the fruit is harvested correctly."

I had not yet met Diakono Abeldorff or any of the brotherhood members who harvested pinkberries. I had planned to visit that section of Dumont Abbi on my next trip. I was curious about how they turned the pinkberries into alhiney. If he was the best farmer among them, then his death could be a big loss for the brotherhood.

Diakono Copperwith barely ate his dinner. I sensed he was affected by Diakono Abeldorff's illness.

"I will have to return to Dumont Abbi first thing in the morning," he said. "Also, you should know . . . Diakono du Vann has asked me to join the Dumont Brotherhood after Diakono Abeldorff leaves us."

My jaw dropped. "Are you serious?"

Diakono Copperwith nodded. "But don't worry. He knows that I must finish out the journey with you. He believes you will fulfill Oscar's prophecy and does not want to get in the way of that happening."

"What about Mrs. Copperwith?" I interjected. "Is she not coming back?"

Diakono Copperwith sighed. "I hope so. And I explained to Diakono du Vann after our last prayer today that I miss my wife. I plan on reuniting with her soon. He understands my position, and while she could not live at Dumont Abbi with the other brotherhood members, he will make special accommodations for her."

"Do you want to become a Dumont Brotherhood member?"

Diakono Copperwith nodded. "I do."

"Why?"

His eyes bulged at my question. I did not think he'd expected it.

"I feel at home in Dumont Abbi," Diakono Copperwith started. "As you know, my goal was to become morrim of the kahall of Santa Sophia. I thought that was the position Kammbi and the Eternal Comforter wanted me to fulfill. However, I met your Aunt Maxina, and she told me about having a copy of the Book of Kammbi in your city. It was Oscar Ortega's copy, and I knew my path would be different from that moment."

I had forgotten about Aunt Maxina for a bit after the news about Diakono Abeldorff. "I found out today that she donated a copy of the Book of Kammbi to Heidelberg University here in town. I did not know she had another copy."

Diakono Copperwith stared at me for several seconds before replying, "I gave it to her. She told me that she had started to read the one left in your city by Oscar Ortega. Your aunt became interested in Oscar's story and wanted to have a copy of her own."

"Did she start to become a believer and follower of Kammbi?"

Diakono Copperwith managed a smile. "I don't know. But she was interested in having a copy of the Book of the Kammbi. But if she donated the copy to the university, then I don't know if she declared her belief."

"She wrote a note in the donated book saying that I would come to Terrance. How could she know that?"

Diakono Copperwith closed his eyes and rocked in his seat. "I told her before she returned to Charlesville that you would have to travel to both regions of this land in order to fulfill Oscar's prophecy."

I placed my left hand over my mouth before replying. "You already knew before you met me that I would have to travel to both regions of the land?"

He nodded.

"What else did you know before I arrived in Charlesville?"

"That you would be the one to fulfill Oscar's prophecy," Diakono Copperwith answered. "I lost a chance at becoming morrim of the kahall of Santa Sophia—the only thing I desired other than my wife. I might lose my title as diakono because of the power you have inside of you. I would never have imagined anything like that. But I have believed in the guidance of the Eternal Comforter for my entire religious life. One of the basic tenets of being a believer and follower of Kammbi is learning to do what you are being guided to do, not what you want."

"But I don't get why Kammbi would take away the only thing you have desired in life. Being the morrim of the kahall of Santa Sophia was an honorable thing to desire. I would think that Kammbi would be eager to guide you to that position."

Diakono Copperwith nodded. "Diondray, human beings are naturally selfish. Selfishness does have a negative connation to it, especially in the context of being a follower of Kammbi. However, I have had to learn over the years as a diakono to give my life to my beliefs. I learned that lesson early, as a second esperah, after graduating from the University of Issabella. It is what Kammbi through the Eternal Comforter wants for my life, not what I want for my life. Our perspective through selfishness is limited. Kammbi sees our entire lives. Many people who are not believers don't understand this, or they refuse to accept it."

"I remember Second Esperah Carranza's words after I first met you in Santa Sophia," I said. "I questioned him about not having his own opinion. He said that a second esperah's role is to be a servant. One can't be a leader without being a servant. Kammbi was the greatest example of being a servant leader."

Diakono Copperwith grinned. "Second Esperah Carranza told me about that conversation. He said you were stunned by that comment. I explained to him that it's rare for people like himself to become servants. Especially young people. Most human beings want to be leaders, and as we have seen many times throughout this journey, human beings glorify being a leader and denigrate being a servant."

His comment rang true. Human beings did have an inherent selfishness and wanting to serve others like Second Esperah Carranza seemed counterintuitive.

"I only knew that my life would change for the good after your arrival, Diondray. And now I have met the Dumont Brotherhood, and I know by the guidance of the Eternal Comforter that I belong with them."

I sighed and knew that he was telling the truth. Diakono Copperwith was a straight shooter, and I had never suspected any kind of deception from him throughout the entire journey. He was the closest thing I had to a father figure in my life. And his life had changed since meeting me.

"Some of the people in this city believe that I'm a god after what happened on the beach," I said softly. "I don't know why Omari gave me this Boma Essence. But it has appeared in unexpected ways, and there is no way I could be a god."

"That is correct. You are not a god. But you are the bridge between those like me who believe in and follow Kammbi, and those who do not believe in and follow Kammbi. Oscar Ortega was meant to become the first bridge builder for Kammbi. However, his act of passha and attempt at reconciliation derailed him from what Kammbi wanted for his life. We have been given a second chance through you, Diondray Azur. You are meant to walk this path, and I hope the guidance of the Eternal Comforter becomes stronger in you than the guidance of those things that are outside of Kammbi's influence."

I took another drink of brownberry juice, trying to let his last comment sink in. I had never seen myself as a bridge builder. I had gained a thought for my next themily and would see if I could use it for the contest at Bremen Park.

"You will become the next Dumont Brotherhood member," I said.

"I know. But I want Annalisa with me. I cannot do this without her."

Chapter 22

Barron and Otto brought me to the Heidelberg University Library a couple of days later. Heidelberg University was in the Anndora District of the city. The Anndora District was considered one of the wealthiest in Terrance. Most of the upper-class citizens lived here and in its neighboring district to the east, Ammaro. I could tell the difference immediately as Barron drove us to the university. The homes here were newly built half-timbered houses. I did not see any duplexes, triplexes, or quadplexes here. People did not hang out on the street corners like they did in the Haddoe District.

As we drove, I learned that Heidelberg University was one of the two main universities in the city. Nancy University in the Ammaro District was the other one, and the schools had a long-standing rivalry with each other. Otto explained that both universities claimed to have the city's best students and had made that declaration publicly in the city for many years. Barron and Otto admitted their bias toward Heidelberg University, but they acknowledged that Nancy University was an excellent school too.

The library was a massive building in the southeastern section of the university. It reminded me of the Stuttgarte in the city's center—a resemblance that was explained when Barron remarked that the university had built it as a replica of the Stuttgarte.

As we entered, the librarian greeted us. She was a tall, stout woman with a well-trimmed treetop hairstyle, and she wore an orange maxi dress that hugged her body. Most people I knew with a treetop hairstyle blew it out instead of trimming it. I thought it looked nice on her.

"Two of my favorite former professors have arrived," she said after hugging Barron and Otto. "Both of you are still on time despite being retired. I wish our students and some of the other professors understood that principle."

"Elexi, we would always be on time for you," Barron replied and smiled warmly at the librarian.

Otto laughed and rolled his eyes at Barron's flattery. He knew Barron's routine out in public and played along with him. Otto had told me on the drive over here that Elexi Lannion and Barron had a long-standing friendship and had dated in their early days as professors.

"You should have been married a long time ago, Barron Roche," Elexi countered as we followed her into another room of the library. "Your kind of sweet talk should have captured someone by now."

Otto laughed. "Barron Roche married . . . that will never happen!"

"Watch your tongue, partner!" Barron shot back. "I don't need to be married to appreciate a beautiful woman and the best librarian in the city."

Elexi had a deep laugh that sounded like it came from her stomach instead of her mouth. I chuckled at her laugh as she walked behind a large desk. I was holding onto my travel bag. It had the Book of Kammbi as well as a writing pad of the themilys I had written during the journey.

The librarian pulled out a book with a black cover and gold lettering that clearly said *The Book of Kammbi*. "The woman who donated this book said she had a nephew she believed would unite both regions of the land through a declaration at the end of the book. She claimed her nephew and a blond-haired man would arrive in this city to share the writings inside the book with our citizens."

Aunt Maxina had definitely been in Terrance. Elexi's comment confirmed that Diakono Copperwith had given her this copy of the Book of Kammbi. I opened my travel bag and pulled out my copy. "My aunt, Maxina Azur, was the one who donated that book. When did you receive it?"

Elexi stared at me for several moments before answering. "I can see the resemblance in your nose and mouth. She came at the end of the first month, Nayur. She did not tell me her name. She had to secretly leave Charlesville and did not want anyone here to know who she was."

Her remarks troubled me. Why would Aunt Maxina have to leave home secretly? Did Uncle Xavier and Mother know that she had helped me leave Charlesville?

I placed my copy of the Book of Kammbi on the desk next to the one Elexi had received.

"Your copy is much older than the donated copy," Otto replied.

"True, partner," Barron added as he touched the covers of both books. "But they are the same book."

I nodded and asked, "Was there a letter placed inside the book?"

283

Elexi opened the book to reveal a letter written on beige paper. She handed me the letter. I rubbed the letter for several moments before reading it. I did not know Aunt Maxina had quality paper like this in her possession.

My Nephew,

If you have received this letter, then everything Malcolm Copperwith said is coming true. He wanted me to have this copy of the Book of Kammbi and write a letter to prove he was making the right decision in believing that you are the one who will fulfill Oscar's Prophecy. Malcolm studied and taught about Oscar's prophecy for all his adult life. But no matter how much one believes in the words written in a sacred book, human beings always need a sign that what they believe is true. Even Kammbi wrote that believers can trust him to a certain point, but they still need evidence. We do not have the capacity to trust blindly. Our perspective is limited, and we cannot see what a god sees. Signs have to be provided at the right time to reveal what we believe in all of life is true. Malcolm needed that sign, and you reading this letter will reveal that you are the one to fulfill Oscar's Prophecy

I know from the letter I (Should this be "received"?) when you escaped Charlesville that you had a lot of questions. I'm sure you have even more questions as you read this letter. Let me answer one: Uncle Xavier and Olivia know that I helped you. They were furious with me and had

*me thrown in the holding cell I freed you from.
Don't worry, my nephew. I'm well, and nothing
my siblings can do will hurt me. I was able to
escape because I had to get this copy of the Book of
Kammbi to Terrance. As you said in the themily I
heard at Aliki Park, "Truth is Freedom." And this
truth will set all of us free. I love you, my nephew.
Fulfill the path that has been laid out for you. Our
land needs a bridge builder. You are it.*

My hands shook after reading the letter. She was correct
that people needed a sign. Trusting in words without evidence
was difficult for most people. The letter reiterated Diakono
Copperwith's comment about me being a bridge builder. Yet,
even he needed a sign that he was doing the right thing for
Kammbi by traveling with me. To me, it finally made sense why
he had stuck with me after finding out I had the Boma Essence
inside of me. Now I had gotten the ultimate sign that this land,
both north and south of the Great Forest, was connected.

"I have to keep this copy of the Book of Kammbi and
report it to the konzill because it's an official donation," Elexi
said to break the silence in the room. "However, I believe you
should keep that letter. And do you have a Malcolm Copperwith
with you?"

"Diakono Malcolm Copperwith of Santa Sophia has
traveled the entire journey with me. I would not be here without
him."

The librarian smiled at me. "Your aunt was prescient, like
most women are."

Or she had gotten guidance from the Eternal Comforter,
I thought. I believed Aunt Maxina had become a believer and

follower of Kammbi. I wondered if Uncle Xavier and Mother knew that as well.

"You must enter the contest at Bremen Park," Barron said as I placed the letter inside my copy of the Book of Kammbi.

"I will," I said while closing my travel bag. "I have been preparing a themily for it."

"We will help you make it the best one for the contest," Otto added.

"I will be there as well," Elexi said. "Barron, my friend, you were right when you told me this young man is something special and change is coming to our city. I want to be a part of it too."

Barron had gotten tickets to see his favorite singer, Cassandra Applebaum, later that evening. Elexi was going with him, and he invited me to come along. At first, I wanted to stay in my hotel room for the evening and work on my themily for the contest at Bremen Park. However, I changed my mind and accepted Barron's invitation.

Cassandra Applebaum was performing at the Mannheim nightclub in the Apollonia District. The Apollonia District was in the northwestern part of the city, and it hosted the city's nightlife, which began at the intersection of Avenue Hendric and Avenue Kammarice. Avenue Kammarice continued west for several miles and was home to the majority of the city's nightclubs. The area reminded me of the Roxie and Penelope District in Walter's Grove. The Mannheim was one of the largest nightclubs in the district, and it competed with the Rochelle nightclub just a few blocks further west on Avenue

Kammarice to get the best Kammarice singers and musicians in the city.

We were served dinner before Cassandra Applebaum's performance. I had choux mixed with sliced pinkberries and grilled bluefish. I was pleased to see bluefish on the menu. The pinkberries added a sweetness to offset the crunchy texture of the choux. I thought the mixture of the two was excellent. It was the best meal I'd had outside of the hotel cafeteria since being in Terrance.

Barron and Elexi had yellow mashed potatoes, choux, and grilled sausage. Their dinner was called the Nante in honor of the settlers who had come with Phillip Nante across the Kammara Sea. Elexi explained that Philip Nante was the second sailor to come across the sea after Hendric Terrance Goltz. Nante was from the land of Rennes, a neighboring world to Hamburg. Rennes and Hamburg were rival lands from the old world and always tried to one-up each other throughout their history.

We were seated a few rows back from the right side of the stage. I sat in a chair with my back facing the stage. Barron and Elexi were across from me and talked to each other like people who dated in the past. I moved my chair around to face the stage. The waitress bought a new bottle of alhiney and poured it into our glasses.

The lighting in the nightclub dimmed, and a spotlight appeared in the middle of the stage. It beamed on a microphone as a well-dressed man in a gray suit accentuated with a pink tie and chest pocket grabbed it.

"Hello, ladies and gentlemen! I'm Cedric Mentz, your host for this evening's special performance. Welcome to the Mannheim!"

The audience clapped loudly. I glanced at my companions to see both of them grinning and clapping as well. I sensed this was going to be a rare performance by Cassandra Applebaum, and the audience was already showing their appreciation.

"Let's get on with it!" Cedric Mentz continued after the applause faded. "She has been called the Queen of Kammarice, with songs like 'Do You Belong To Me,' 'I Have Never Met Anyone Like You,' 'Brownberry Wishes,' and her outstanding remake of Walter Leonardo Fuente's classic, 'Kammara, Kammara.' Please join me in giving Cassandra Applebaum, the Queen of Kammarice, a big Mannheim welcome!"

The audience erupted with applause as a slender, dark-skinned woman with a trimmed treetop hairstyle appeared on stage. Cassandra Applebaum wore an aqua-green sequined dress that stopped at the knees. It was accentuated with a thick white pearl necklace and matching bracelets on both wrists.

Barron rose from his chair with a look of awe on his face. Elexi stood as well and placed her arm around her former lover.

"Please be seated," Cassandra Applebaum said with a delicate voice. "Thank you all for coming tonight. It has been a while since I performed at a nightclub like the Mannheim. However, I felt it was right to return to my roots as an upcoming Kammarice singer in the tradition of Walter Leonardo Fuente, Harrie Einstein, and my mentor, Pilar Meldorf."

The audience roared with applause. "You sing real Kammarice music!" someone yelled out.

Cassandra Applebaum laughed at the comment and added, "I sure do."

The audience continued with their applause.

The singer waved her hands. "I have a special guest to join me this evening. You know this great musician from his classic song 'Mango Surprise' and many, many other songs played on his guitar. Please welcome Ruben Davar!"

Barron and Elexi smiled at me. They'd known Ruben Davar was going to play with Cassandra Applebaum for tonight's performance. I returned the smile and appreciated their gesture of bringing me to the Mannheim to see him.

Ruben Davar started playing his guitar softly as the spotlight illuminated the entire stage. Behind him and Cassandra were a dark-skinned, heavyset drummer and an attractive brown-haired woman holding a horn.

"As many of you know, I lived on the beach in the Megaro District," Cassandra said to the audience while the guitarist played. "And I have seen and heard about a lot of things that happened there. But several days ago, a friend told me about an event that surprised me. He told me a young man who looked to be about the age of my son, Maxwell, had stopped a sudden rainstorm. My friend believed that Megaro, the sea god, brought the rainstorm. As you know, most of us who lived on the beach still believe in the gods."

The singer raised her hands like she knew some of the audience would object to her comment. "I know. The gods left us long ago. But my friend was convinced after a leopard ran toward this young man after he stopped the storm that he was descended from the gods. At first, I did not want to believe my friend. However, I began writing a tune about someone being able to stop a rainstorm. I called this song, 'The One Who Made Rain Go Away.'"

I cut my eyes at Barron, and he nodded at me. Had he told Cassandra Applebaum what happened on the beach? The singer's deep, powerful voice began to sing.

I heard about someone stopping a
rainstorm that came from the sea.
A storm believed by some to come from the sea god.
But I was told the sea god had left us
during the time of Syonne.
Syonne said the people must believe in themselves
In other people
Not gods who want to control humankind.
And if we stopped believing in them
They would leave us.
But how do you explain my friend's claim about
The One Who Made Rain Go Away?

The horn player began a solo that sounded like the sea. I looked around at the audience on each side of the table and saw many surprised looks. They had not come to the Mannheim tonight to hear this kind of song from one of their greatest and most beloved singers. The audience wanted to hear her version of 'Kammara, Kammara' or 'Brownberry Wishes' or 'Do You Belong To Me' instead of this song. Barron had explained the city's wealthy came to the Mannheim as their choice of nightlife. Because of their patronage of the club and its singers, this clientele had expectations. Expectations of music that made them feel good. Expectations of music that acknowledged their status. Expectations of music that made them feel longing and nostalgia.

The rain came out of nowhere
The beachgoers fled the beach for cover
But there was one who walked toward the rain
One with skin as dark as mine

One with hair thick and kinky as mine
One who went to the rain
One who made it stop
And how do you explain
About the One Who Made Rain Go Away?

Cassandra Applebaum finished the second verse, and I noticed a sorrowful look on her face. The Queen of Kammarice knew her audience would not be happy with a song reminding them of a past they had been taught to leave behind. However, I felt her performance was changing something in this city. From now on, things would not be the same.

"Thank you for listening to this song," she said while the musicians continued playing. "It's time to give you what you came for. Let's do it, band!"

Ruben Davar strummed the guitar with a faster tempo, and the horn player provided several blows of the horn that changed the audience's mood instantly. Cassandra Applebaum started singing "Do You Belong To Me," and the audience clapped with approval. I scanned the crowd again and noticed big smiles all around. The Queen of Kammarice had given them what they came to hear. They would try to forget about "The One Who Made Rain Go Away" for the rest of the evening and delight in the songs Cassandra Applebaum had made famous.

"Are you all right, Diondray?" Barron asked after Cassandra finished singing "Do You Belong To Me."

Barron and Elexi looked concerned. "Did you tell her about what happened on the beach?" I asked.

Barron shook his head. "Even though Cassandra Applebaum is my favorite singer, I don't know her personally, and there is no way I could have told her. And for her to write a song about it . . ."

"Was unexpected," Elexi interjected. "Her singing about it will get the attention of the konzill."

"And Jules Raymond," Barron added.

"She has those kinds of connections?" I asked.

"She is called the Queen of Kammarice for a reason, my friend," Barron replied. "Look at this audience. There are members of the konzill here in attendance along with those from the upper classes. She is their singer, and her song will be discussed."

Barron pointed out some members of the konzill—several silver-haired men wearing white suitjackets and sitting at a table a few rows to the left of us. The konzill members were focused on the Queen of Kammarice and her band. I could tell they were enjoying the performance.

"If her song gets discussed by the konzill, what will that mean?" I asked after turning my attention back to our table.

Barron and Elexi stared at each other for a moment before he responded. "The konzill will investigate what happened on the beach."

"And if it's corroborated by enough people, they will try to find out where the person who actually stopped the rainstorm is located," Elexi finished.

"Then what?"

The former lovers exchanged a look. "The konzill will try to stop it from happening again. They don't want people, especially the lower-class citizens, to believe in the gods," Barron answered.

"Then why have the Stuttgarte?" I replied as Cassandra Applebaum finished another song. "I saw people going there to worship those large paintings."

"A harmless ritual," Elexi said. "Jules Raymond and the konzill know they cannot get rid of the city's oldest landmark. So they allow the people to show their allegiance to the gods only in that setting."

I glanced at my companions and then looked over at the konzill members again. The waitresses at their table bowed to them while serving glasses of alhiney. It seemed at that moment that the konzill wanted the people to treat them like gods instead of those that had existed in the past. I gathered their agenda was more about about where the people's worship belonged. If you believed in the gods, then you could not totally submit to the authority of the regnator, Jules Raymond, and the konzill. They wanted control over the people in every facet of their lives, not only legally but spiritually too. How could belief in Kammbi survive in this city? The Dumont Brotherhood lived in the southernmost part of Terrance, and their influence was limited to alhiney making. Since the brotherhood had decided not to proselytize the people of the city, they were not a threat to the regnator and the konzill. But what Diakono Copperwith and I had come here to do might be.

Cassandra Applebaum's song was going to be discussed by the konzill, and I still had over twenty days left in the city. What if they found out I was the one the city's greatest singer had described in her song? What would happen? I sipped on another glass of alhiney as the music ended.

"We are taking a short break," Cassandra Applebaum announced. "Thank you again for coming, and we will back shortly."

The audience stood and applauded the Queen of Kammarice and the band. I got up from my chair and walked away from the table.

"Diondray, where are you going?" Barron called out.

"I need some fresh air," I replied. "I will return."

The professor nodded, and I headed for the exit. Just before I walked outside, I felt a tug on my right arm. I turned to see a person I'd thought I would never see again.

"My beloved, I thought it was you."

"What are you doing here, Darcie?"

"I came here to find you. I could not let that good-bye from days ago be our last parting. I had to find you. Let's go outside."

I looked at her, and all my desire came rushing back. She was wearing a tight sea-blue maxi dress that showed off her hips. Darcie Fendlewiesen smiled, and I followed her out of the Mannheim.

We walked across the street and made it down to the Rochelle nightclub. Darcie wanted to dance. I was trying to figure out how she had found me at the Mannheim.

"How did you know I would be at the Mannheim?" I asked as we stood in line to get into Rochelle.

Darcie smiled seductively. "We will talk later. I found you. I'm happy. Let's dance."

She grabbed my hand as we entered the nightclub. The atmosphere of the Rochelle was completely different than the Mannheim. Guanamamma music pulsated through the nightclub. People were dancing everywhere as we walked to the dance floor.

"I hope you have not forgotten everything I taught you," Darcie remarked.

We found a spot on the left side of the dance floor, and she grabbed my hands to place them in position to dance Guanamamma. I moved my right hand to the small of her back as taught by Ciscoe. However, Darcie moved my hand down to her backside and smiled.

"Ciscoe is not here," she said. "You can touch me, my beloved."

A new song came on. It had a heavy drumbeat like I'd heard when I first arrived in Walter's Grove. I began leading Darcie in dancing Guanamamma. She followed along perfectly. The back-and-forth motion, the spins and turns came back as we danced. Darcie's cheeks flushed, and she had a joyous smile on her face. *I want you to remember that more than one woman loves you.* I remembered her comment to me as I got on the autobus to come to Terrance. Did she really love me? She would not have come here to find me if that was not the case.

The song ended, and we faced the stage as a chubby, dark-skinned man wearing an orange jumpsuit appeared. "Glad you all have decided to come to Rochelle! Rochelle is the place in Terrance where you can dance the night away. We don't just sit on our backsides and listen to music like most people in town. Especially at that other nightclub across the street. We move our backsides to Guanamamma music like they do in Walter's Grove!"

The audience roared, and Darcie playfully bumped me with her ample hip. I smiled at her as a new song came on.

"Let's go!" she said and pulled me away from the dance floor.

"Where are we going?"

She looked back at me with a big smile, and I followed her out of the Rochelle. We walked outside, and an autobus was parked in front of the nightclub. Darcie gave the driver some money, and we got inside.

"Alsace Hotel," she said.

"Darcie, I came with some people," I protested. "I cannot leave them."

"Were they a couple?" she asked.

"In the past," I answered. "Just friends now."

She grabbed my hands and placed them on her hips. "We are friends too. And it's time we enjoyed each other's company."

The autobus driver left the Rochelle, and Darcie pulled my face close to her. We kissed, and we did not stop until we got to the Alsace Hotel. Desire was all that matter in that moment.

Chapter 23

Darcie and I made love after leaving the Rochelle nightclub. It was the first time I had made love since Mara back home in Charlesville. Desire overflowed from me like I had not experienced it before, and it felt good being inside of Darcie. She gave her body willingly and at the height of pleasure, she told me how much she loved me. However, I had to admit to myself that I did not feel quite the same.

Several days later, I thought back to that night and pondered what had happened. I enjoyed dancing Guanamamma with Darcie. Dancing at the Rochelle with her had felt right—in the sense of being dance partners. But I did not have the same feeling of love toward her that she did for me. I grabbed Maisa's letter from my travel bag and held it in my hand. What if Maisa found out about my tryst with Darcie? Would I lose her for good?

I sighed as I sat at my hotel room desk, working on my themily for the contest at Bremen Park tomorrow. Barron had called my hotel room several times that night after I left the Mannheim. He and Elexi were worried that something had happened to me. I called him the next morning and explained that I'd met an old friend and spent some time catching up.

The former professor was relieved and invited me over to his duplex to go over what I had written for the contest. Our visit would be today.

However, my mind was not focused on the themily or the contest at Bremen Park. I knew I had crossed a line with my night of desire with Darcie. I heard Diakono Copperwith's warning loud and clear in my mind: *"You cannot go back to that temptress again. You are going to get burned. Maybe that magic inside of you will protect you from her."* Where was the Boma Essence when Darcie had come to me? I had not felt anything stirring inside my body after the beach incident. Did the Boma Essence believe it was okay that I had made love to Darcie?

I knew I had to tell Diakono Copperwith. I did not want him to be angry with me, but it would not be right to keep it from him. I imagined what would happen if Mrs. Copperwith found out about my tryst. She had made sure that I was not alone with Maisa during our journey through the cities north of the Great Forest. *"At night, an unmarried man and woman should not be in the same room together."* Maisa had been in my hotel room in Santa Teresa, and Mrs. Copperwith had seen us embrace. She had immediately claimed that her husband had a rule that we could not be together at night. She wanted to make sure I did not get distracted from fulfilling Oscar's prophecy.

I had broken that rule. Mrs. Copperwith would have scolded me if she were here. She had admitted that I had become like a son to her and Diakono Copperwith. She had gone back to Issabella as a sacrifice so that her husband could stay with me on the journey. I felt like I had let her down too.

I managed to write some more of the themily and got enough words on paper to make a sufficient draft. I hoped it would be good enough to at least make an impression on the audience at the contest. I placed the themily in my writing pad and got dressed for breakfast. I had not seen Diakono Copperwith for a couple of days. He had been spending all his time at Dumont Abbi helping Diakono du Vann with the brotherhood member who was sick—but this morning I knew he was back, and waiting for me to come down so we could eat together. I had always looked forward to eating breakfast with Diakono Copperwith. This time would be different.

Diakono Copperwith and I sat down to a breakfast of freshly baked boissants, grilled sausage, and glasses of brownberry juice. The pleasant aroma from the boissant did not help me overcome the sense of dread I felt.

"Diakono Abeldorff died yesterday."

I looked up from eating and saw a sorrowful look on my friend's face. "My condolences to you and all the members of the Dumont Brotherhood."

Diakono Copperwith nodded and looked away from our table. "He served as a Dumont Brotherhood member for forty years. Diakono Abeldorff helped Diakono du Vann become the leader of the brotherhood. They had a close relationship, and Diakono du Vann has taken his death hard."

I did not know what to say to comfort Diakono Copperwith. Death was something I had rarely dealt with in my life. The only person close to me who had died was Uncle Barfield, Aunt Maxina's husband. I was nine years old when he died, but I knew it was difficult for Aunt Maxina. They had been married for less than a year when he got very sick and died at the hospital days later. Aunt Maxina told me when I got older that Uncle Barfield was the only man she had ever loved, and his death changed her. Outside of that experience, I did not have much of a connection to death, other than that I knew it was something we would all face.

"Diakono du Vann asked me to give the eulogy at his funeral tomorrow," Diakono Copperwith said. The tone of his voice was flat and soft. "I barely knew him, but I'm honored that the brotherhood would ask me to do this. I hope the Eternal Comforter will give me the proper words for the occasion."

I managed a weak smile at Diakono Copperwith and continued eating the rest of my breakfast. "I have that contest at Bremen Park tomorrow. Should I withdraw to join you for Diakono Abeldorff's funeral?"

"That's okay, Diondray. You should go to the contest," Diakono Copperwith replied. "I believe something is meant to happen at that contest, and you will be the reason for it."

I felt relieved that I did not have to attend the funeral. I did not want to go, and being in that kind of environment would have been tough.

"Are you okay?" Diakono Copperwith asked.

I took a deep breath. "I have to tell you something. And I know you are going to be angry with me."

Diakono Copperwith looked concerned. "What is it?"

"I ran into Darcie Fendlewiesen a couple nights ago. I did not expect to see her again after we left Walter's Grove. We went dancing and . . . spent some time together."

I stopped talking.

"You made love to her," Diakono Copperwith said.

I nodded. "I know I let you down. I know I let Mrs. Copperwith down."

I got up from the table and began pacing.

"Sit, Diondray!" Diakono Copperwith ordered. "I knew from the Eternal Comforter that the temptress would come back into your life. I believe she was sent by the evil one to keep you from fulfilling Oscar's prophecy. While I do not agree with sex before marriage, there was no way I could have protected you from that kind of temptation. You have not declared your belief in Kammbi. And without the protection of the Eternal Comforter, that kind of temptation will take down most men. I consider you a son. I have to tell the konseho of Kammbi about this tryst, and I know they will ask me to return to Issabella. However, I will not go. Because I know you are the one to fulfill Oscar's prophecy, and that belief is why I'm still here with you."

I sighed with relief. But I noticed the look of disappointment on Diakono Copperwith's face. I had let him down. But I still did not understand everything. How could he know from the Eternal Comforter that I would become intimate with Darcie? And if he knew, why did not he stop me from going out that evening with Barron and Elexi?

"You will have to make an act of aphemmia before this journey ends," Diakono Copperwith continued.

"But I'm not a believer and follower of Kammbi," I replied.

Diakono Copperwith stared at me for a moment before answering. "That will have to change. You will have to declare your belief in Kammbi before this journey ends. And your act of passha has made that even more apparent."

I looked down at my empty plate and interlocked my fingers. Diakono Copperwith said I had committed an act of passha. I had heard that term throughout our journey together. It was said about Oscar Ortega and his affair with Mother Adrianna. It was said about Teresa not wanting to marry Leopolde. It was said about Dexter and his defiance toward the river god of the city of Alicia. Now it was said about me, even though I had not become a believer and follower of Kammbi. I felt the sting of those words as I became the latest to wear that label.

I arrived at Bremen Park a couple of hours before the contest. I had spent most of the prior evening with Barron and Otto at Barron's duplex. They had me read my themily several times and made suggestions on how it could be better. I trusted their suggestions and corrected the themily.

The former professors could tell I was not in the right frame of mind during the practice session, so after we had worked a little while, they asked me if something was wrong. I explained to them about my night with Darcie Fendlewiesen and the consequences of my action in regard to fulfilling Oscar's prophecy. Even though I was not married like Oscar Ortega, I had committed an act of passha. Fulfilling Oscar's prophecy would be in jeopardy unless I converted to believing and following Kammbi.

Both former professors thought that belief was antiquated and out of touch with the reality of what goes on between a man and a woman. They explained that most belief systems wanted their followers to achieve some kind of purity status. But if human beings were flawed in some aspects of their character, then how could a belief system expect purity? It did not make sense in their eyes.

I shared with them that Kammbi's sacrifice had taken on all the acts of passha that humanity committed in order to give people a relationship with him. Believers and followers had a path to reconnect with Kammbi by performing an act of aphemmia. It seemed he understood our flawed nature and wanted to remain connected to humanity regardless.

Barron and Otto did not understand why a god would have to sacrifice himself for humanity. Was not a god higher than humanity? I had thought the same thing when I first heard Diakono Copperwith explain the concept. But I had begun to think differently after hearing him tell me that I had committed an act of passha. I could not explain why I felt this way.

My discussion with the former professors did not resolve the conflict I felt within me. However, I was able to focus for the rest of the practice session and was soon ready to deliver my themily for the contest.

The audience began to come toward the stage at the back end of the park. All the contestants were behind it, and most of them were going over their themilys as a last-minute preparation. A tall, slender man with brown hair gave every contestant a number. I received the number three on a sheet of paper. The man said I would be the third contestant. I nodded and walked away from the rest of the contestants. I needed some space before I read my themily.

I held the two sheets of paper in my hands, and I read the themily in my mind a couple of times. I was trying to process what had happened on my journey through the cities south of the Great Forest. I had received the Boma Essence from Omari in the city of Adrian because of my connection to Reuel. I had learned of family members who shared my last name in that city and were the biggest producers of javann in Adrian. However, I had also discovered Eduardo's hatred of the Boma-Men because of his belief that they had killed the woman he loved. My relative had told me before I left Adrian that he would never befriend the Boma-Men despite the contrary evidence about what had happened to his fiancée.

Next, I had arrived in Walter's Grove and learned how to dance Guanamamma. That style of music had been born out of the rejection of Walter Leonardo Fuente's lifestyle of having two wives, which was forbidden in Terrance. Despite his status as the greatest Kammarice singer in Terrance's history, he had been forced to leave his birth city. Because of that rejection, he had built a city, some said with the help of the goddess Apollonia, based on his new style of music and dancing. In Walter's Grove, there would be no rules to keep people from how they wanted to live.

With that as a backdrop, I had met Darcie Fendlewiesen, a nightclub owner and immigrant from Santa Teresa. She had grown up in Santa Teresa under the teachings of the Book of Kammbi and was due to get married at twenty-one like all the women of that city. But instead, Darcie rejected that mandate and left her birth city. Like Walter Fuente had many years before, she came to Walter's Grove and remade herself in a place with no rules. Darcie had rejected the teachings of the Book of Kammbi and wanted me to do the same. She believed that people should not be controlled by outdated beliefs, especially if they forced women to get married whether they wanted to or not.

While in Walter's Grove, however, I had met Ciscoe and Latisha Maldonado, a dancing couple who had gotten a copy of the Book of Kammbi due to Darcie's past relationship with Ciscoe. Ciscoe had read the Book of Kammbi and believed in its teachings despite having no support from the people in Walter's Grove. How could a person believe in something without any way to confirm his beliefs—at least, until our arrival in that city?

Finally, I had made it here to Terrance. A city where gods used to reside and rule until the people were forced not to believe in them anymore. Humankind was the highest plane of existence, not gods. However, there were people in this city who still believed in the gods, and I had been labeled as a reminder of that past.

All of these thoughts had gone through my mind over the past few days, and I had tried to capture them within the themily. What was the connection? I hoped my themily succeeded in capturing everything I had experienced on this part of the journey.

I had gotten so lost in my thoughts that I did not hear the first contestant read his themily. The lukewarm applause from the audience got my attention.

"You are up next, Number Three," the man who gave out the numbers said to me.

I nodded and followed him to the area where the contestants stood before heading onto the stage. I looked out through an opening to the stage and watched a striking, blond-haired man read his themily.

Terrance is the greatest city in this region
Terrance is the city that has the most history
Terrance is the city that has the most culture
Unlike that city west of here
Where they believe culture is about
music that makes you dance

The audience laughed. He would score points for civic pride. Also, he had a good stage presence and engaged with the audience.

There are some people in our city
Who continue to believe in the past
They believe the life we had in the past is
better than the one we have currently.
However, I believe you cannot live life in the rearview mirror
Humankind must progress forward each and every day
And let the things of the past
Remain in the past.

The audience clapped loudly for the second contestant's themily. I liked his delivery and how his themily had appealed to the greatness of the city.

"Thank you, Contestant Two, Michael Augsburg from the Apollonia District," the man who had given out numbers said on stage. "Our next contestant comes from the city of Charlesville. We like the fact that our contest attracts members from outside our city, especially when they are people of importance. Please give a big welcome to Contestant Three, Diondray Azur of Charlesville!"

The introduction caught me off guard. Did the announcer know of my status back home? I walked past Contestant Two onto the stage. The announcer smiled and gave me a pat on the shoulder for encouragement. The audience clapped politely as I scanned the crowd. I noticed Barron, Elexi, and Otto to my left. They all gave me warm smiles, and I read Barron's lips saying to take a deep breath and be genuine. I looked to the right and saw three men dressed in white suits with the letter

"K" embroidered on the right chest pocket. Members of the konzill were here. They knew about me. Barron had mentioned last night that the konzill's investigation after Cassandra Applebaum's performance had come to him and Otto. They had told the investigators about what had happened on the beach, including telling them about me.

I glanced away from the members of the konzill and saw a familiar face blowing me a kiss. Darcie had a big smile on her face as she stood near the front of the stage. I felt a rush of desire come upon me as I noticed her hip-hugging yellow dress. I knew she wanted another round of lovemaking. I did too, even though I had committed an act of passha with her.

I sighed and looked away from Darcie. Further back, Diakono Copperwith was standing in the middle section of the audience with Diakono du Vann and a few members of the Dumont Brotherhood, I wondered why they were there. Weren't they supposed to be doing the funeral for Diakono Abeldorff? I smiled at Diakono Copperwith, and he nodded his acknowledgement. His gesture got me to relax as I pulled the themily out of my pocket.

Sometimes a journey can take you far away from home
It can take you far away from what you believe
From the only world you had ever known
And make you realize how much we are connected to each other
Also, how divided we can be.
Whether it's one city against another, like Terrance
against all the other cities in this region,
Or one region against another, like those north of the
Great Forest against those south of the Great Forest
Or vice versa

Whether you believe in a god or gods or humankind
Or even people within our own families
I have seen it all on this journey
And I have to come believe
More than anything
We need a bridge builder.
A bridge builder to bring cities of the same region together
A bridge builder to bring regions together
A bridge builder to bring those who believe in a god
Whether Kammbi or the gods of the past in this city
With those who believe in no god.
A bridge builder is needed to remind us of how we are connected
Instead of focusing on what divides us
A bridge is needed to remind us of how we are connected
And can come together as one

I have been called a lot of things on this journey
A Non-believer
One who will fulfill Oscar's prophecy
A Special Person
A Lover
And most recently a God
I do not think I'm any of those labels
My hope as I read this themily
Is that I embrace the true label for myself
A bridge builder

The audience was silent. However, I did not feel any discomfort in their silence. It seemed they were trying to absorb what my themily meant. I took a deep breath and saw Elexi wiping tears from her eyes. Barron and Otto smiled like I was one of their students who had done well on an exam. Darcie's eyes watered as well, and she blew me another kiss. I glanced at Diakono Copperwith and the other members of the Dumont Brotherhood and saw small smiles on their faces as well.

"Diondray Azur," one of the members of the konzill said. "Can you please come with us?"

Before I began to walk toward the konzill members, I felt energy stirring inside of me. I dropped to one knee. The energy flowed through my body like a river raging during a storm. I had to compose myself before I could leave with the konzill.

"Stand up, Diondray."

I knew that voice. I obeyed Omari's command.

"You are not going with the konzill," he continued. *"Just stand and receive the Boma Essence."*

Omari's voice left. I straightened my posture and continued to follow his command.

"He is a god!" I overheard one of the konzill members saying. "His skin is glowing!"

I looked over at my right arm and saw blue light just above my skin. I was glowing.

"I saw him on the beach!" someone in the audience yelled out.

"Me too!"

"Ammaro has returned!"

The audience continued to chatter about me as I heard a familiar growl coming from the east.

"The leopard from the beach! It has returned!"

I turned to my right and saw that Reuel had joined me on stage. It felt right that he would be here. The leopard growled at the konzill members, who had stepped back from the stage. I rubbed Reuel's head to calm him. I knew the konzill members had to speak to me. The leopard stopped growling after a few rubs on his head.

"Konzill members, I know you have something to say to me," I announced. My voice echoed through the crowd. The audience looked around, trying to determine where my voice had come from.

The three konzill members came back onto the stage. They walked slowly toward me but had their eyes on Reuel.

"Reuel will not harm you," I said as a token of reassurance.

The tallest of the konzill members came the closest to me and spoke. "Diondray Azur of Charlesville, we have learned through our investigation that it was you whom our beloved Queen of Kammarice, Cassandra Applebaum, sang about during her performance at the Mannheim."

"Correct," I replied.

"As you know, we have decided as a city that the gods are a thing of the past. We cannot have someone like yourself residing in our city."

"He stopped the rainstorm from Megaro on the beach!" someone from the audience yelled out.

The three konzill members continued to look down at Reuel. The leopard purred as I continued to rub his head. "People of this city continue to worship the gods," I said. "I surmised that from the scene at the Stuttgarte, as well as from the statue of Megaro on the beach."

"You are correct, Diondray Azur," the shortest konzill member said. "But we are asking you to leave our city in a peaceful manner. We cannot have any representation of the gods here."

I raised my hand and saw the blue light move with it. "I will leave Terrance before my time in this city is done—but only on one condition. My companion, Diakono Copperwith, is amongst the Dumont Brotherhood." I pointed my friend out in the crowd. The konzill members looked out at the audience and saw my blue light glow over Diakono Copperwith.

"He needs to have a kahall built here in this city with the assistance of the Dumont Brotherhood. As a city, you have minimized the Dumont Brotherhood's influence. They have served you with their ability the make the best alhiney for everyone to drink. Now it's their turn to share their beliefs with the city they have served. Having a kahall will give them more of an influence. People of this city have the right to listen to their beliefs and accept or reject them as they choose."

The konzill members nodded, and the shortest one answered, "We can accommodate that request. As long as they will not force their beliefs on the people of this city, the konzill will make sure their kahall is built."

I took the blue light off Diakono Copperwith. A big smile rested on his face. That request was the least I could do for him after everything he had done for me on this journey. Even though I had not become a believer and follower of Kammbi, he had become the closest to family that I had outside of Aunt Maxina. Family took care of each other.

"I'm not a god, as I stated in my themily. I'm a bridge builder. And I have one more bridge to erect before my journey is done," I announced.

I rose off the ground with Reuel at my side. I'd heard the old adage that *you can never go home again.* Well, I was going to put that old adage to the test.

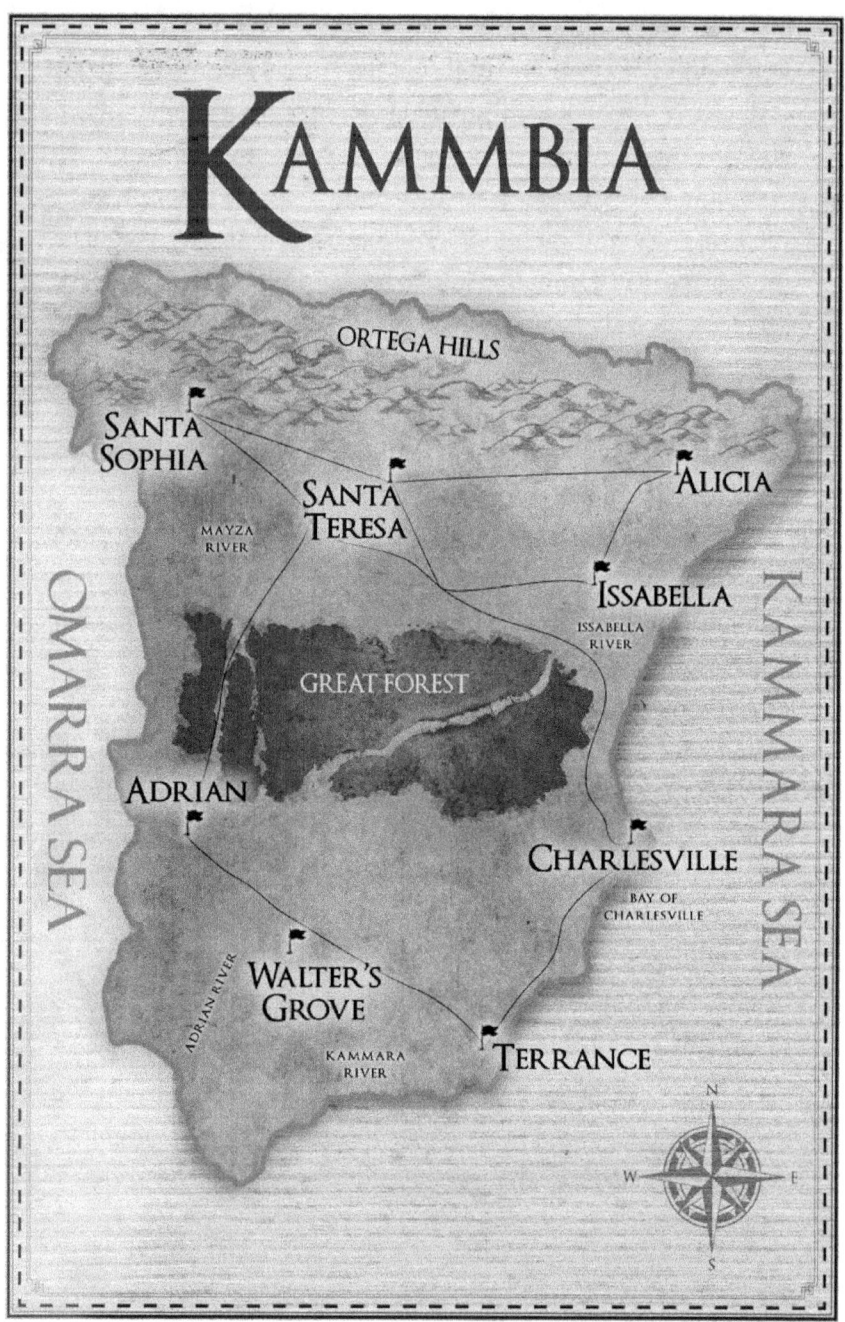

KAMMBIA

ORTEGA HILLS

SANTA SOPHIA

SANTA TERESA

ALICIA

MAYZA RIVER

ISSABELLA

ISSABELLA RIVER

GREAT FOREST

OMARRA SEA

KAMMARA SEA

ADRIAN

CHARLESVILLE

BAY OF CHARLESVILLE

WALTER'S GROVE

ADRIAN RIVER

KAMMARA RIVER

TERRANCE

N
W   E
S

Thanks for reading ***Diondray's Roundabout***, the third and final of The Diondray's Chronicles and joining him on his adventure in Kammbia.

If you enjoyed it—and if you haven't read the previous two books—you'll want to learn all about why Diondray started down the road to adventure. His travels began in *Diondray's Discovery*, Book 1 of The Diondray's Chronicles.

His adventures continue in *Diondray's Journey*, Book 2 of The Diondray's Chronicles.

Ciscoe's Dance is my latest novel set in Kammbia that takes place after the events of The Diondray's Chronicles. Ciscoe's Dance is the first book in a duology called the Dance and Listen Series. The second book, Cassandra's Revelation will be released in the fall of 2023. However, each book in this series can be read as a standalone story.

If you are an avid reader, you can check out my Marion's 25 Book Review series. I have been a book review blogger since 2011 and have reviewed over 200 books on my blog, marion-hill.com. I have created a book series featuring 25 books I have reviewed that I consider as favorites. I believe in reading widely from genre to literary fiction to non-fiction.

Reading is the easiest way to travel to new worlds and feed your curiosity!

Marion's 25 Volume 1
Marion's 25 Volume 2

If you want to keep up with all things Kammbia, then go to Marion's webpage: https://marion-hill.com/

Instagram: @marhill31

Goodreads:
https://www.goodreads.com/author/show/8202665.Marion_Hill

Bookbub:
https://www.bookbub.com/profile/marion-hill-e4d3343b-634b-45e9-bcdf-294c03430436

www.ingramcontent.com/pod-product-compliance
Lightning Source LLC
Chambersburg PA
CBHW060944120726
47910CB00002B/482